AWAKENED

THE LEPIDOPTERA VAMPIRE SERIES
BOOK TWO

BY

SUSAN HODDY

Prologue

THE STORY SO FAR....

After the death of their mother and father, and the disappearance of their brother, Stephen, sisters Violette and Danielle move to Bagnolet with their foster parents, Emily and Adrian, and into a lavish lifestyle.

Settled into her new life in France, Violette meets Michael Gramaze and soon discovers a world of danger and secrecy, where rival vampire dynasties fight for power, and where the very existence of the human race hangs in the balance, which Violette now realises that she has a role to play in.

As the Lepidopteras continue to fight the Debauched vampires, and then regroup, there is one final surprise: Violette's full transformation into a vampire shows that she is a direct descendent of Queen Talitha. Not only does the Gramaze coven plan on eliminating the Debauched vampires, but they must also protect their princess, Violette, who is next in line for the throne.

Violette also faces a future where she must live in two worlds: that of school, friends, and family, and that of the underworld of vampires.

Whilst gathering other coven members worldwide, so that they can protect their princess, Violette's brother Stephen, resurfaces and soon she realises he is a Lepidoptera too. With the Gramaze coven finding it hard to protect Violette from the Debauched vampires on a daily basis, William, who is head of the France Lepidopteras, tries to convinces his good friend, Adrian, who is a warlock, and his wife Emily to let Violette move into the Gramaze household.

Chapter One

"I don't want to hear excuses. Just get it done. Otherwise you will be the next one to die," said Nicholas scowling, and holding the sentinel up by his shirt until his feet were off the ground. "Am I making myself clear?"

"Yes, sire," said the young sentinel swallowing hard. Fearful of the repercussions, he was anxious to please his master.

Nicholas let go of his shirt and watched the sentinel immediately fall to the ground.

"Where do I get good soldiers around here?" shouted Nicholas, walking away.

Picking himself up off the floor, the frightened sentinel bowed his head to his leader, Nicholas once and headed for the doorway. He certainly had a lot to learn about being a Debauched vampire. One thing he was sure of, he only wanted to make his master proud.

With his operations being immobilised at every turn by the Gramaze coven, Nicholas wondered what he could do to prevent these assaults and lose of soldiers. He knew he needed to come up with a plan of attack, and soon.

It's a pity the drugs that we injected into William Gramaze last year didn't work for long. I would love to see that vamp go down in a big way. I want that bastard to pay for all the Debauched vamps he has killed. Let alone my houses that he has torched, thought Nicholas.

Hearing a knock at the door, he bellowed, "Come."

"Sire…" said Prometheus, as he walked through the wooden, double-door entrance to Nicholas's lounge room.

"What do you want?" said Nicholas abruptly, with his back to Prometheus.

"Sire, I have some good news," said Prometheus, hoping his master would be pleased with him.

"What is it, Prometheus?" snapped Nicholas.

"We have been told that a new multi-coloured female Lepidoptera vampire has been born to the Gramaze coven," said Prometheus.

"Who told you this?" said Nicholas, with his eyebrows furrowed. The disbelief on his face was apparent.

"We have an insider who has given us this information, sire," said Prometheus.

"Is this a reliable source?" said Nicholas, turning around.

"Yes, sire. Very reliable," said Prometheus, thinking back to his previous conversation he had with the new assistant principal at Lycee International.

"See if you can find out where she is being held. I want to meet this beauty," said Nicholas, walking over to the window, with a smirk of sheer happiness on his face.

"Yes, sire," said Prometheus, as he ran out of the room, like a dog with his tail between his legs.

Hmm… so they have a multi-coloured female. Oh, what I could do with her blood. If I can get my hands on her then I would be unstoppable, thought Nicholas looking out his window and off into the distance.

Taking his phone from the pocket of his long, black coat, Nicholas rang his driver.

"Bring the car around."

Campbell knocked on the door to Nicholas's office.

"Come," bellowed Nicholas.

"Your ride is here master. Did sire need me to come along for protection tonight?" said Campbell.

"Yes. Organise two others to come with us as well," said Nicholas, walking towards the door.

Stepping into the limousine, Nicholas instructed the driver to take him to the brothel he owned down town in Paris, whilst Campbell and the other two soldiers followed behind in the black SUV.

Pulling up outside the house of ill repute, Campbell instructed the two soldiers to stand guard whilst their master was in the brothel. Looking around to make sure all was good to go, he then opened the limousine door for his master to step out.

"Sire, the two soldiers will wait out here and guard the place, and I will come inside to protect you," said Campbell, standing in front of Nicholas.

"Right," said Nicholas, pushing past Campbell, and continuing on inside.

"Why... hello Nicholas. What, pray tell, brings you here? Do you fancy one of my best girls tonight?" said Rose, taunting him.

"Upstairs... now... business first, and then maybe we can discuss the ladies," said Nicholas authoritatively. "Campbell, you stay here at the elevator and don't let anyone else come up here. Are we clear?"

"Yes, sire," said Campbell, stony faced.

As the metal doors shut to the elevator, Nicholas pressed the first floor button, which was for Rose's office. "How has business been, Rose?"

"Well... it hasn't been too good Nicholas, since the Gramaze vamps decided to pay us a visit last month. It seems that they have scared a lot of our regular clientele away," said Rose, looking up to Nicholas.

"Those fucking bastards don't give up, do they? I am going to have to do something about them," said Nicholas, frustrated that once again, one of his businesses had been ruined by William and his coven.

The elevator door opened and they stepped out into Rose's office, which looked more like a boudoir, than an office. Nicholas grabbed Rose tightly around her waist and pulled her in close to him.

"Did you miss me, baby?"

"Silly question… I always miss my most favourite man," said Rose provocatively, as she wrapped her legs around his waist.

Carrying her over to the desk, Nicholas bent her over, face down, and held her in place with his hand, as he ripped off her panties and proceeded to penetrate her aggressively.

Panting, she groaned as his shaft continued its onslaught of pleasure.

"Oh baby, keep going. I'm nearly there," said Rose breathing heavily.

Rose was Nicholas's lady of the night, whom he nailed every time he came to the club. There was never any kissing or fondling in their relationship, just unadulterated pleasure. He preferred it that way, and she loved the way he was always rough with her.

When the deed was done, they recovered their clothes and got straight down to business. Nicholas was not one for small talk and Rose liked it that way.

"Tomorrow night we will be bringing by some ice for you to sell to the customers who want that little something extra,

Rose. Please make sure you have plenty of guards on the doors, as we don't want anything going wrong," said Nicholas sitting in the chair behind the desk.

"Yes Nicholas," said Rose, perched on the side of the desk with her sheer black pantihose garter showing, as she crossed her legs.

As they were talking business, Nicholas' phone rang. Taking it out of his jacket pocket, and looking at the screen, he answered, "Yes."

"Sire, I have some good news. We have located the female. Did you want us to bring her to you tonight?" asked Prometheus.

"No… I want you to find out over the next couple of days where she will be during the daylight hours, and we will take her from there. No one will ever expect this to happen. Do you understand me?"

"Yes, master, I will get straight onto it," said Prometheus, his voice shaky.

"You have done well, Prometheus, and you will be rewarded, once we have the female in hand," said Nicholas. As Nicholas hung up, he pondered on what he would be able to achieve, once the female was in his hands.

I need to contact Tsoukalos, so he can start organising what we need for our experiment when we seize the female. If we can acquire the female's DNA and most of her blood then we should be able to produce a multicoloured female Debauched vampire of our own. These Lepidoptera bastards think that they have got it all sewn up; well, we will see who is master of all, soon enough, thought Nicholas as he dialed the number.

"Tsoukalos, I need you to get the lab ready for a multi-coloured female Lepidoptera. We will be extracting her in a couple of days," said Nicholas.

"Yes, sire. Are you sure you have found a multi-coloured female Lepidoptera?" said Tsoukalos, curiously. He knew that a new female Lepidoptera hadn't been seen in many years.

"Don't question me… just do as you are told and get on with it now, Tsoukalos," said Nicholas authoritatively.

"Yes, sire," said Tsoukalos, nervously.

As Nicholas hung up his phone and put it in the pocket of his jacket, the elevator door pinged, and then opened. Looking up, he noticed his guard, Campbell, running towards him.

"Sire… we need to get you out of here. The Gramaze vamps are in the area," said Campbell, with his eyes widened and his fists clenched.

"Let's go," said Nicholas, watching Campbell return to the elevator. "Good night, Rose."

"Goodbye, Nicholas. I am sure we will catch up again, real soon," said Rose, raising her eyebrows and smiling sweetly at him and remembering their sexual encounter.

Nicholas and Campbell took the elevator down to the night club, and slipped out the side entrance, where the limousine was waiting for them in the side alley. Speeding away, Nicholas instructed the sentinel to take them to his mansion. The black SUV followed not far behind them.

Whilst out on patrol, William, Grayson and Brock, vampires from the Gramaze family, decided they would pay a visit to some of the night clubs in the area. Entering the night club, which they knew Nicholas owned, they scanned the room for any Debauched vampires. As they walked through and came upon the bar, Rose approached them.

"Good evening, gentlemen. Anything we can get you tonight?" said Rose, gesturing for them to look around.

"Rose, isn't it?" said Grayson.

She nodded.

"Point us in the direction of the owner. We want to have a word with him," said Grayson.

"He isn't here tonight. May we interest you three charming gentlemen in a bit of entertainment?" said Rose, as she pointed to the establishment ladies.

"We are not here for that," grunted Grayson, annoyed.

"Pity… we can offer you fine gentlemen some fun for the night," teased Rose.

"Don't try playing us, Rose. Now where is Nicholas?" said William, irritated, as he jumped the bar to stand directly in front of her.

"I told you; he is not here tonight," said Rose, gulping.

"When he returns… you tell him William Gramaze is looking for him," said William, forcefully pulling Rose by her clothing, until she was very close to his face.

"Yes, sir. I will let him know," said Rose, taking a deep breath and shaking.

"Let's get out of here," said William, with his nostrils flaring, as he released Rose and walked towards the front entrance, with Grayson and Brock. He despised women like Rose, and what she stood for.

Standing on the pavement outside the night club, William said, "We will scan the streets from the rooftops for any sign of Debauched vampires and the trouble they could wreak on the human race tonight."

"Yes, sire," said Grayson and Brock, simultaneously.

William scaled the side of the building with ease. When he reached the rooftop, his thoughts returned to the night he was taken prisoner by Nicholas and his soldiers. *I would love to catch up with one of those fuckers that kidnapped me last month. How good it would feel to torture them bastards instead?* thought William. His fists were clenched, as he looked out over the rooftops.

"Every dog has its day, sire," said Grayson, hearing his thoughts, and placing his hand on William's shoulder, supportively.

"That they do," said William, looking around to see Grayson and Brock standing beside him.

Tortured, and injected with an experimental drug the Debauched vampires were trying out, William's abilities had been slowly taken from him over several hours. Luckily, his good friend, Susan, a healer, had come to help him gain his abilities back. It had taken about two weeks to fully recover, and in that time, William thought he would have to relinquish his leadership and would become a human again. The thought of it sickened him, as he had been a Lepidoptera vampire for over three thousand years. He couldn't even fathom becoming a human again. Luckily, he had the love of his life and partner, Renee, to reassure him that he would overcome this sickness and would go on to destroy the Debauched and what they stood for.

As they jumped from one roof to another, Grayson spotted two Debauched taunting a human woman.

"Hey guys… have a look over there. Looks like we might see some action tonight, after all," said Grayson, pointing to the road below.

William and Brock stopped quickly in their tracks and looked in the direction Grayson was pointing. They could see a woman being harassed. Jumping down off the roof top, Grayson and Brock watched and waited to see what the two Debauched were going to do with the human.

As the Debauched pushed and shoved the human slowly into a corner, in a side alley, she was pleading with them to leave her alone. But they weren't listening.

"You guys need to pick on someone who can fight back," said Brock, as he and Grayson stood in the entrance to the alley, behind the two Debauched vampires.

"Mind you own business, fuckhead," said the first Debauched, turning around.

"Fuckhead. Ha. We'll see who is a fuckhead," said Grayson, running towards the first Debauched and punching him in the face and then in the stomach. "Take that, you moron!"

Recovering from the attack somewhat, the Debauched vampire ran straight for Grayson and wrestled him to the ground. But he was no match. Grayson was a powerful vampire who knew how to look after himself. Once Grayson had the Debauched vamp face down on the ground with his hands behind his back, William appeared from the shadows, took his sword out of its sheath and swung it in a downward motion, to cut off his head. The young, inexperienced Debauched didn't see what was coming, and disintegrated in an instant.

The second Debauched vampire watched out the corner of his eye, whilst battling Brock, and he knew he would be next if he wasn't careful. But before he could get the situation under control, Brock had forced him to the ground, so that William could swing his sword righteously to cut off his head. His body disintegrated as well.

With the battle over, William and Brock scanned the immediate area to make sure no other Debauched were hiding in the shadows, whilst Grayson headed for the human woman, to see if she was all right.

With her back to him, and crouched down beside a dumpster, she sobbed uncontrollably. As Grayson bent over to touch her shoulder, she slowly turned around to face him.

"Are you OK, mademoiselle?" said Grayson, kneeling beside her.

Wide-eyed, she flinched away from him. Her heart hammered in her chest, and her whole body shook from what she had just witnessed: the beheading of what she thought were humans.

Reading her thoughts, Grayson said, "It's OK, mademoiselle. I am here to help. I won't hurt you."

"What just happened?" she said, her face tear-stained, smudged with mascara, as she looked up into Grayson's eyes and trembled.

He didn't answer. Instead he put his hand out in front of him, and helped her to her feet.

At first she hesitated, wondering if she could trust him. But then she placed her hand in his.

As they stood up together, Grayson said, "It's OK."

Slowly, he pulled her in close and placed his arms around her, for comfort. She struggled, trying to break free, but then felt his soothing embrace calm her.

Pulling away from their embrace, Grayson looked into her eyes and said, "What is your name?"

She choked back a sob. "Samantha… my name is Samantha."

"Hi Samantha. My name is Grayson. Don't worry, I will take care of you and make sure you get home safely. OK?"

"Thank you. That would be good," said Samantha. But she still didn't entirely trust him, because of what she had just seen.

"You are most welcome. I am just glad we were here at the right time to help you. So… what were those guys saying, anyway?" said Grayson.

Wiping her face, she gathered her thoughts, and said, "Well… I had just finished my shift at that restaurant, over there. I only started waitressing there tonight. When I came outside, I walked over to the bus stop, and this is when they approached me and asked if I would like a lift. When I said, 'No,' they got all weird and said things like, 'We want to drink from you; we want to screw you.' I just thought that they were possibly drunk and were out of their minds. But after a few minutes, I could see they were serious."

Shaking, Samantha started to cry again.

Grayson could hear from her thoughts that she was scared and wanted to return to her apartment where she felt safe.

"Bastards… I am glad we were here to stop them. Don't worry Samantha, I will make sure you get home safely," said Grayson, rubbing his hand up and down her arm.

"Hello mademoiselle. My name is William and this is Brock. Are you going to be all right?" said William.

"Yes. Thank you so much, the three of you. I think some-one was looking over me tonight," said Samantha, looking towards the sky and wiping her tear-filled eyes.

"You are most welcome," said William.

"I promised Samantha that I would get her home safely. Do you mind if we meet up later?" said Grayson.

"No problem, Grayson. Just give us a call when you are ready to be picked up," said William.

William said to Grayson through mind talk, *Make sure you wipe her mind.*

Grayson nodded once in agreeance.

William then caught wind of her scent.

"Samantha, you have blood on your neck. Have you been injured?" asked William.

"I don't know," said Samantha, feeling her neck and looking at the blood on her hand. "I didn't even realise I'd been cut."

"Let me have a look," said William. Lifting her hair to get a good look at the wound, he noticed that Samantha had a faint outline of a butterfly tattoo on the back of her neck. *Lepidoptera*. His eyes widened, at the thought of yet another female being found.

"I think we should take you to the hospital to get that looked at, as it looks like you may need stitches," said William.

"It's funny you know, I didn't feel any pain in my neck at all, until now. But now it's hurting so much that I have a headache as well," said Samantha, rubbing her temple.

"I will go get our car and be back in a few minutes and then we can drop you and Grayson at the hospital. OK?" said William.

"Thank you. That's very kind of you to offer. But... I am not sure I should be..."

Before Samantha could finish her sentence, her vision blurred and she fainted. Moving quickly, Grayson caught her before she hit the ground.

"What happened?" said Brock.

"I think the shock of it all has caught up with her. It's a lot to take in, what she has seen tonight. Let alone the blood loss from her wound," said William.

"Luckily you were there to catch her, bro," said Brock.

"I can't believe we have found another female Lepidoptera Vampire. Once she is feeling better, Samantha will need to be protected by our family," said William. "Oh, and by the way Grayson, I think she is attracted to you and that is why her butterfly outline is showing up."

"Hmm... I think you could be right, because I am feeling the same way," said Grayson, holding her in his muscular arms.

Chapter Two

The automatic doors opened inwards as Grayson carried Samantha into the emergency area of the hospital.

"Can someone help me? My friend has been injured," said Grayson, approaching the front nursing station desk.

"Come this way," said the doctor, gesturing to a private room.

Following him into the room, Grayson laid Samantha's well-toned body on top of the hospital bed gently. Pushing her dark hair away from her face, he couldn't help but notice her velvety smooth skin and her sensual lips. Even her scent of lavender seemed to welcome him in.

"Stand back, please," said the doctor, touching Grayson on the shoulder.

"Hmm... OK... is she going to be all right?" asked Grayson.

"She has a nasty gash on her neck. How did this happen?" asked the doctor, looking over Samantha's injuries.

"I don't know. I found her like this," said Grayson.

"Right...well... if you would like to wait outside," said the doctor.

"I am not going anywhere," said Grayson, knowing he must guard this new Lepidoptera at any cost.

"Stay out of the way then, whilst I sew her wound up," said the doctor walking over to the cupboard and retrieving some medical supplies.

Samantha's eyes opened to find Grayson sitting in a chair, next to the bed.

"Hello, sleepy head," said Grayson.

"Where am I?" said Samantha, slowly looking around the room.

"You are at Mercy Hospital and this lovely gentleman brought you into emergency," said the doctor, gesturing to Grayson. "You had a nasty laceration on your neck and you had lost a lot of blood, so I would say that is why you became unconscious."

Samantha felt her neck, which had now been bandaged, and remembered the night's events. With her brow furrowed, she took a deep breath to calm herself.

"Don't worry, you are going to be all right. You have a few stitches though. In about one week's time you will need to see your local doctor to get them taken out. How are you feeling?" said the doctor, checking the pulse on Samantha's wrist.

"My head is banging, and my neck hurts," said Samantha rubbing her temple. "Otherwise, I don't feel too bad."

"I will ask the nurse to bring you in some pain relief. But we will need you to stay here for a couple of hours so that we can continue to do checks on you," said the doctor.

"Oh, OK. Thank you," said Samantha, nodding.

"Do you remember anything about what happened to you tonight or even how you got your injuries? I need to do up a police report," said the doctor.

"Umm... no... I don't remember. It's all a bit of a blur," said Samantha. She looked from the doctor to Grayson and gulped.

"Right... well... we can deal with that later. For now, you just need to get some rest," said the doctor, placing her chart on the end of the bed.

She nodded, and watched him walk towards the doorway.

When the doctor left the room, Samantha turned to Grayson and said, "Thank you for bringing me in here. I probably would have died if it wasn't for you and your friends tonight."

"You're welcome," said Grayson.

"So… you brought me in here and you haven't left. Well… that's a first. Any other guy I've ever known would have run a mile by now," said Samantha.

"I did say to you before you fainted that I would get you home safely. So I am not going anywhere, and as promised, I will take you home once they release you. OK?" said Grayson smiling.

"OK. Thanks. Such a gentleman," said Samantha, breathing a sigh of relief.

"So where do you live, Samantha?"

"I live not too far from the Eiffel Tower actually. I have only just moved into my apartment, and still have some unpacking to do. What about you Grayson; where do you live?"

"I live in Bagnolet, with my family," said Grayson.

"Family… so you are married and have children, then?" said Samantha, trying to hide her disappointment.

"No… oh I see, you thought when I said family, I meant married with children."

"Well… yeah," said Samantha.

"I live with William and Brock and a few others. I class them as my family," said Grayson.

"Ah, OK. That makes sense. Where are they anyway, Brock and William that is?" asked Samantha.

"They have returned home," said Grayson.

"Right," said Samantha, confused.

As they were talking, a nurse walked into the room with a clear bag of fluid in her hands. Walking over to Samantha, the nurse said, "I am going to feed this pain relief medication through the intravenous cannula they put in your arm previously, Samantha. The medication should kick in soon. You just need to rest."

"Je vous en remercie," said Samantha, in appreciation.

A few minutes after the nurse administered the pain relief, Samantha's eyes became heavy and she drifted off to sleep.

"Thank you," said Grayson to the nurse.

"You are most welcome… I will be back later to check on her. Until then why don't you get some rest yourself?" said the nurse, walking towards the doorway.

"Probably good advice," said Grayson. "Once again, thanks."

Leaning back in the lounge chair, Grayson watched Samantha sleep. He wondered where she had lived previously and what she had done with her life. Intrigue had set in and he wanted to find out as much as he could about her.

Samantha woke as she heard the nurse's white shoes squeak on the vinyl floor when she entered the room. Standing beside the bed, the nurse checked Samantha's vitals. "Well, you seem OK now. I think you can go home. Once you get dressed, meet me at the nurse's station in the hallway, and I can give you some more pain relief medication to take home with you. I am guessing this gentleman is taking you home?" said the nurse, indicating to Grayson.

"Yes, I am taking her home," said Grayson, as he opened his eyes.

"Great. We can't release Samantha unless someone is going to look after her tonight," said the nurse.

"No problem," said Grayson.

Samantha looked at Grayson and said, "Are you sure? I don't want to put you out."

"Yes, I am sure. Now let's get you all sorted with the nurse and I can take you home," said Grayson, standing.

It was a twenty-minute ride to Samantha's apartment, and she was starting to feel tired from the medication and the events of the night. Relaxed, she put her head on Grayson's shoulder and fell asleep. When the cab pulled up, Grayson paid the driver, and then carried Samantha up the stairs, to her apartment.

Approaching her apartment doorway, she said, "You can put me down if I am too heavy."

"You're not heavy. Where is the key to your door?" said Grayson.

Samantha fumbled through her purse and found the key.

"Here you go," she said, looking into his mesmerising eyes and watching how his hair glistened in the dim light.

"Thank you," said Grayson, taking the keys from her hand.

Lowering her onto the couch, he asked, "Where can I find a pillow and blanket?"

"Just over there, in that cupboard," said Samantha.

Retrieving the pillow and blanket, Grayson then propped her up with the pillow behind her back.

"You need to rest," said Grayson, as he covered her with the blanket and breathed in her beautiful scent. *Lavender. Mmm… god, wouldn't I like to kiss those luscious red lips?* Mentally slapping himself, Grayson shook his head. *Get a hold of yourself, man.*

"Thank you, Grayson. You are so kind," said Samantha, watching his every move.

"You're welcome. Would you like some water?" said Grayson, trying to calm himself.

"No thanks. Actually, I am feeling tired. I can't seem to keep my eyes open," said Samantha, lying down flat on the couch and closing her eyes.

"That's OK. It's probably the medication. You rest," said Grayson, watching her closely, as he sat on the coffee table in front of her.

As the street light shone in threw the window of her apartment, Grayson admired her glossy, long, brown hair and how her flawless skin was like satin. All he wanted to do was stroke her hair, but he dared not touch Samantha for fear of waking her. *I wonder why this beautiful woman has appeared in my life? And why now? I never thought I would find my life partner.* Grayson couldn't comprehend the instant attraction he felt for her either. These type of feelings were foreign to him. His life had always been about battling the Debauched and nothing else. Over the years, he never had even looked twice at a woman, let alone been romantic with one. A new chapter was about to start in his life and he wasn't sure he even wanted it or was prepared for it yet.

Listening to her breathing and heartbeat, Grayson could tell she was going to be all right, so he thought it best that he leave and let her get some rest. He was sure William was probably wondering where he was, anyway.

As he kissed her forehead goodbye, she stirred, but didn't wake.

Slipping quietly out of Samantha apartment, Grayson rang William.

"Ready for collection, sire."

"We'll be there in five," said William.

"How is the young lady?" said William, as Grayson climbed into the back seat of the car.

"She is all right. Nothing a good night's sleep won't fix," said Grayson.

"That's good news. I have Annabelle guarding her apartment tonight. So she should be safe, until we can work out some arrangements for her," said William.

But Grayson already knew Annabelle was there guarding Samantha. The minute he had left her apartment, he had seen her waiting on the other side of the road in the shadows.

"Great. Thank you, William. So where are we going to now?" said Grayson, expecting to go back out on patrol.

"We are going home. It's pretty quiet out tonight," said Brock.

"Right," said Grayson. He was glad to be going home, so he could burn off some extra energy in the combat room.

On the ride home, Grayson's thoughts were of Samantha and how he would like to get to know her better. But he also wondered how she would feel about their world. Time would tell.

Chapter Three

Damn… thought Violette as she stepped out the limousine and heard the bell ring. She was already late for her first class of the second semester at Lycee International. "See you later, sis."

"Yep. See ya!" shouted Danielle, running off in the opposite direction to Violette.

With seconds to go before the final bell rang for classes to start, Violette arrived at the classroom. Noticing that the professor, who had flared nostrils, was looking at her, and then at his watch, she heard him think, '*Young lady, you are late, and it's only the first day.*'

"Sorry," mouthed Violette quietly, hunching her shoulders and giving a cheesy smile, as she stood at the front of the class.

Looking around the classroom, Violette saw that the seats were divided up into five rows down the room, each six deep, with the professor's desk situated at the front of the room. Feeling like all eyes were on her, she quickly discovered an empty chair in the front row and took her seat. She took her books out of her bag, and spotted the words 'Maths 3A', written in chalk, on the black board behind the professor's desk. *Phew. Yep, I am in the right class room.*

"Everyone… quieten down please," said the professor standing in front of his desk, waiting for his students to become silent. "Today we will be having a pop quiz so that I can see what level each of you is at."

The professor then proceeded to pass out the test papers to each person sitting in the front row, so they could pass them backwards to the other students.

Most students in the class muttered under their breath at how this was unfair and that they hadn't had time to practise maths over the holidays.

"When you have your test papers, turn them upside down until I say to start," said the professor.

Once the professor advised the class that they could start, Violette turned over her pages and started going through each question. Some of them were multiple choice and some required extended answers.

Too easy. Most of these questions are on equations I have learnt at my old school in LA, thought Violette looking through the test.

Breezing through the quiz in record time, Violette placed the papers at the top right hand corner of her desk and leaned back in her chair. As she waited for the bell to ring, Violette's mind wondered off, with thoughts of how much her life had changed in such a short time, since the death of her parents. The move to Bagnolet certainly wasn't one she had expected, nor had she realised its full advantages and disadvantages yet. With thoughts of her life partner, Michael, Violette closed her eyes and smiled for a brief moment until she was interrupted by the Professor standing next to her desk.

"Mademoiselle Castell… I see you have finished," said the Professor, picking up Violette's quiz paper and reading through the answers.

"Yes sir," said Violette, startled by his voice. Sitting up straight, she gulped hard. "How did I go?"

"Hmm, not bad. Though, your working out is a bit different to what I have taught you last semester," said the Professor, looking over his glasses at her.

"Oh. OK," said Violette. *As long as I come up with the same answer, who cares?*

Returning Violette's quiz to her desk, he continued to walk throughout the class and watch students take the quiz. Occasionally he stopped and looked through their quiz papers as well.

Forty minutes later, the bell rang to finish maths. "Please hand in your test papers to me. Oh, and make sure your name is on it," said the Professor, watching all of his students pack up their bags for their next classes.

Violette's next class was English 3D, and by the time she had finished this class she had already been given her first assignment for the semester. Luckily it was only a small assignment and wouldn't take her long to plough through it that night. The rest of day went by fast for Violette, and by the time 4.30pm came around to finish up for the day, she was glad. She had forgotten how exhausting schoolwork could be.

As Violette was getting her books out of her locker, Annabelle put her head around the door and said, "How was the first day; not too hectic I hope?"

"Hi Annabelle… yeah, the day hasn't been too bad, as far as first days go. I am looking forward to getting home though. I am feeling a little bit brain drained today."

"Oh, OK. By the way, William has worked out a roster for you, Violette. It looks like I will be collecting you each day from school. He was thinking that you should be safe at school during the day, so we won't have anyone guarding you. And at night, when you are actually at your house, it will either be Grayson or Michael. Whoever guards you at night will also bring you to school in the morning as well," said Annabelle.

"Right. Sounds like it's all been sorted then," said Violette, shutting her locker door and locking it with the padlock.

"Does Danielle want a lift home as well with us today?" asked Annabelle.

"I am not sure. She should be here in a minute or so. Her locker is next to mine and you can ask her yourself," said Violette, pointing to Danielle's locker. "Actually, here she comes now."

"Hey, sis. Hi Annabelle. Are you joining us at school now Annabelle?" joked Danielle, opening her locker.

"Hi Danielle… no. My days of school are over. I am here to pick up Violette. Would you like a lift home today with us as well?" asked Annabelle.

"No thanks, Annabelle. I am going to study at the school library this afternoon with a couple of new friends I made today. I will probably get a lift with them. If not, I will ring Emily and ask if the chauffeur can come and collect me. But thanks for asking anyway; maybe another day," said Danielle.

"Sure. No problem," said Annabelle smiling. "Well, we had better hit the road, Violette. See you later, Danielle."

"Yeah, see ya," said Danielle. "See you at home sis."

"Bye," said Violette, slinging her bag over her shoulder.

Violette walked by Annabelle's side and as they approached the car in the school parking lot, Violette said, "Nice car. Audi V8 isn't it? Wow… whose car is this?"

"It belongs to all of us actually. We get to drive whatever car is available in the shed each day," said Annabelle, unlocking the doors with the key fob.

"You are so lucky," said Violette, hoping in the passenger's seat and looking around inside the car. She had secretly always wanted a nice car like this.

"I will have to take you down to the garage when you come over next and show you what cars we have. Besides our SUVs, we have some other really valuable cars like this one," said Annabelle, smiling.

"OK," said Violette, trying to comprehend the enormity of how many cars the Gramaze family had.

"So how are you feeling now?" said Annabelle, as they drove off out the carpark and away from the school.

"Today has been the first day that I haven't needed blood. So far so good," said Violette.

"That's great. Maybe your transformation is complete," said Annabelle.

"Hope so... Annabelle, I wanted to ask you... what happened to all the Debauched and Lepidoptera vampires that we rescued last time I was taken?" said Violette, with her brow furrowed.

"William has brought in some specialists and healers to deal with the situation. As of this morning they have managed to turn all the Lepidopteras back into vampires, but they haven't had any luck with the Debauched vamps. Only time will tell, and in the meantime, William has allowed the Debauched bastards to stay in our house. But they are confined to one part of the house and have guards on them. Most of us Lepidoptera aren't happy about this at all. We have also had to remove the queen from our premises, and hide her in another location, just in case the Debauched find her. I suppose one consolation is that they are currently human and can't cause us much trouble," said Annabelle, gripping the steering wheel hard in frustration.

"Do you reckon it would be OK if I was to visit the Gramaze house?" said Violette.

"I can't see there being any problems with that, Violette. You know you are always welcome," said Annabelle, as she pulled up to Violette's house and put the car in park.

"Great… well, thanks for the lift, Annabelle. I will see you tomorrow afternoon after school," said Violette, getting out the car.

"OK. See you tomorrow, Violette," said Annabelle, smiling.

Violette finished her homework and looked over at the digital clock next to her bed, which was showing six-thirty. It had taken her longer than expected to finish, and her shoulders were crying out in pain. As she packed up her books, there was a tap at her window. Looking over to the double-door windows, she noticed it was Michael.

"Hello. Can I come in?" said Michael through the glass.

"Shhh," said Violette, putting her finger to her lips. "Yes, come in and I will shut my bedroom door before anyone hears us."

As she was shutting the bedroom door, she felt Michael put his hands on her shoulders and started to give her a neck and shoulder rub.

"Oh, that's just what I needed. Thank you, Michael," said Violette, feeling a bit more relaxed.

"De rien," said Michael. Turning her around he pulled her chin up to his mouth, and kissed her ever so tenderly.

I have missed you today, Violette, and I couldn't wait to see you, thought Michael.

I know what you mean. It's been hard to concentrate today at school. Do you have to go out on patrol tonight? thought Violette, as she enjoyed the taste of his lips.

Slowly pulling away from their embrace, he said, "No. You have me all to yourself tonight. What would you like to do?"

"What if I ask Emily if you can stay for dinner and then we can cuddle up on the sofa and watch a movie or something?" said Violette.

"Or something. Now that sounds good," teased Michael, as he tried to wrap his muscular arms around her waist.

Violette smiled mischievously and quickly pulled away from him. "Cheeky... give me a minute and I will go and ask Emily if you can stay for dinner. You had better go hide and then you can turn up at the front door when you hear what Emily says," said Violette.

Michael nodded, quickly gave her a kiss on the forehead and left via the window again.

Violette ran down the stairs in search of Emily and found her reading in the sitting room.

"Would it be all right if Michael comes over for dinner tonight and then stays awhile?" asked Violette.

"As long as you have finished your homework dear, that is fine with me," said Emily, firmly.

"Yes, I have finished it. I'll go and let Lamiae know that we have one extra for dinner tonight. Thanks, Emily," said Violette, eagerly running off.

As Violette entered the kitchen Lamiae said, "Hello Violette. How was your first day back at school?"

"It was great, Lamiae. Thanks for asking. I hope it's not too short notice, but Michael is coming for dinner tonight," said Violette.

"Yes. I know dear. I have made plenty of food," said Lamiae.

"Oh. Right... thanks, Lamiae," said Violette, remembering Lamiae could read minds, too.

"How are you and Michael getting along now anyway?" asked Lamiae, as she checked on the meat in the oven.

"He is such a wonderful guy and I just love him to bits," said Violette, sitting down on the leather stool at the island bench.

"He deserves someone nice like you too, Violette. I am sure he loves you as well," said Lamiae, standing next to the bench.

"At the moment we are waiting for Emily and Adrian to let us know if we can live together," said Violette.

"Wow… you must love him a real lot then," said Lamiae, her eyebrows raised.

"Yes, I love him very much, Lamiae; in fact, so much, that I know we will marry one day," said Violette.

"Hmm, that is serious. Do Emily and Adrian know how you both feel about each other? Maybe if you tell them, they will take that into account, and might let you live together."

"I am hoping so. Well… I will leave you to it, Lamiae. I am just going to go upstairs and take a shower before Michael gets here. I will see you later."

"OK, dear. Dinner will be at the usual time," said Lamiae, watching Violette walk away.

Chapter Four

Violette's eyes opened wide, and goose bumps formed over her body, as she pulled her conditioner-covered hair out from under the hot water shower head. The voices she heard were clear in her mind, and she wondered how close the three Debauched soldiers were. Wiping the soap from her eyes, she stood still to listen to their chatter more closely, only to realise they were walking past the front gates.

Remembering the conversation William had had with Adrian, about putting up some wards around the house, so the Debauched wouldn't be able to detect her presence, Violette quickly washed off the conditioner from her hair and turned off the faucet. Opening the glass shower door, she stepped out and hastily dried herself off. As she pulled her denim jeans on, she listened as the three Debauched continue to walk past the house without hesitation or knowledge of her existence.

Phew, thought Violette, breathing a sigh of relief and rolling her eyes. *Must be working. I wonder what they are doing in the area. Coincidence…? I don't think so.*

Putting her blouse on, Violette heard a familiar voice in her mind. *Michael.* Smiling, she quickly brushed her wet hair and headed down stairs. When she entered the sitting room, she noticed Michael talking with Adrian.

"Hello, Michael," said Violette.

Standing, Michael walked over to Violette and gave her a kiss on the cheek. "Hello, Violette."

"How was the first day back at school, Violette?" asked Adrian, watching them embrace.

"Umm… it was good. Bit of a brain-drain, though," said Violette, trying to gather her thoughts after Michael's initial interaction.

"Hmm… yeah can get that way, I suppose," said Adrian smiling. "Well, dinner is nearly ready. Are you hungry?"

"Oh, OK. Famished," said Violette, remembering she didn't have lunch. Even though she was a Lepidoptera now, she still enjoyed her food.

Michael, did you realise that there were Debauched soldiers outside the front gates, just now? thought Violette.

Yes… we are not sure why they are in the area, though. But don't worry, Grayson and Annabelle are following them now to see what they are up to, thought Michael, placing his hand in hers.

Nodding once, Violette smiled, knowing she was well guarded by her Lepidoptera family.

Entering the room with Danielle, Emily said, "Hello Michael. I didn't know you were already here."

Bowing his head once to Emily, Michael said, "Good evening, Emily, Danielle."

"Michael has only just arrived. We were just catching up, my dear," said Adrian.

Nodding, Emily said, "Dinner is almost ready and Lamiae has set up the table for dinner. So we may as well go into the dining room."

"OK, my love," said Adrian standing.

"So, Violette… we wanted to ask you if you would like to do anything for your seventeenth birthday next week?" said Emily, taking her seat at the table.

"It's your birthday next week… you never told me that," said Michael.

"Yeah, I just figured that it's just another day," said Violette, reaching for Michael's hand. "To be honest with you, I haven't really thought much about it at all, Emily."

"What about if we all go out for dinner? Maybe the Eiffel Tower restaurant?" said Emily.

"I would love to," said Violette excited.

"OK. I will make the booking tomorrow," said Emily smiling.

"Will it be all right if I could invite a few friends, though?" said Violette.

"Yes dear. That will be fine. How many did you have in mind?" said Emily.

"Will five be OK?" said Violette.

"That will be fine. We are going to invite William and Renee as well," said Emily.

"Sounds good. Thanks, Emily and Adrian. This is so nice of you," said Violette.

"You're welcome, dear," said Emily.

My first birthday without Mom and Dad. I wish they were still here.

Taking a deep breath, Violette's shoulders slumped as she remembered back to how her mom had always baked her a birthday cake each year, and how her dad had always played the prankster in front of her friends. She had always enjoyed the fuss they made over her on her birthdays.

Danielle watched Violette's stare off into the distance. She knew that look all too well and what Violette was thinking. Placing her arm around Violette's shoulder, Danielle said, "I miss them too, sis."

Violette leaned on Danielle's shoulder. "One of the many things I miss about Mom and Dad."

After dinner, Michael asked Violette, "Would you like to go for a walk in the gardens, to get some fresh air?"

"Sure," said Violette.

Overhearing their conversation, Emily said, "It's a gorgeous night outside. Enjoy yourselves."

"Thanks," said Michael and Violette together.

"You look beautiful tonight," said Michael, steering Violette over to a heart-shaped wooden love seat, near the pool.

"Thanks," said Violette, sitting down.

As Michael sat next to Violette he pulled a box out of his jacket pocket and opened it.

"I was in the city today, and we were passing this jewellery store, when I saw this and thought of you," said Michael.

"Oh, wow. It's amazing," said Violette, when she saw the silver bracelet with a multi-coloured butterfly hanging from it. "Thank you so much, Michael."

Placing the bracelet on her wrist, he said, "You are welcome, Violette."

Violette couldn't believe how lucky she felt to receive such a lovely bracelet. Moving her wrist left and right, she watched how it sparkled in the moon-light and moved up and down her forearm.

"Thank you, Michael. I love it," said Violette, snuggling into his shoulder.

With his arm around Violette's shoulder, Michael watched Emily and Adrian walking towards them.

"Do you both have a minute? We would like to talk with you," said Adrian, as he and Emily sat across from them.

"Sure. What's up?" said Violette, sitting up straight.

"You know… we can see that you both love each other and want to spend time with each other, but we are not sure about the moving in thing yet. Both Adrian and I are a bit worried about your studies Violette, and Michael, we really don't know you that well, yet," said Emily, with her brow furrowed, as she looked from Violette to Michael.

"What would you like to know about me?" said Michael.

"How would you provide for Violette if she lived with you? What intentions do you have? These are the sort of things we would like to know, Michael," said Adrian, knowing Violette would be safe and welcomed at the Gramaze residence, especially now her transformation from human to vampire was complete. But he wanted to hear it from Michael's mouth, how he intended to look after Violette and her future.

Hmm, that's heavy. Here goes, thought Michael.

"Well… as you know, I am working for William at the moment, at his security business. This is how I would support Violette, if we were to live together. But more importantly, I too, want Violette to finish her studies. That way she can follow her dreams of becoming a teacher and I do want to support that. Like you both, I only want what's best for Violette. I love her, very much… I don't know what else to say, besides that, if you give us a chance to live together, I will not let you down," said Michael, as he looked from Adrian to Emily and watched their reaction to his answer.

"Well… you certainly have thought about this a lot, haven't you, Michael? We do appreciate you being honest about your feelings," said Adrian, feeling a little more at ease, knowing Michael had good intentions towards Violette. He only wanted what was best for his family.

"Can I make a suggestion?" said Michael.

"I am all ears… what are you thinking?" said Adrian.

"What about if Violette initially comes to live with me for one month, as a trial?" said Michael.

Emily and Adrian looked at each other and paused.

"Hmm… I don't know if that is a good idea," said Adrian.

"Please… just give it a try," pleaded Violette.

"It's not totally a bad idea," said Emily, looking at Adrian.

"Well…," said Adrian pausing. "I suppose we could try it for one month. It's not as though we won't see you either, Violette, as you will only be living a few houses away."

"Yeah, and we can speak with William and Renee today and see if it's OK for Violette to move in Saturday, on a trial basis," said Emily.

"At least, this way, if it doesn't work out, then Violette can shift back here," said Michael.

"Sounds like a good plan to me," said Violette.

"Thank you, Emily and Adrian. You won't regret your decision," said Michael, standing and walking over to shake Adrian's hand.

"Emily and I will go and give William and Renee a call now to let them know what we have discussed tonight," said Adrian, standing and shaking Michael's hand firmly.

"I can't believe they just agreed to that, Michael," said Violette standing, and walking over to Michael.

"Neither can I. But I can't wait to get you to my house where I can have my way with you anytime of the day or night," said Michael, with a smirk on his face, as he pulled her in closer.

"So you think you are going to have your way with me, hey? Shame on you, Michael Gramaze," said Violette, slapping him gently on the arm.

Michael laughed and pulled Violette in even closer for a passionate kiss.

Slowly pulling away from their embrace, Michael breathed in her alluring frangipani scent. She was intoxicating to his heightened sensors.

"I suppose I had better look like I am going home now. But as per usual, I will be climbing in your window for the night and guarding you."

"Right… is that what you call it?" said Violette, with raised eyebrows.

Michael smiled and they walked inside arm in arm together.

Standing in the doorway of the sitting room, where Emily and Adrian were seated, Michael said, "Good night, Emily and Adrian."

"Good night, Michael," chimed Emily and Adrian together.

"Thank you for being so understanding about Violette moving in. See you tomorrow," said Michael.

"You are welcome. Just don't let us down," said Adrian seriously.

"I don't intend to," said Michael.

Giving Michael a kiss good night at the front doors, Violette whispered, "See you soon, gorgeous."

After Michael left, Violette decided she would speak with Emily and Adrian and reassure them that they had made the right decision.

Sitting down across from them on the sofa, Violette said, "Thanks, Emily and Adrian, for agreeing to me moving into the Gramaze house. I really do appreciate how much you care for me and only want what's best for me. Don't worry, I won't let you down."

"You're welcome. As long as you realise this is only a trial, Violette. If this doesn't work out, then we will expect you to return home again. Are we clear?" said Adrian, with his brow furrowed.

"Yes sir. I do understand," said Violette, fidgeting with her hands.

"Who would have believed that you are nearly seventeen years old? You certainly have grown into a level-headed young lady, who knows what she wants," said Adrian, standing.

Violette stood up too, and gave Adrian a warm hug.

"Yes, we sure will miss your bubbly presence in the house. Just remember that we are always here for you," said Emily standing.

"I sure will miss you both, too," said Violette hugging Emily. "Well… I am feeling a bit tired. So I might go off to bed now. See you in the morning."

"Good night," said Emily and Adrian together.

Running up the marble stairs, with a smile from ear to ear, Violette couldn't contain her excitement. She was looking forward to living with the Gramaze family coven, where she felt she belonged, and wanted to learn about the Lepidoptera traditions. Even more than that, she was eager to spend a life time with Michael, her partner.

As Violette put on her pyjamas, she heard Michael's thoughts. *I'm here.* Pulling back the curtains, her face lit up and her pulse quickened, when she saw him through the French windows. Opening them inwards, Michael stepped into her bedroom. Smiling, he placed his arms around Violette's waist, and pulled her in closer.

With her heart racing, she took a deep breath and steadied herself. His scent was intoxicating, and she was yet to figure out what his alluring perfume was, which smelled like sweet tropical fruit.

Michael leant in and kissed her forehead first, then her eyelids, and eventually her warm lips. As his tongue entered her mouth, she melted in his arms and felt the world slip out of her thoughts, if only for a minute.

Eventually pulling away from her embrace, to catch a breath, Michael said, "So… how are you feeling? Do you need any blood or are you OK?"

"You know I haven't even thought about it today," said Violette, looking into his eyes. But I do feel like I need a top up."

"Would you like to drink from me tonight or did you want me to go home and get you some blood and bring it back?" asked Michael.

"Will you be all right if I take some of your blood?" said Violette, remembering what happened last time she drank from him.

Michael paused for a brief moment to think about it, and then shifted his head to one side. As Violette stepped towards him, Michael stood rigid, with his nostrils flaring, because he felt the presence of another vampire.

"What is it?" queried Violette.

Putting his finger to his mouth, Michael said, "Shh."

Walking over to the window, his suspicions were confirmed.

"Hey… down here," said Grayson, trying to get their attention.

"What are you doing here?" said Michael.

They then read Grayson's thoughts. *I have blood for Violette.*

"That's what ya call great service… thank you Grayson. You didn't have to come all that way for me," said Violette.

"No problem, Violette; anything for family," said Grayson, jumping up onto the balcony and handing her the bag of blood. "I believe you are going to be staying with us for one month. Well, isn't that going to be interesting?"

"You are shameful, Grayson. You really do need to get yourself some action," said Violette, bumping him on the shoulder.

He smiled and said, "Well, I had better get out of here and get back out on patrol. See ya later on Michael. See ya Violette."

"Bye," said Violette.

Michael nodded once and watched Grayson jump down from the balcony and run off.

Sitting on her bed, Violette opened the container and drank the blood. Within minutes, she felt her body relax again.

"Do you feel better now? asked Michael, as he closed the window and sat next her.

"Yes. Much better," said Violette. Cuddling into Michael's muscular body, she felt a warmth emanate over her and the need for sleep. Pulling back the covers, Violette climbed into bed and yawned.

"Good night, my sweet man. Thank you for the bracelet."

"Good night, my sweet princess. See you tomorrow morning," said Michael, as he cuddled in next to her.

Chapter Five

Between going to school, homework, and of course her life partner, Michael, the week had slipped by fast and before she knew it, it was Saturday. The day to move into the Gramaze house.

Violette had never lived apart from Danielle before, and she was going to miss her sister. They had already been through so much together, since the death of their parents, but they always knew that they had each other to rely on. But things had changed since she'd met Michael and become a Lepidoptera, and Violette was concerned that their closeness as siblings would be lost.

Pulling up to the Gramaze house with Violette's belongings that Emily, Adrian and Danielle had helped her pack up, Adrian said, "The welcoming committee."

He indicated to everyone that was waiting outside the front door to welcome Violette to her new home and help take in the boxes.

Craning her neck towards the front windscreen of the limousine, Violette's eyes lit up and she whimsically smiled, as she heard the many voices in her head welcoming her.

Welcome, Princess.

Thank you, thought Violette.

Once they were inside the Gramaze house, Annabelle thought to Violette, *We have cleared a space in Michael's wardrobe and his bathroom for your clothes and toiletries.*

Thanks, Annabelle, thought Violette, as she nodded once to Annabelle.

"Would you like to stay for a coffee, Emily and Adrian?" asked Renee, as she closed the front door.

"That would be lovely. Thanks, Renee," said Emily.

"Let's go into the sun room," said Renee, indicating the way.

"I will show Violette upstairs, so she can put her stuff away," said Annabelle.

"OK dear," said Renee.

"Come on, sis, you can come too," said Violette to Danielle, as she took her by the hand and pulled her towards the staircase.

Taking a seat in the sun room at a timber stained outdoor setting, Adrian said, "William and Renee, we wanted to thank you for taking Violette into your lovely home. We have already spoken with you about the money that we will send you each week whilst she is living here, but if you need any more please don't hesitate to ask. Or even if this arrangement doesn't work out, please just let us know and we will come and collect her."

"Thank you Adrian, but I am sure that this living arrangement will work out. You have our word; if it doesn't, then we will contact you. Don't worry, she will be in safe hands here, and Violette will be treated like our own daughter," said William.

"Thank you William; that is comforting to know," said Emily.

"We will also give you regular updates on how Violette is going with her studies," said Renee.

"That is one thing we are worried about. We don't want Violette falling behind in her studies either. So if you can let us know how she is going weekly, that would be most appreciated," said Adrian.

"Of course, my friend," said William. "By the way, I would like you to put up some wards around our house before you go today."

"Yes… I was going to ask you if you needed an incantation or ward done," said Adrian.

"Maybe we can go and organise that now, whilst the ladies have a chat," said William, standing.

"Sure," said Adrian.

With the wards now in place, Emily and Adrian were ready to go home. As they stood at the front door saying their goodbyes, Emily said to Violette, "Don't be a stranger. Remember to come and visit sometimes, or even just to ring. We will miss you terribly." Emily and Adrian then hugged her.

"I will miss you both too, and don't worry, I will keep in contact," said Violette, with a creased brow and sorrow in her heart. Ever since the day she had met Emily and Adrian, in the foster home, Violette had always felt loved and cared for by them.

She then turned to Danielle.

"I sure will miss you, sis. But I will see you at school anyway, and I can come and visit sometimes as well," said Danielle, placing her arms around Violette for a warm hug.

"You can't get rid of me that easy, sis," teased Violette, as she hugged Danielle and the tears welled in her eyes. Releasing Danielle, she turned to Emily and Adrian and said, "I really am going to miss you all. But don't worry, we are only a few houses away, and I won't forget to visit sometimes. I love you all very much."

Am I doing the right thing by leaving them and moving into the Gramaze house? thought Violette, as she stood on the front door step and watched them drive away.

Renee heard Violette's thoughts. "Don't worry, dear girl. You will be OK here, and we do love you like our own."

"Thanks, Renee," said Violette. But she was still torn between the two families.

"Michael, why don't you take Violette up to your room and help her get settled in?" said Renee.

"OK, Renee. Come on," said Michael, taking Violette by the hand.

Walking into Michael's room, Violette said, "Has William said who will be guarding me tomorrow night when we go out for my birthday dinner at the Eiffel Tower?"

"Why? Are you worried," asked Michael, walking behind her.

"No," said Violette turning around.

"As William, Renee and myself will be at the restaurant with you, we are sure you will have enough protection. Plus Adrian is going to put a ward up around us all. So we should be safe. You don't need to worry Violette, your safety is our number one priority. Should be a good night. Are you looking forward to going?" said Michael.

"I sure am. I have been looking at the menu on line, and I think I already know what I might have," said Violette excited.

"Yeah, I believe the food is meant to be really good," said Michael.

"Michael, would you mind if I have a lie down for a while? I am feeling a bit tired," said Violette.

"You OK?" asked Michael.

"Yeah…" said Violette.

Truthfully, Violette was exhausted. She hadn't slept well the previous night. Her mind kept going over and over all of the events in her life since her parents had passed away. And becoming a Lepidoptera had weighted heavily on her mind.

"Sure… make yourself at home," said Michael, gesturing to the bed.

"Thank you."

At about 1.30pm Violette was awakened by Michael kissing her on her forehead. "Lunch is ready sleepyhead… how are you feeling?" said Michael, looking into her eyes.

Pulling herself up into a sitting position, she said, "My heart is sad for leaving Emily, Adrian and Danielle, but I know it's for the best if I stay here. I just miss them. I will need to make some adjustments, that's all."

Michael put his arm around Violette and kissed her temple.

"Don't worry, everything will be all right. We can go visit whenever you feel like it."

Snuggling into Michael's chest, she said, "Yeah, I know. Thank you for being so supportive, Michael."

"How about we go and get some lunch? Are you hungry?" said Michael.

"A little bit," said Violette.

As they walked towards the dining room for lunch, Violette noticed everyone had gathered at the entrance and a banner that said 'Welcome Home Violette'. Her heart melted and tears of joy streamed out of her eyes. She was so overwhelmed.

"Thank you everyone for making me feel at home. I love you all very much," said Violette, looking around the room.

One by one they all came over and gave her a warm, welcoming hug.

As she sat through lunch, Violette looked around the table at each of the faces in her newly found family, and realised that she had done the right thing moving into the Gramaze house. Each one of them made her feel welcome, and in the past, had either rescued or helped her through one situation or another. There was no doubt in her mind that this was the kind of family she had been missing since her parents died. They all seemed to love her very much and treated her like their own.

Deep in thought about her new family, Violette soon realised William had sat next to her, when he placed his hand on hers. Looking upon his face, she wondered what he had come to speak with her about.

"Violette, we were wondering if you would like to start learning how to use your abilities tomorrow?" said William, looking into her eyes.

"I am a bit nervous, but yes, I would like to learn," said Violette, taking her hand from under his.

Putting his hand on her shoulder, he said, "No need to be nervous, my dear. We are all here to help you."

She smiled and gave William a warm hug. "Thank you William. You are so kind to me."

Violette could feel that William was a bit taken aback by her hug, as he pulled away quickly. *Maybe it's not a done thing hugging the leader of the Lepidoptera vampires,* she thought to herself.

"We are all here to help you adjust Violette, so please don't hesitate to ask for help when you need it," said William, standing and returned to his seat at the head of the table, next to Renee.

Smiling, Violette nodded once.

"I don't have to go out on patrol tonight until about ten o'clock, so what would you like to do, Violette?" said Michael, placing his arm around her shoulder.

"Umm… not sure. Why?" said Violette. Her mind was still on the conversation she'd just had with William.

"I was thinking we could watch a movie together or something," said Michael.

"Sounds good," said Violette, snuggling into his shoulder.

"What are your plans for this afternoon?" asked Michael.

"Actually, I was going to ask Annabelle if she could come shopping with me today after lunch, as I need some things," said Violette, sitting up.

"Ah, OK," said Michael.

"Sorry to eavesdrop Violette… that is a yes. I would love to go shopping with you. Where would you like to go?" said Annabelle.

"I need to get some personal things, and I want to buy some more clothes. But I am not sure yet on where the best places are for that, so I will let you choose," said Violette.

"OK. We can decide in the car anyway," said Annabelle.

"What are you going to do all day, Michael?" asked Violette.

"Well I could go and do some training, or I could guard you from a distance if you like," said Michael.

"To know you are guarding me from a distance would be great, Michael. You are just too good to me, and I don't know what I did to deserve a great guy like you," said Violette hugging him. She always felt safe when he was around.

"I only want what's best for you, and I would be honoured to guard you. My world would not be the same without you in it."

"We had better go now though, Vi, as I need to be out on patrol by seven o'clock tonight," said Annabelle. "As long as this is acceptable with you, William?"

"Yes. But keep a watch out for the Debauched," said William, wanting his lineage to continue.

"Yes sire," said Annabelle and Michael together.

"OK. Are you ready to go Michael?" said Violette.

"Give me five minutes and then I will be ready to guard you," said Michael.

"I need to get my bag from my room. I will meet you both out the front, in the limo," said Annabelle, standing.

Arriving at the shopping centre, Michael hopped out of the limousine and checked the parking lot was safe for Annabelle and Violette to go inside.

"So what did you need to buy, Violette?" said Annabelle, as the car pulled up outside the side door entrance of the shopping centre.

"Well... I need to buy some tampons, deodorant, shampoo, that type of thing," said Violette.

"OK. We can go into the Centro shop over there to get those type of personal items," said Annabelle, pointing to a doorway on the side of the building.

"Hey Annabelle... before we go inside, I wanted to ask you if you could help me with something," said Violette.

She looked at Violette perplexed, then smiled, as she already knew what Violette was going to ask her.

"Yeah, it's just that I don't want everyone listening to my thoughts, and I would like to select the times when I want people to hear what I am thinking, because sometimes, well... it's private," said Violette.

"You don't have to explain to me, Vi. I am only too happy to help you with that. But we are better off doing this at home, as it takes a lot of practice at first," said Annabelle.

"OK. Thanks, Annabelle," said Violette.

The chauffeur opened the door to their car and extended his hand to help them out from the car. Out the corner of her eye, Violette saw Michael leaning on a wall next to the entry. As they approached him, he entered the shopping centre, but kept his distance.

"Now we have your personal items, where to next?" said Annabelle, following Violette out of the supermarket.

"I wanted to buy some nice lingerie for Michael. Also I need some new knickers and bras."

"Oh, right. Well… there is a great shop over there that sells bras and things and they will have what you are looking for, Vi," said Annabelle, pointing to the doorway, across the mall.

As Annabelle and Violette walked into the shop, Violette spotted Michael out the corner of her eye. Winking at her, he mouthed the words, "Thank you."

Rolling her eyes, and sighing in annoyance, Violette looked over at Annabelle. *See what I mean? I can't keep anything a secret.*

Annabelle then thought to Michael, *Go away… this is meant to be a surprise and you are spoiling it.*

Whoops… sorry, thought Michael.

"Men," said Annabelle to Violette, rolling her eyes.

Violette snickered and said, "That's just one of many reasons why I need your help with blocking anyone from hearing my thoughts."

"We can work on that when we get home," said Annabelle.

After trying on a few items she had chosen from the racks, Violette called out over the change room door to Annabelle, "Would you like to go and get a coffee after we finish here?"

"I would love to Violette, but we had better not push the boundaries," said Annabelle.

"What?" said Violette confused by her answer.

"The shopping centre is crawling with vamps and Michael is telling me it's time to go. Rain check though for another day," said Annabelle, opening the door to her change room. "You nearly finished?"

"Almost," said Violette, hurriedly putting her shoes back on and gathering her handbag. Unlocking the door to her change room, Violette quickly followed Annabelle to the counter to pay for the items she wished to purchase. With the sound of her heart beating fast in her ears, Violette glanced around the shop quickly for any sign of the Debauched.

Placing her hand on Violette's arm, Annabelle said in a low voice, "It's all right Violette. You are safe with Michael and me."

Composing herself, Violette felt the injection of calm enveloping her mind and body from Annabelle's touch.

"Thanks, Annabelle."

Stepping into the waiting limousine, Violette took her seat next to the window and scanned for Debauched. Turning to Annabelle, she said, "You will have to show me how you knew that there was vamps here. I didn't even detect them."

"You have plenty to learn Vi, but all in good time," said Annabelle.

Closing the door and seating himself across from Annabelle and Violette, Michael's nostrils were flared and his eyes were dilated, as he breathed a sigh of relief. He was relieved to finally have Violette in a safe environment and on their way home. "Let's go, driver," said Michael, looking into the rear vision mirror at the driver.

"Yes, sire," said the driver, as he pulled away from the shopping centre.

"You ladies like to play it a bit too close to the line," said Michael, looking from Annabelle to Violette, with his brow furrowed. "Annabelle, you should have known better than to keep shopping whilst those fuckers were hanging around. You know what they will do to Violette if they get their hands on her; let alone yourself."

"Sorry, Michael. I wasn't thinking. It won't happen again, I can promise you," said Annabelle, feeling guilty for enjoying herself.

Stony faced, Michael looked Annabelle in the eyes. He was furious with Annabelle for placing their princess in danger. *Where the fuck do you get off putting Violette in harm's way? You know how valuable she is to our coven; let alone to me*, thought Michael to Annabelle.

Annabelle looked down at her lap and sighed. She knew he was right. Instead of protecting Violette, she had, for once, let herself be distracted by the one thing she loved to do. Shopping.

The car seemed to be silent as they pulled away from the curb, and when Violette looked from Michael to Annabelle, she realised that Michael was mind talking to Annabelle, instead of talking out loud. Frustrated, she watched his mouth twitch, and his eyes narrow. To her it seemed like he was chastising Annabelle.

Violette put her hand on Michael's knee and said, "Stop that. Don't chastise her. I am as much to blame as Annabelle. Talk out loud please, as I want to hear what you are saying."

"She put your life in danger, Violette," said Michael, pulling away from her hand. "There is no excuse."

"But…"

"There are no buts, Violette," barked Michael, with his arms crossed over his broad chest.

Violette then knew not to take the conversation any further.

The drive home was silent, but Violette suspected that Michael was still chastising Annabelle, even though she had asked him not too.

Stepping out the car in front of the Gramaze house, with her bags from shopping, Violette said to Annabelle, "Sorry to get you into so much trouble. Can we meet up later on to go over the mind talking thing?"

Annabelle gave Violette a hug and said, "It's OK, Vi. Michael was right. I needed to protect you instead of enjoying myself. And yes, give me about one hour and then come to my room and we can start some training on the mind talking."

"Thanks Annabelle," said Violette, releasing Annabelle and walking towards the front door.

Walking into Michael's room, Violette placed her bags down on the bed and said to Michael, "I know I have a lot to learn, Michael, but that was really uncalled for, chastising Annabelle like that. She didn't deserve to be dressed down."

Sighing, Michael tried to compose himself before he spoke. *Women can certainly be infuriating. Calm yourself, Michael. You don't want to show Violette a side of yourself she will find hard to accept.*

"Violette, you need to sit down, so that I can try and explain to you how valuable you are to the Debauched vamps. Then when you understand it, you will know why I chastised Annabelle."

"Michael, I already know about the Debauched vamps, as William has told me. But that doesn't give you the right to talk to Annabelle the way you did," snapped Violette, with her brow furrowed.

Even though you are an infuriating princess, and my life partner, you really can get fiery when you're passionate about something, thought Michael to himself. But he wasn't about to back down either, and no way in hell was he going to apologise for keeping her safe.

"You will learn to do as you are told, Violette. This is not something that is up for discussion. We are just going to have to disagree on this one," said Michael, in a heated voice, with his arms crossed over his chest.

"Don't tell me what to do, Michael," barked Violette. Turning her back on him, Violette stomped over to the closet to put her new items she had bought away. "I don't want to talk about this anymore." She was seeing a side of Michael that she didn't like and thought he was over reacting to the situation.

"Fine…," said Michael, throwing his hands in the air and walking towards the doorway. "I'll come back when you are ready to talk."

Michael left the room feeling annoyed, as he knew from experience what would happen if the Debauched vamps got hold of Violette or Annabelle. He couldn't fathom why Violette wasn't listening to him and needed to cool off before he said something he would regret, so he decided to go for a walk.

Violette sat on the edge of bed and ran through the whole conversation with Michael and what had happened at the shopping mall. As realisation hit her as to why Michael was acting the way he was, she started to feel ashamed for the way she had treated him. With tears welling in her eyes and then forming droplets on her cheeks, she laid face down on the bed thinking about what she was going to do. She was not one for confrontation. It made her feel anxious and uncomfortable.

"Knock, knock," said Annabelle, tapping on the open door as she entered the room. She could see Violette sobbing into her pillow. "Please don't cry Violette, and please don't fight with Michael either. He had every right to be furious with me. He really loves you Vi, and this is why he is so angry. He couldn't stand for anything to happen to you." Annabelle sat on the edge of the bed, next to Violette.

"But I had you with me Annabelle and Michael was there as well. So I had plenty of protection," said Violette, sitting up.

"That's just it Vi, you didn't have enough protection. There were at least twenty vamps at the shopping centre and we could never have handled that many without one of us getting hurt or worse yet, kidnapped," said Annabelle.

"Why were there so many vamps at the shopping centre?" asked Violette.

"I would say that the Debauched bastards could sense that you have just turned into a Lepidoptera. Then once a few of them sensed you, they called their buddies," said Annabelle matter-of-factly.

"Hmm… now I understand why Michael was so angry. But why didn't he just tell me all this? Instead I had to hear it from you Annabelle," said Violette, as she choked back a sob.

"Men are not good at communicating, Vi. You will learn this the more you hang around the male Lepidoptera," said Annabelle, jokingly.

"I guess I am not experienced enough with men yet, so I have a bit to learn. Would you mind if I could take a rain-check on the mind talking thing, Annabelle? I want to go find Michael," said Violette.

"Sure kiddo. I have to go out on patrol soon anyway. I can help you with it tomorrow, if you like," said Annabelle.

"Thanks. That would be great Annabelle, and by the way, thank you for coming shopping with me today," said Violette, hugging Annabelle.

"No problem. Anytime. Well, see you later on then," said Annabelle, walking toward the door.

As Annabelle was leaving the bedroom, she bumped into Michael in the doorway and they exchanged a quick glance at each other. "Sorry Michael," said Annabelle, as she kept walking.

"Humph," said Michael, entering the bedroom, and spotting Violette on the bed.

"Violette… can we have a chat?" said Michael, walking over to the bed.

As he sat next to Violette, she put her arms around Michael and said, "Sorry, Michael."

"I'm sorry too. I don't like it when we argue," said Michael, placing his arms around her shoulders and listening to her thoughts. "You and I are so alike, you know. We are both hot headed and won't back down when it comes to fighting about something we are passionate about." Pulling away from their embrace, he looked into her soulful eyes and gently caressed her cheek. "I do love you for just being you, so don't ever change. But you do need to understand the importance of the situation you and Annabelle put me in today. You were in danger and both could have been killed."

"You have my word that this won't happen again, Michael. The sooner I learn how to detect the Debauched vamps when they are close, the better," said Violette, with a creased brow.

"Yes, that would have helped… so … what would you like to do for the rest of the day?" asked Michael.

"Well… I was going to have a shower," said Violette.

"Why don't we go down to the combat room and do some training?" said Michael.

"Sure. Sound like a good idea," said Violette. "Wait... what is that I just heard?"

Twisting his head sideways, Michael listened. "It seems we are needed by William. Let's go," said Michael, getting up off the bed and holding his hand out to Violette.

Entering the operations room, Violette and Michael were the last ones to take their seats around the long wooden conference table. William stood at the foot of the table looking anxious, until everyone quietened down.

"Right... we have just had word that Nicholas has a large shipment of cocaine being delivered to his night club, later tonight. Grayson, Michael, Taiven and James, you will come with me tonight and we will put a stop to these fuckers. Once and for all. Everyone else, I want you on standby," said William authoritatively.

They all nodded in agreeance, as William laid a plan of the night club out on the table, and went through his plan of attack with the four Lepidoptera he was taking on the mission.

Standing at the back of the room, Violette watched in anticipation, and wondered when her first real mission would be. Or whether she would never be able to go on a mission, considering her status of princess. She knew that she still had a lot to learn, but was eager to help out her new family.

Reading her mind, Michael looked over his shoulder to where Violette was standing. Smiling at her because he didn't know what else to do, he knew one day soon, he would have to explain to her that she would never be able to go out on a mission, because she was too valuable to their kind.

Looking up from the plans, William said, "I want the rest of you to make sure our weapons are ready for tonight's raid. Annabelle, you should be able to explain to Violette on what to do. So I will leave that in your capable hands."

"Yes, sire," said Annabelle, nodding in William's direction. Taking Violette's hand, she led her out of the operations room.

See you later on, babe, thought Michael to Violette.

Bye, thought Violette.

"That was really intense in there," said Violette, walking down the stairs with Annabelle.

"Yeah. I wish I was going on this mission tonight. I hate those Debauched vamps. Bloody fuckers need to be exterminated from this world," said Annabelle, with clenched fists.

"I wish I could go on the mission too. Not sure when I will be ready for combat, but I hope one day soon," said Violette, looking to Annabelle for reassurance.

"Mmm." Annabelle didn't acknowledge what Violette had just said. She knew it wasn't her place to tell Violette that she would never be able to go on any mission. So she just changed the subject as they entered the weapons room. "Come on, let's get these blades sharpened and then I will show you how to clean up the other equipment."

Taking a machete from the wall, Annabelle showed Violette how to sharpen the blade with a thick steel file.

Dirty and worn-out from all the work they had had to do in the weapons room, both Annabelle and Violette went up to their rooms for showers, before dinner was served.

Standing with her hands on the tiles and her head under the shower, soaking up the hot water on her aching body, Violette felt like she needed some blood. Whilst she hadn't been a vampire long, she did have ravenous feelings more often than most.

Hearing the door click open, she turned around to see Michael standing in the doorway. "Can I come in?" said Michael.

"Sure," said Violette, pulling him into the shower with vampire speed. "Can I drink from you, Michael?"

"Yes. Take what you need, my love," said Michael, feeling her need for blood and pulling her in close.

Biting into his neck, she sucked a little bit of blood from Michael. Coming up for breath, she looked into his eyes, licked her lips and said, "Mmm… you taste really good."

"Take some more if you need it, Vi," said Michael, wanting to please her.

"Are you sure?" asked Violette.

He nodded his head quickly.

Taking another bite, but this time from his forearm, Violette sucked the blood from his body with speed. She growled as she took gulps of his blood and let it run through her body. Pushing him against the tiles with vigor, she sucked harder.

"Violette… stop… you need to stop," said Michael, pushing her away with force, when he realized she was in need of more than he could give her.

With fangs extended and blood dripping from them, she panted heavily. She realised, after a few seconds, what had just happened, and looked at Michael's face and saw the hurt in his eyes. "Oh god… sorry, Michael. I couldn't help myself," said Violette, placing her hand over her mouth, and feeling ashamed for what had taken place.

Pulling her chin up, he said, "How long since you have had blood?"

"I... I don't know... I haven't been keeping a count on when and how much I have been drinking," said Violette.

"You could have killed me, Violette. You are lucky it was me you took a drink of," said Michael irritated.

"I am so sorry Michael. Forgive me... please," said Violette, placing her arms around his waist and cuddling into his chest.

Putting his arms around her body, he said, "So that this doesn't happen again, I will monitor you more closely now. I wasn't aware you hadn't had a drink for a while. You really need to get a handle on this, Violette."

"Yes Michael. I know," said Violette. She knew he was right, but at the same time, she didn't want him telling her what to do and when to do it. He was meant to be her boyfriend, not a father figure.

"Come on let's get washed up, because dinner is being served down stairs in the dining room," said Michael matter-of-factly.

Violette could hear in his tone of voice that he was not happy with her. Nodding, she said, "OK."

Violette sat next to Annabelle at the long dining room wooden table. "How are you going?" asked Annabelle. She knew from reading Violette's thoughts upstairs what had happened.

"I'm OK. But I am not sure about Michael. He seems mad with me," said Violette.

"He was right you know," said Annabelle.

"Yeah, I know," stated Violette angrily.

Placing her hand over Violette's, Annabelle leaned in said, "Sorry... but you need to be aware that you could have easily killed him. Being that you are a female multi-coloured Lepidoptera, Michael has to give you blood when you need it. He doesn't have a choice either. If you ask for it, he has to give it to you. No matter if you are his life partner or not."

Looking astonished and feeling guilty, Violette finally understood what all the fuss was about. "Oh god… really…"

Nodding, Annabelle put her arm around Violette and said, "Yes, really. So keep an eye on it, OK? I am here for you always if you need help figuring out when to drink. So please don't hesitate to ask me."

"Thank you, Annabelle. You are kinder than I deserve," said Violette.

"You're welcome," said Annabelle smiling.

"What are you two chatting about?" asked Michael, as he looked from Violette to Annabelle.

"Women's business. How are you feeling?" asked Annabelle.

"I will be OK. After dinner, I will have a drink of blood. I should be all ready to go then for the mission tonight," said Michael, with his head held high.

"That's good," said Annabelle.

On the drive to the night club, William gave instructions on the plan of attack. Pulling the SUV over to a side street, two blocks from the night club, so that the Debauched vamps wouldn't sense them, William and Grayson jumped out the van and took to the roof tops, whilst Michael, Taiven and James walked the pathway. As they neared the night club alleyway, they spotted a dumpster which they could crouch behind. Located across from the night club side entrance, Michael, Taiven and James waited patiently for any sign of the delivery.

Within minutes of their arrival, a white truck pulled up, and parked down the alleyway, next to the club. Watching the driver in the truck side mirror, Michael saw him make a phone call. When the side door of the club flew open, the driver of the truck got out his vehicle and unlocked the back roller door. Inside the vehicle were pallets of cardboard boxes stacked to the ceiling. One by one the cartons were carried into the night club by five Debauched vamps, as the driver stood guard over his shipment.

Noticing that there was no sign of their leader, Nicholas, William wondered how far away he was, especially as this shipment would be worth millions of dollars. Once the cartons were unloaded and the driver had driven away, William gave the signal to his family to enter the club.

Walking into the club side by side, with their hands on their weapons and ready for engagement, William watched the manager, Rose, stride toward them.

"Good evening gentleman. What can we get you tonight?"

Pushing straight past her without saying a word, William, Grayson and Taiven started to search the club, whilst Michael and James stood guard at the entrance.

"You can't go in there," said Rose anxiously. But when they didn't listen, she ran over to the bar and took out her mobile phone from the drawer. Before she could even dial a number, Michael appeared out of nowhere, and smashed the phone out of her hands, causing it to break into pieces when it hit the ground.

"No you don't. Go and sit over there so we can keep an eye on you," said Michael, pointing to a booth in sight.

"You'll be sorry when Nicholas finds out about this. See how smug you are then," said Rose, sitting down with her arms crossed over her chest.

"Shut your mouth woman, or I will shut it for you," said Michael, not amused by her arrogance.

Returning to the bar, William said to Michael, "We haven't found anything yet. The drugs have to be here, because we saw them brought in." Approaching Rose, William picked her up out of her seat, by her hair and asked, "Where are the drugs, woman?"

"I don't know what you are talking about!" screamed Rose, trying to pull her hair free from his grasp.

"You know all too well where they are. Speak, woman," said William holding his sharp machete to her throat.

"Let her go, Gramaze," said a Debauched vamp, holding his stance near the bar.

"Tell me where you stored the drugs, and I might let her live," said William.

"We don't have or sell drugs here. Now let her go," said the Debauched vamp, trying to sound authoritative.

Before he could say another word, Grayson came up from behind him and cut his head off. The Debauched vamp disintegrated.

Rose screamed in fear for her life.

"You will pay for this."

"You had better tell us where the drugs are, or you will be next," said William, pressing the blade further into her neck until it bled.

"All right... all right... they are upstairs," said Rose.

"You had better be telling us the truth, woman," said William, taking the blade away from her neck and letting her fall back down to her seat.

"I am telling you the truth. The elevator is in the corridor to your right," said Rose, with tears streaming down her face and holding a hand over her neck wound.

With vampire speed, William, Grayson and Taiven took the elevator to the next floor. Not knowing what to expect when the doors opened, they prepared their weapons for battle.

They knew that at least four Debauched vamps were in the club still, but they hadn't seen them yet.

With weapons drawn as the doors opened, Grayson and Taiven ran out into the room, but to their surprise, not a vamp or soul were in sight. Stepping out the elevator, William signaled to Grayson and Taiven to listen. Hearing some voices coming from another room straight ahead, they quietly walked over to two semi-closed, wooden double doors and looked through the cracks.

There inside the room, was a long black table, with large bags of cocaine sitting on top. The cardboard boxes they had seen taken out the truck, were now empty on the tiled floor. Assessing the situation, William detected that there were eight Debauched vamps sorting the cocaine into smaller plastic bags and getting them ready for distribution.

Giving the signal to attack, William rushed into the room with his men, and cut the head off two Debauched before they could get hold of any weapons. But the other six were fast and before they knew it, William, Grayson and Taiven were backed into a corner and fighting for their lives. Outnumbered, and wondering how they were going to fight their way out, William saw Michael and James enter the room. With swift precision, the Gramaze family slaughtered the six remaining vamps. The battle was finally over. They could breathe easy now.

While taking a good look at the cocaine, William heard a sound coming from a closet door. Opening the door quickly, with his machete in his hand, ready to strike, he found Nicholas with one of his soldiers, hiding.

"Get out, you fuckers… now…" said William, pointing his machete toward them.

Stepping out the closet, Nicholas said smugly, "Well, well. We meet again, William."

"Hmm… you call yourself a leader? Well I suppose hiding in cupboards is one of your cowardly traits then," said William.

But before Nicholas could answer, William beheaded him, then his soldier. As he watched their bodies disintegrate, William felt powerful, knowing he had just killed not only the leader of the Debauched, but also the asshole that nearly took away his empire and vampire powers. Finally, his revenge was accomplished.

"What would you like to do with all this cocaine?" said Grayson to William.

"Call the police. They can sort it out. Let's get the fuck out of here though, before they arrive," said William, sliding his machete back into its sleeve on his belt.

Chapter Six

Grayson walked up the stairs to Samantha's apartment, wondering how she was feeling that morning. As he knocked on the door, thoughts flooded back to him of the night they had met, and how he was instantly attracted to her. Would she welcome him into her life, considering she now had had time to think about what she had been through and seen that night?

Looking through the peephole in her door, Samantha was surprised to see Grayson standing there. Smiling, her heart beat quickened as she opened the door.

"Hello Grayson."

"Hello. May I come in?" asked Grayson.

"Sure, come in," said Samantha, waving him in. "Umm, I was just making a coffee. Would you like one?"

"No thanks. I have had my quota this morning already. But thank you for the offer," said Grayson, entering her apartment.

"No problem... I must admit, I didn't think I would ever see you again, Grayson. I am so glad you came by," said Samantha, shutting the door.

"Why?" said Grayson, with a raised eyebrow.

"Well... first you had to rescue me, and then you had to take me to the hospital. And finally, you brought me home and

I fell asleep on you. Nice host I am," said Samantha, trying to gauge his reaction.

"You needed your rest last night, Samantha. Once I could see you were all right, I then went home myself. How is your neck today, anyway?" asked Grayson.

Lifting her hair and peeling back the bandage to show Grayson the wound, he could see it was healing nicely. But what took him by surprise was the butterfly tattoo was now starting to show its colour: orange.

"Well... it's a bit sore. How does it look to you?" said Samantha.

"It looks like it's healing really well," said Grayson, touching her neck to look at the wound.

His touch was mesmerising, and Samantha felt her heart skip a beat.

"I can't remember thanking you properly last night Grayson. So thank you very much for all you did for me," said Samantha, looking into his eyes, and then leaning in to kiss his cheek.

Grayson read Samantha's mind and knew she was attracted to him. So as she was about to kiss him on the cheek, he turned to face her, and their lips met briefly, for the first time.

Pulling away slowly to gather her thoughts, Samantha didn't know what to think. But she did enjoy their brief encounter.

Quickly placing his arms around her waist, Grayson pulled her in closer for a passionate kiss.

She didn't pull away this time. Instead, she melted in his arms.

"Mmm... that sure was nice," said Samantha, coming up for a breath. Looking into his mesmerising brown eyes, she couldn't restrain herself anymore, so she kissed him again.

Slowly Grayson drew away from her alluring lips.

"So… are you working tonight or do you have the night off?"

"I am only working from 1.30 until 5.30 today. So yes, I have the night free," said Samantha. "Why?"

"Would you like to maybe go out to dinner or movies or something with me tonight?" asked Grayson, noticing, for the first time, her deep blue eyes.

She stood there for a moment, thinking what to say. Samantha couldn't afford much, so dinner and movies were out of the question for her.

"I can make us dinner if you like, and maybe we can watch a DVD. How does that sound?" said Samantha.

"That sounds great. I look forward to it," said Grayson. He didn't care what they did. Just as long as he could spend some more time with Samantha, getting to know her.

"What type of food do you like Grayson?" asked Samantha.

"I eat most things. But I don't like eggplant, though," said Grayson.

"What to do you like to drink?"

"I like most drinks. My favourite at the moment is Corona. What about you. What do you like to drink?" said Grayson.

"I like most drinks, as well. At the moment my favourite is a White Russian," said Samantha.

"What about if I bring some drinks with me tonight?" said Grayson.

"Sound good. I'll make the dinner if you bring the drinks. Deal," said Samantha, smiling.

"You got a deal," said Grayson. "Well… I had better go and let you get ready for work."

"OK. So what time will you be coming by tonight?" said Samantha.

"How does 7.30 sound?" said Grayson.

"Yep. That sounds good," said Samantha. *At least I will have plenty of time to prepare the food.*

Opening the door to her apartment, Grayson turned and pulled her into his arms and kissed her passionately. *Beautiful... lavender, Oh baby, the way you make me feel.*

Coming up for air, she took a deep breath and gazed into his eyes, as she ran her hand down the side of his face.

"You had better go, before I change my mind. I could kiss those gorgeous lips of yours all morning," said Samantha, smirking.

Raising his eyebrows and grinning, he said, "See you tonight, then."

"You shall," said Samantha, gently pushing him backwards out the doorway.

Standing in the shadows across the road from Samantha's apartment, Grayson kept watch on the woman he hoped to spend the rest of his life with. From the time Samantha left her apartment for work, until she returned home again, it was his job to guard her and make sure that the Debauched vampires didn't kidnap the newest female Lepidoptera, who would hopefully one day make a great addition to the Gramaze family coven.

Hearing Samantha lock her apartment door and push the chain across, Grayson took his phone out of his jeans pocket and called Brock.

"Hey man... can you guard Samantha for a while?" asked Grayson, watching her silhouette move about, through the apartment window.

"Sure, bro. I'll be there in five," said Brock.

Within what seemed like seconds, he heard Brock's thoughts, as he came around the corner to greet Grayson.

"How goes it?" said Brock, placing his hand on Grayson's shoulder.

"All quiet here," said Grayson. "I shouldn't be too long, man. Just need to freshen up and then I will be back to relieve you."

"Take your time… by the way, William has instructed me to keep guard whilst you are having dinner with Samantha tonight," said Brock.

"Right… any reason?" asked Grayson.

"You have to ask…? Can't you smell her from here? If I can smell her scent, then the Debauched will too, bro," said Brock. "The sooner she is under our roof, the safer she will be. Don't you agree?"

"Her lavender scent is intoxicating, isn't it? I thought I was the only one who could smell it… she sure does take my breath away. But yes, you are right. She needs to be living with us, so we can keep her safe," said Grayson.

Samantha heard someone knocking at her front door. Checking the peephole, she saw Grayson standing on the other side. As she took one last glance at herself in the mirror, she took a deep breath to steady her nerves and opened the door.

"Hi…come in," gestured Samantha, smiling.

"Hello. These are for you, lovely lady," said Grayson, smiling as he handed her a bouquet of flowers.

Smelling them, she breathed in their beautiful perfume of sweet honey, jasmine and rose.

"Thank you. That's so thoughtful of you," said Samantha, as she kissed Grayson on the cheek.

Samantha's one bedroom rental apartment was quaint, but very small. The front door led straight into the lounge room. She had a faded, floral three seat couch, two plain single chairs, and light veneer coffee table, all over to the left-hand side of the room, near the window that faced the street. The kitchen was off to the right, and the only thing that separated the lounge room from the kitchen was the cream laminate kitchen bench, which had three chrome and black bar stools under it.

"So... what have you made for us? It smells divine!" said Grayson, walking in and sniffing the air.

"Thanks. I have made lasagna and a garden salad. And for dessert, apple pie and cream," said Samantha, delighted with her efforts.

"Mmm, you sure know the way to a man's heart and stomach," said Grayson, smiling.

Noticing he had a bottle of wine in his hand she said, "You can put the wine in the fridge, if you like."

Following her into the kitchen, he said, "Sorry... I didn't buy the ingredients for your favourite drink because I thought we could try this new wine everyone has been raving about. Apparently it's meant to be really nice... where do you keep your glasses?"

"That's OK, Grayson. It's always good to try something else, every once in a while. The glasses are in the cupboard above your head, to the right."

When he pulled open the wooden laminated cupboard door, Grayson noticed that she didn't have a big selection of glasses; in fact, her cupboards didn't have much of anything in them at all. Taking two odd glasses out, he poured them both a glass of white wine and put the half empty bottle in the fridge. Taking a seat at the kitchen bench, Grayson pondered on how quickly his life had changed, since meeting Samantha the day before. If anyone had told him that he would be having dinner with his life partner that night, he would never have believed them. He had always thought that he was destined to be alone and would eventually, one day, start a coven of his own.

Grayson was originally born in the early 1700s in Dubrovnik, Croatia, to a well-known fisherman's family, and was destined to follow in his father's footsteps. At the age of twenty-four, he was stuck down with smallpox. After many days of using a local medicine called peach blossom, to fight the disease, his family were told he was eventually going to die. Knowing his life was ending, Grayson took solace in his god. As he sat in his local church praying, Talitha, the Lepidoptera queen, heard his cry for life, and decided to turn him. Since that day he had always been indebted to her and had served and protected his queen.

Samantha opened a cupboard up, which was next to the sink, to get a vase out for the flowers. Arranging the flowers, she sniffed their perfume and then put them on the middle of the coffee table in the lounge room. "Penny for your thoughts," said Samantha, as she watched Grayson staring off into the distance.

"Hmm… sorry… what?" said Grayson, as he remembered where he was.

"Thank you for the wine," said Samantha, sitting next to Grayson at the bench. *Mmm, yum this is nice*, she thought.

"You are welcome. So… how was work?" asked Grayson.

"Busy… but at least I got home safe today. Just wish this cut would hurry up and heal. It's still a bit sore," said Samantha, placing her hand over the bandage. As the oven timer started to beep, she walked back into the kitchen to check the lasagna. "Nearly ready."

Samantha placed the lasagna back into the oven and closed the door, and was then greeted by Grayson, who had snuck up behind her, to give her a cuddle from behind. Leaning back into his body as his arms wrapped around her waist, she lay her head on his shoulder. She took a deep breath in and then out, and closed her eyes, as she felt Grayson kiss the side of her temple.

"I think I could grow to love this sort of treatment," said Samantha.

Mmm, I hope so, thought Grayson, smiling.

Placing the dished-up meals onto the table, next to the bench, Samantha said, "Take a seat. I will just get the cutlery out the drawer."

"OK," said Grayson, taking his seat at the head of the table. "So… tell me a little about yourself."

"What would you like to know?" said Samantha, as she sat next to Grayson and handed him his knife and fork.

"Anything," said Grayson shrugging.

"Well… when I was born I was adopted into a middle-class family. My father's job took us all over the world, and eventually we settled here in France. But when I was about ten years old, my adoptive parents split up, and I had to choose which parent I wanted to live with. Eventually I made the decision to live with my dad, because my mom moved back to, Chicago, Illinois, our home town."

"Oh, wow. That must have been hard, choosing which parent to live with. I bet you missed your mom?"

"Yeah, I sure did. Life was different without her growing up."

"Did you go to university when you finished schooling?" said Grayson, cutting into his food.

"Yeah, my dad paid for me to attend Sorbonne University to study children's medicine. But when I was about twenty, my father died suddenly of a heart attack," said Samantha, remembering how devastated she was and how it had changed her life's path.

"I'm sorry for your loss, Samantha," said Grayson, placing his hand over hers.

"Thanks… I still miss my dad, everyday… I think one of the worst things that came from my dad passing away was that I had to fend for myself because he didn't have any insurance and what little money he did have in the bank, well… it didn't last long. I ended up having to get a job to support myself. A few months after my dad passed away, I found it very difficult to work and study, so eventually I had to quit university too. My mother never had any money to support me either. So I couldn't rely on her," said Samantha, wondering if she would ever be able to finish her university degree. Secretly she had hoped that one day her situation would change, so that she could finish her studies and open her own practice.

"Wow, life hasn't been kind to you, has it?" said Grayson.

"Not really… well, enough about me and my sad little story; what about you?" said Samantha, pushing her food around the plate.

Grayson spoke to her about how he worked in his family security business.

"Sounds dangerous," said Samantha.

"Not really. You just need to know what you are doing," said Grayson, as he read her thoughts. "Are you feeling all right?"

"Actually, I was feeling fine, up until about thirty minutes ago. But my head is starting to throb," said Samantha, rubbing her temples.

"Do you still have the pain medication that the hospital gave you last night?" asked Grayson.

"Yeah, it's just over on the counter," said Samantha.

Grayson went over and poured some water into a glass, and then retrieved the tablets.

"Here we go. Take these with the water, and go and lie down on the couch," said Grayson, as he handed them to her.

"Thanks Grayson," said Samantha. After taking the medication, she walked over to the couch and lay down. With her eyes closed, she soon felt Grayson's presence as he knelt on the ground in front of her and then rubbed her forehead. "That feels really nice. So soothing… thank you."

"You're welcome. How do you feel now?" said Grayson.

"The headache has just about gone. But I feel a bit drained though," said Samantha, opening her eyes.

"Why don't I head off home so you can get some rest?" said Grayson.

"No… don't leave. I am enjoying your company. Anyway, you haven't had the dessert yet. It's still in the oven warming," said Samantha, with a creased brow, as she placed her hand on his arm.

"OK. I will stay, but only if you let me dish up the dessert," said Grayson, smiling.

"Oh, all right… it should be ready now anyway. So all you have to do is dish it up. The pie is in the oven and the whipped cream is in the fridge. Are you sure you don't mind?" asked Samantha.

"I don't mind. Only too happy to help out. You lie there and I will dish it up," said Grayson, walking over to the oven.

After they had eaten their dessert, Samantha regained her strength and was starting to feel good again. As Grayson took the dessert plates over to the sink for washing, Samantha couldn't help but notice his physique. *Mmm, so yummy. Cute butt too.* Smiling, she sat at the table in disbelief of how lucky she felt to have met Grayson.

"Would you like to watch a DVD?" asked Samantha.

"Sure. What do you have in your collection?" said Grayson.

Seated next to each other on the sofa, as they waited for the movie to start, Grayson intertwined his fingers slowly into

Samantha's. Hearing her heart beat quicken, he listened to her thoughts about how she was nervous, but attracted to him. He breathed in her lovely scent, lavender, and felt a desire and attraction to her, too. Actually, he couldn't believe how intoxicating she was to his heightened senses. As he turned his head towards Samantha, she looked at him so mesmerisingly. Without hesitation, he leaned into her and kissed her lips ever so tenderly. As she melted in his arms, and he felt her trust, Grayson enjoyed the sweet taste she provided. He knew from her thoughts that she was enjoying how he held her in his arms tightly, and how his sensual kiss was turning her on.

Pulling away for a breath, Samantha said, "Would you like to move this to my bedroom?" She couldn't hold back how she felt any longer.

She didn't need to ask Grayson twice. He quickly picked her up in his arms and carried Samantha to her bedroom, which was next to the lounge room. He put her down on top of the bed, and stood at the side of the bed watching her in awe, as she undressed.

What am I doing? I can't do this to her. Stop…

Was he out of his mind? He had to let Samantha choose for herself if she wanted to become a Lepidoptera vampire. Having sex with her now would surely start her transformation. But how was he going to explain this?

"Are you sure you want to do this Samantha?" asked Grayson, gingerly.

"Yes. Stop talking," said Samantha, breathing heavily. She pulled Grayson onto the bed and started to take off his shirt. As she took off his denim jeans and his boxer shorts, and threw them to the ground, his penis sprang free. In the darkened room, Samantha couldn't believe how good he smelt, and she couldn't help but throw herself onto his penis. As she sucked his penis with vigour, she looked up at him to see if he was enjoying their encounter.

Grayson watched her every move and threw his head back with enjoyment of the pleasure she was providing him. As she twirled her tongue around the head of his cock and then sucked it hard, he began groaning in sheer delight.

Samantha knew if she didn't stop now, he would blow, and she didn't want that to happen, just yet. Pulling herself up off his cock, she started to make her way up his abdomen, kissing it softly and biting as she went. This tormented Grayson to no end.

Gently, Grayson pushed Samantha onto the bed, so that she was lying flat on her back. "My turn now," said Grayson, as he knelt over her and slid down her belly, kissing it slowly as he went.

The relentless way he tortured her with his tongue and lips made her quiver all over. Samantha had never felt pleasure like this in her whole life. When he reached her clitoris, he massaged it just enough to make her orgasm. Gently caressing her nub with his tongue, he put his finger into her vagina, she moaned in sheer delight and had her second orgasm. Her body was overwhelmed with emotions and she felt she couldn't take this much longer. Samantha was so turned on by him, that she just wanted him to fuck her.

But he didn't.

Sitting up quickly on the edge of the bed, he placed his hands over his nose and mouth. *I can't do this,* thought Grayson.

"What are you doing?" said Samantha, anxiously.

"I don't think we should take this any further," said Grayson, getting off the bed and putting his boxer shorts back on.

What the fuck? What is going on here? thought Samantha.

"Why?" she said, sitting up on the bed.

"I want to talk with you some more first, about what happened last night and what you saw," said Grayson, with his back to her, as he pulled his jeans on.

"Who cares about that? Not me," said Samantha. She didn't want to talk about that. It frightened her.

Samantha sat on the edge of the bed with her bare back to Grayson, and breathed a heavy sigh. Not knowing what to say, she heard her bedroom door close. Realising Grayson had left the room, she got off the bed and dressed herself quickly, and then followed him into the lounge room.

"What is going on here?" said Samantha, with her hands on her hips, as she entered the lounge room.

"Do you remember what you saw happen last night? You know; what we did to those guys?" asked Grayson, calmly.

"Yes. But I would prefer not to talk about it… Grayson, I don't understand why you are bringing this up. Weren't you enjoying yourself in the bedroom with me?" asked Samantha, as she sat in front of him on the veneer coffee table.

"Don't get me wrong, Samantha, I would love to fuck you. Your body is so exquisite, and I love the way we feel together. It's just that I need to try and make you understand about what happened last night. Then, once you are clear on things, if you want to, we can still have sex," said Grayson, looking into her deep blue eyes.

Samantha felt confused. "OK. I am all ears," said Samantha, as she crossed her arms and legs, waiting for his explanation.

Looking into his eyes, Samantha heard Grayson say, *How am I going to explain this to her?* But his lips didn't move. She thought she was hearing things.

"Did you say something?" said Samantha, looking at Grayson astonished, and shaking her head.

"You heard me. Oh fuck, I forgot about that," said Grayson now realising she could hear his thoughts.

She looked at him, perplexed.

"You forgot about what?"

"Well here goes… do you have a hand mirror?" said Grayson.

"Hmm, what do you want that for?" asked Samantha, impatiently.

"Can you just get one?" sighed Grayson, exasperated.

Samantha stood up with her hands on her hips and sighed heavily. Walking into her bathroom, she searched through her cabinet to find the mirror. As she came across the mirror, she felt Grayson's presence behind her.

"Here you go. But what do you need that for?" said Samantha, handing Grayson the mirror.

"Stand still, facing the vanity mirror and I will show you," said Grayson. His heart was pounding.

Grayson lifted her hair off the back of her neck, and peeled back the bandage so she could see the outline of the butterfly tattoo in the mirror.

"Where did that come from?" questioned Samantha, feeling the tattoo.

"You were born with it. And when you meet your life partner it then starts to show an outline, and eventually it colours itself in," said Grayson, hoping she would understand. But he only confused her more.

"Trust me to hook up with a Looney Tune like you. Well… I think it's about time for you to leave, Grayson, as I have heard enough bullshit for one night," said Samantha, walking out of the bathroom and towards the front door. Opening the door for Grayson to leave, she was surprised to find William and Annabelle standing there.

"Hello, Samantha. May we come in?" asked William.

With her heart pounding in her chest, she felt a bit apprehensive, but let them in anyway.

"Come in," said Samantha, as she stayed close to the open door.

"So I believe Grayson has told you about the butterfly tattoo on the back of your neck," said William, watching her reaction.

"Yes. But he said something about life partners. I am not sure I understand any of this... hang on, how did you know that?" asked Samantha, her brow furrowed. She was becoming increasingly anxious.

"May we sit?" said William, gesturing to the table. He was trying to keep the situation calm.

"Umm... I suppose," said Samantha. Leaving her front door open, she followed them to the table.

Once they were seated, William proceeded to tell Samantha about their kind and how she would eventually turn into a Lepidoptera vampire.

As she sat there listening to William, Samantha started to remember the events of the previous night, of how she saw Brock and Grayson fighting with the two Debauched vampires and how William beheaded them and then they turned to ash.

Terrified, she ran screaming to the front door. But as she got to the doorway, Annabelle appeared in front of her, and prevented her from leaving. Annabelle then held Samantha in a tight embrace until she stopped kicking and punching. Before she knew it, Annabelle had carried Samantha in her arms to the couch.

"Annabelle, is any of this true what they are saying? I am having a hard time believing any of it," said Samantha, shaking. Her mind was racing.

"Yes, it is true. But we are all here to help you through your transformation, once it starts," said Annabelle, placing her hand on Samantha to keep her calm. Eventually it all became too much for Samantha and she fainted. Annabelle felt Samantha's body go limp, so she lay her down on the couch and put a blanket over her, which was still there from the night before.

"Let us know when she wakes," said William to Grayson, as he approached the front door.

"Yes sire… can Annabelle stay nearby, just in case I need her to come and calm Samantha down again?" asked Grayson.

"Yes. I will take Brock with me and Annabelle can guard Samantha tonight," said William.

After they both left, Grayson went over to the window and saw the exchange take place between Brock and Annabelle across the street. Backing away from the window, he sat on the coffee table in front of Samantha and watched her sleep. After a while, he picked her up in his arms and carried her to the bedroom, and waited patiently for her to wake.

Sitting in the small chair near her bed, he hoped she would wake soon, because he wanted to try make her understand their kind. Grayson knew it wasn't going to be an easy task because he could tell from Samantha's mind that she was very methodical and there was no way that this would make sense.

Samantha slept through the entire night, and as the sun came up Grayson decided to go back to the Gramaze residence. Annabelle had been instructed to keep guard throughout the day by William until Grayson could return.

Chapter Seven

Waking from what she thought had been a bad dream, Samantha slowly got out of bed and pulled the curtains open to her bedroom window. Looking outside, she noticed the sky was a brilliant blue and the sun was shining brightly. Down on the street, she noticed a blonde-haired female standing across the road, who was standing in the shade, but she was looking directly at her. The name came to her mind: *Annabelle*. Samantha took in a deep breath, her eyes widening, as she backed away from the window, remembering how she knew Annabelle. With her heart pounding, and her breathing accelerating, she sat back down on the bed. She shook her head in disbelief. *Why is she standing out there looking up at me? Maybe I should ring the police and let them sort her out. What am I going to do?*

Startled, Samantha heard a knock at the door. Not knowing whether to answer it, she tip-toed quietly to the front door and looked through the peep hole. She recognised Annabelle standing on the other side of the door.

"Go away. I am not letting you in, Annabelle," said Samantha, with her back now resting on the door, as her whole body shook.

I won't hurt you, Samantha. Please let me in, thought Annabelle.

Sensing in her mind what Annabelle had just said, Samantha felt anxious about opening the door. She leant on the door, looking up at the ceiling, and didn't know what to do.

I am here to keep you safe, Samantha. Please let me in, thought Annabelle.

After a few minutes, Samantha began to open the door. After all, she did have her phone in her pocket, so if anything went wrong, she would call the police.

"Hello. May I come in?" asked Annabelle, as the door opened.

"No… I would prefer you didn't at this stage," said Samantha, defiantly.

"Oh, OK. How are you feeling this morning?" asked Annabelle.

"None of your business. Why are you waiting outside my apartment, across the road?" asked Samantha.

"I am here to guard you. Do you remember what William and Grayson told you last night?" said Annabelle, with raised eyebrows.

"Yes…" *But I thought I dreamt that.* "So, you are saying it is true. I'm a Lepid… can't pronounce the word… vampire?" asked Samantha, with her hands on her hips.

"Yes… may I come in to explain?" said Annabelle, reaching through the doorway to touch Samantha on the arm lightly.

"I told you, the answer is no!" shouted Samantha, trying to pull away from Annabelle. "Umm… I don't know… maybe… all right."

She felt dazed from Annabelle's touch, and couldn't seem to stop her from entering the apartment.

Walking into her apartment, Annabelle said, "Can I take a seat and we can talk about the Lepidoptera family?"

Shutting the front door, Samantha indicated for her to sit at the kitchen bench.

"I know this is a bit daunting, Sam. Can I call you Sam, or do you prefer Samantha?" asked Annabelle.

"Either is fine… daunting. Yes, you could say that," said Samantha, standing on the opposite side of the bench to Annabelle.

"I remember feeling the same way when I found out I was a Lepidoptera vampire. I couldn't wrap my head around it at first. But I soon leant to live with it. And you will too," said Annabelle.

"Look Annabelle… you are nice and everything, but I don't believe a word of this shit you are all telling me. Vampires don't exist in real life, only in the movies, and it's a bit farfetched, the stories you are describing to me."

"So you are telling me after everything you saw the other night when you were attacked by the Debauched vamps, that you still don't believe vampires exist? Come on. Think about it," said Annabelle, with raised eyebrows.

"I don't know what I saw that night. It all seems like a blur to me. Everything happened so fast, and before I knew it, Grayson was standing there helping me. You are going to have to convince me a lot more than that Annabelle. You know, evidence. That's what I need to see," said Samantha, with her nostrils flaring.

"Humph…fine," said Annabelle, smirking. "Keep watching the front door." With her mind, Annabelle placed the chain lock on the door and took it off again. Then she unlocked the door and opened it up completely.

"Look any magician can do those tricks. Sorry, you will have to do a little better than that to convince me," said Samantha.

"OK, sure. But can any magician do this?" said Annabelle, opening the fridge door with her mind.

"Still not convinced," said Samantha, folding her arms over her chest and snickering.

OK. Can you hear my thoughts? mind said Annabelle.

Samantha's eyes opened wide when she heard the thought in her mind. Frightened, she gulped and said, "Yes."

"Still think it's a parlour act then? No magician can do that," said Annabelle.

"No. But how can I hear you?" said Samantha, confused.

"Only Lepidoptera vampires can hear one another," said Annabelle, reading Samantha thoughts. Walking around the bench, she placed her hand on Samantha's shoulder. "You will be OK."

Her heartbeat started to slow down and her mind calmed. "What did you just do?"

"I have the power to calm you with my touch," said Annabelle.

Astonished by what was happening, Samantha took a seat in the lounge room on the couch.

"You have a power to calm people? Wow…" With the realisation that Annabelle could be telling her the truth, Samantha started to wonder about what it would be like to be a Lepidoptera vampire. "What else can you do?"

"I am very strong, so I can now protect myself and others. Like you, I mean," said Annabelle.

"Will I be like you one day?" asked Samantha.

"It all depends on the colour of your butterfly tattoo. Each colour has different powers. But yes, you will be strong," said Annabelle. "Are you working today?"

"Yeah. I start at 2.30 and finish at 6.30," said Samantha.

"Don't worry, I will be waiting for you when you finish work. I will make sure you get home safely," said Annabelle.

"Thanks, Annabelle. Would you like a drink?" asked Samantha.

"Umm, maybe a coffee, if that's all right," said Annabelle.

"Sure. No probs. How long have you been outside for?" said Samantha, walking back into the kitchen.

"I have been guarding you since Grayson arrived at your apartment last night," said Annabelle.

"Really... aren't you exhausted?" asked Samantha, frowning.

"No. Vampires don't feel exhaustion. And I am only too happy to guard you, anytime," said Annabelle.

"Wow... thanks. I still don't understand how any Debauched vampires would know that I am in transition, as you all call it," said Samantha.

"They can smell it. As soon as you meet your life partner the transition from human to vampire starts with the black outline of the butterfly on your neck. I think also, because there haven't been too many new female Lepidopteras for hundreds of years, that the Debauched can detect your smell straight away. But you do understand that the full transformation doesn't take place until you have sex with Grayson?" said Annabelle, with raised eyebrows.

"Oh, OK. No, I didn't know that. But that explains a lot," said Samantha, thinking back to when Grayson told her he didn't want to have sex with her just yet.

"There has been another way that it could happen. Apparently, if you get extremely agitated, it can bring the transformation forward. This did happen just recently to one of the other females," said Annabelle.

"Right," said Samantha, placing the coffee cup in front of Annabelle.

The more questions Samantha asked, the more she became increasingly apprehensive about her future. It seemed that her life would be all planned out for her. She wasn't ready for this life. She still had plans to become a doctor in children's medicine. Feeling trapped and confused, her anxiety rose.

"Are you all right?" asked Annabelle, placing her hand on Samantha's shoulder.

"Not really. I feel like my heart is going to jump out of my chest. It's beating so fast," said Samantha, trying to slow her breathing.

Annabelle walked around the kitchen bench, and stood in front of Samantha. Placing her arms around her for a hug, Annabelle could feel Samantha's anxiety building up and tried to calm her.

Within seconds, Samantha pulled away from their embrace. With her hand held up against her mouth, she said, "My teeth are hurting and I can taste my own blood."

Annabelle knew what that meant. Placing her hand on Samantha's arm, she said, "Stay calm… I think we need to get you to the hospital for a transfusion."

"What… what are you talking about? It's just a toothache," said Samantha, shaking her head at Annabelle.

"Where is your bathroom?" asked Annabelle.

"Through there. Why?"

"Come with me," said Annabelle, forcefully taking her by the arm and walking with her to the bathroom.

Turning the light on as they entered the bathroom, Samantha said, "What is going on? Why are we in here?"

"Look in the mirror and open your mouth up," said Annabelle, indicating to the mirror.

Frowning, but doing as she was instructed, Samantha stood in front of the mirror and opened her mouth. Her eyes widened when she spotted them. Big white pointy fangs hanging down from the top of her gums. "What the fuck… why do I have these?" said Samantha, pulling her top lip out to look at her gums.

"They are your vampire fangs. I am not sure why you would have them now. You haven't transformed yet, and from what I know, they only appear when you start to transform from human to vampire. Strange…" said Annabelle, with furrowed brow.

Feeling nauseous, Samantha held onto the vanity cupboard bench top to steady herself. "I feel sick," said Samantha, walking quickly past Annabelle to the kitchen.

She didn't get far before she passed out. Luckily, Annabelle caught her before she hit the ground.

Samantha opened her eyes slowly. Looking around the room, she wondered where she was or even how she got there. She noticed that a drip was attached to her, and when she looked up at the monitor, she saw that it was giving her blood. She then noticed Annabelle, who was sitting in a chair next to her bed.

"You are in the hospital. How are you feeling?" asked Annabelle.

"I don't know, to tell you the truth. Why am I hooked up to a drip?" asked Samantha.

"Your transformation has started. So you will need to have A+ Blood for the next coming week. It's so that you don't become a Debauched vampire," said Annabelle, watching Samantha's reaction and placing her hand on her arm to calm her. "Believe me, I know this is a lot to take in, but you will be all right."

"How is it possible that I have started my transformation? I am not ready for this, Annabelle. I have a life, you know…" said Samantha, as her tears spilled over onto her cheeks.

"We are not sure how or why this has happened now. But William said he is going to speak with our queen, Talitha, about it. He hopes she might be able to shed some light on why you have transformed so quickly. By the way, your butterfly is starting to colour itself in as well. It's orange," said Annabelle.

"You know I have been thinking; I have always felt that there was something on the back of my neck. But I thought it was a scar, not a butterfly tattoo. What will my abilities be?" asked Samantha.

"You can create illusion," said Annabelle smiling.

Processing the idea of an ability, she said, "Wow... that sounds like a cool power to have, hey?"

"Sure is," said Annabelle, realising Samantha was relaxing. "You know Grayson has been waiting outside for two hours. He came to the hospital as soon as I rang him. He really cares for you, Samantha. Can I let him in now?"

"OK. You can let him in," said Samantha, excited that someone actually cared about her. She had never felt like anyone cared about her since her father passed away. Yes, her mother was still alive, but she didn't pay much attention to her daughter. She was too consumed with her own life.

Annabelle waited outside the room, so that Grayson and Samantha could get better acquainted.

Entering the room, Grayson could see Samantha was quite calm. Walking over to her bed, he said, "Hi. How do you feel?"

"I would feel better if I could get a hug," said Samantha, with her arms held open.

Leaning in, Grayson hugged Samantha, and as he pulled away, their cheeks grazed against each other. Looking into each other's eyes, they both leaned in and he kissed her lips gently.

"How do you feel about becoming a Lepidoptera vampire, Sam?"

"It's a lot to process. In a way, I feel cheated. I have always wanted to become a children's doctor, but now, well... I don't think that will ever happen," said Samantha.

"Of course you can still become a doctor. What makes you think you can't?" asked Grayson, frowning.

"Well... one - I won't be able to work. So that means no income coming in to support myself. Two - no income means I won't be able to save for my tuition to go to university to study. Plus, from talking with Annabelle, she indicated that I would have to go on patrol sometimes, or even guard people. It seems like I won't have any time for anything I had planned in my life. So forgive me if I am feeling a bit ripped off at the moment," said Samantha.

"I can speak with William about your study if you want me to. Life won't be as bad as you think it will," said Grayson. "How are you feeling, anyway?"

"I'm not sure. For the last couple of minutes, I have felt like I want to rip my skin off. Feels like something is crawling under my skin. I can't stop itching. Plus I can hear people's thoughts in the hospital. It's starting to drive me crazy, as I can't block it out," said Samantha, nervously.

"The blood will start to work soon, and some of the symptoms will go away. But not completely. You will eventually get it all under control," said Grayson, holding her hand.

"I hope so. How long have you been a vampire, Grayson?" said Samantha, trying to focus on something else.

"A few hundred years," said Grayson.

"Really? At what age did you turn?"

"When I was about 28 years old," said Grayson.

"And in all that time you haven't had a life partner?" asked Samantha, curious.

"That's correct. I have never had a life partner; nor did I ever think it would happen either," said Grayson.

My, what a lonely existence, thought Samantha.

"No, I haven't been lonely. I have just kept busy. The time seems to go fast when you are a vamp," said Grayson.

Huh… Did he just hear my thought? This is something I will need to get used to, that's for sure, thought Samantha.

"Yes," said Grayson with a smirk on his face.

"What colour are you, Grayson?" asked Samantha.

"I am the same colour as you Samantha. But males have different abilities to the females," said Grayson.

"Can I have a look at your butterfly tattoo?" asked Samantha, sitting up.

Sitting on the bed, he lifted his hair for her to see his tattoo. She traced her fingers over the outline of his butterfly, and felt an instant attraction between them. Leaning in, she kissed his neck sensually.

"Do you know how much you turn me on, Samantha, when you touch or kiss me? My whole body aches for you morning and night since we met," said Grayson, turning to meet her gaze.

"That's funny, because since I met you, I can't stop thinking about you and when we touch my whole body does somersaults," said Samantha, as her heart beat quickened.

Leaning in, Grayson gently pushed Samantha's hair away from her neck. As his lips touched her, it sent shivers up her spine and her breathing increased when his teeth grazed her left ear. She moaned when his hand caressed her breast through her blouse, in anticipation of what he was going to do next. When their lips met, it was like fireworks going off on a still, hot night.

When he pulled back to look into her eyes, she said, "A girl could get used to all this attention." Then she kissed him again.

"Could she now?" said Grayson, smirking as he kissed her back. Just as he said it, he felt her fangs protrude. Pulling away quickly and looking her in the eyes, he thought, *Samantha*.

The look in her eyes was one of prey. Reading her mind, Grayson knew her next move was to feed from him. And he wasn't about to let that happen. "Samantha," said Grayson, shaking her.

"Huh. What?" But as soon as she said it, she knew what the problem was. Touching her fangs, she looked him in the eyes, scared. "I'm sorry."

"It's OK. You just need more blood. I shouldn't have teased you so much, but I couldn't help myself," said Grayson. "I am the one who should be saying, 'sorry'."

Sensing there was some blood in the room adjacent to them, Grayson said, "I will be back in a minute."

"OK," said Samantha, watching him walk out the room.

Within seconds he was back with a cup, and it was filled with blood. "Here, drink this," said Grayson.

"I don't know if I can drink that Grayson. It makes me feel sick just looking at it," said Samantha, looking inside the cup.

"Try. Put the cup up to your lips and close your eyes. Maybe if you don't see the blood, it will be all right?" said Grayson. It had been a while, but he knew exactly how Samantha felt, because he remembered feeling the same way the first time he drank blood.

Holding her breath and closing her eyes, Samantha took a sip. As the blood hit her tongue, she couldn't swallow it. Instead she gagged on it and spat it out in a bed pan next to her bed. Wiping her mouth, she said, "I can't drink this. It makes me feel nauseous."

"Try again, my love," said Grayson.

Swallowing hard, trying to keep the saliva from coming up, she took another sip of the blood. As it went down the back of her throat, she closed her eyes in anticipation that she would be sick. But that didn't happen. Instead she took another sip, then a gulp of it. The taste of the blood was metallic at first, but now it was sweet. Drinking down the whole cup, Samantha felt like her body had just come alive.

"How was that?" asked Grayson.

"Can I have another cup full?" said Samantha.

"Yes. You can have as much as you like," said Grayson, pouring her another cup.

Taking the cup from his hand, she chugged it down fast, then gave him the cup to fill once again.

"Thank you Grayson, for persisting with me. Wow… this stuff makes me really feel alive. I have so much energy now," said Samantha.

"Yeah, that's how it should make you feel. Once you get over the first week, then you will only need to drink it once a month. And no, we don't drink from humans. We have a man on the inside here at the hospital, who we get our supplies from," said Grayson, smiling at her.

"OK. That's good to know. I was a bit worried about where I would get my blood from… Grayson… Annabelle told me that I will have to stay at the Gramaze house from now on because the Debauched vamps will try to kidnap me. Is this true?"

Grayson could tell that Samantha was feeling a bit over-whelmed and apprehensive about staying with people she didn't really know, and also that she liked her own space.

"Yes, it's true. But what about if you stay for only a couple of days first to see if you like it and then we can go from there? If you don't like it, I am sure we can sort something out later. OK?" said Grayson.

Truthfully, Grayson didn't know what else they could do later, so he was hoping Samantha would like the Gramaze house.

"Thank you for understanding," said Samantha, as she hugged him.

"You're welcome. How are you feeling now?" said Grayson.

"Yeah, I'm good. The skin crawling has stopped, but I can still hear the voices," said Samantha.

"That will disappear in time. I will show you how to turn them off. So do you feel like you could go home?" asked Grayson.

"I think so," said Samantha.

"Great. I will just go and find Charlie, the morgue attendant at the hospital, so he can give you a few more bags of A+ blood," said Grayson, walking to the door.

"OK," said Samantha.

Chapter Eight

Pulling into the drive way of the Gramaze house, Samantha's jaw dropped open when the house came into view.

"You live here? It's beautiful," said Samantha, looking out the window.

"You could live here too," said Grayson.

Stepping out the car, Samantha felt apprehensive as they approached the house. Squeezing Grayson's hand hard, she took a deep breath.

"Don't be nervous, my love. Everyone here has been through the same as you and they are only too happy to help you through this," said Grayson.

Entering the foyer, Annabelle greeted them and gave Samantha a hug. Feeling a bit calmer, she whispered, "Thanks, Annabelle. I appreciate you doing that for me. It takes the edge off my nerves."

"You're welcome," said Annabelle, smiling.

William and Renee approached Samantha, and Renee said, "Hello, Samantha. My name is Renee and I am William's partner. How are you feeling, my dear?"

"I feel a little bit anxious, Renee. I still don't know what to think about all this, let alone try reason with it in my head. But otherwise I am well; thanks for asking," said Samantha.

"If you need anything dear, don't hesitate to ask as we are all here to help you," said Renee, hugging Samantha.

"Thank you," said Samantha.

"Welcome to our home. When you are feeling better tomorrow, we will introduce you to the other members of our family," said William.

"OK. Thank you," said Samantha smiling.

"Let's take you upstairs to my room and get you settled in for the night. You will probably need some rest," said Grayson.

"See you tomorrow, Sam. Have a good night sleep," said Renee.

"Thank you. Good night everyone," said Samantha.

Entering Grayson's bedroom with her overnight bag they had collected from Samantha's apartment, Samantha noticed the room was wallpapered in light grey tones. In the middle of the room was a huge four-poster, queen-sized bed, which had a black, white and red quilt cover on it. Standing there in awe, she said, "This is your room? Wow… this is not what I expected. This is so lavish, compared to my old apartment. You are so lucky, Grayson."

"This could be yours too, if you want, Samantha. But there is no pressure. You just need to relax and rest so you can feel better. You are safe here," said Grayson, kissing her temple. "You can put your clothes in here; this is my wardrobe."

Walking over to the wardrobe entrance and placing her clothes in the on the coat hangers provided, she thought, *God… look how big this is. Enough room in here for five people's clothes and shoes. Not what I am used to.*

"Through this door here is my bathroom. You can put your toiletries in there, if you like," said Grayson, pointing to the doorway.

When Samantha walked through the doorway, a light automatically turned on. The bathroom had black tiles with a grey fleck in them, that went from floor to ceiling. At the back of the bathroom was a deep, white claw foot bath. And beside it was a shower built for five. Enormous was an understatement. Next to the shower was a grey toned vanity which had two basins. "This bathroom is beautiful. I have never seen anything like it before, except in the magazines," said Samantha, feeling the soft towels on the wall towel rack, as she looked back at Grayson.

"Beautiful bathroom, for a beautiful lady," said Grayson, as he pulled her close.

Smiling, she said, "Thank you."

Leaning in, she kissed his lips with passion. She had never had any man give her so many lovely compliments before.

"Would you like to have a bath or shower before bed to relax?" asked Grayson.

"Would it be OK if I have a bath?" asked Samantha.

"Sure. I will run it now for you. Do you like bubbles?" said Grayson.

"Mmm, that sounds good. Thank you," said Samantha. Sitting on the tiled ledge, she waited for him to fill the bath. She felt thankful that she had met Grayson and was staying at the Gramaze residents.

He hasn't even tried to take advantage of me yet. I know he wants to as I can hear his thoughts sometimes. Maybe I could ask him if he want to have a bath with me, thought Samantha.

"That's all ready for you now, Samantha, and I have put a towel next to the bath for you as well," said Grayson.

"Would you like to have a bath with me Grayson?" said Samantha smirking.

He didn't answer her right away.

Is this the best thing to do, considering the circumstances? I don't want to put her transformation in jeopardy.

Samantha grabbed him by the hand and pulled him into her embrace.

"I do feel good. And you being in here with me is exactly what I need at the moment," said Samantha.

"Are you sure?" said Grayson.

"Yes I am sure," said Samantha.

Samantha watched as Grayson took his shirt off and then his jeans and boxer shorts. She couldn't believe what a muscular, athletic body he had. As he stepped into the bath, he said, "Come on."

With the blood rushing through his body rapidly, Grayson waited in anticipation as Samantha took off her clothes. Her body was beautiful, but he knew that he couldn't make love to her until she was ready. Pushing himself up against the back of the bath, Samantha sat in front of him, and rested her head on his chest.

"Are you comfortable, my love?" asked Grayson.

"Yes. Thank you. This is nice and relaxing. Just what I needed," said Samantha, yawning. She was exhausted from the day's events.

Noticing her breathing had quietened and there was no chatter coming from her mind, he realised she had fallen asleep. Picking her up in his arms, Grayson carried her out of the bath and put her into his bed naked. Samantha was so tired that she didn't even wake when he put the quilt on her to keep her warm. As he stood there admiring her beauty, his body and mind yearned to be near her when he slept. So he got dressed and slipped into bed and cuddled up next to her.

When Samantha woke the next morning, she felt an arm around her waist. Turning around in the bed, she watched Grayson sleeping. Smiling she thought, *God…how lucky am I? I hope I don't wake up and find this is all a dream.*

Opening his eyes, he said, "Good morning. How did you sleep?"

"I slept like a log. Did we …?" said Samantha, looking down at her body which had no clothes on.

Laughing he kissed her forehead and said, "Don't worry, nothing happened. Oh well… besides me eyeing your body off."

"A girl could get used to all these lovely comments you have all the time, Grayson. I don't know what I did to deserve you, but I thank God I met you," said Samantha, smiling.

"Come here," said Grayson, putting his arm out for her to cuddle into him. "Are you hungry, my love?"

"Famished. I could eat a horse," said Samantha.

"Let's get showered and head down for breakfast," said Grayson.

"Do we have to? I am enjoying just staying here cuddling you," said Samantha.

"No, we don't have to. But I won't be held accountable for what will happen if we do stay here. Your body is just so irresistible and beautiful. And all I want to do is fuck you all day," said Grayson, pushing his hard penis into her leg.

"I don't think I am ready for sex yet, Grayson," said Samantha. "I think what I need at the moment is a drink of the A+ blood the hospital gave us."

"You can drink from me, Sam," said Grayson, placing his neck near her mouth.

"Are you sure?" asked Samantha, watching his vein pulsate.

He nodded.

Biting down hard on his neck with her sharp fangs, she tasted his blood for the first time. Sucking his blood quickly sent her into a frenzy.

Hearing her thoughts, he pulled away from her grasp.

"Samantha, you need to stop and pull yourself together before you hit blood lust!" shouted Grayson.

She looked at him with fury in her eyes, and tried to push him down on the bed with the new strength she had acquired.

All of a sudden, Annabelle came running into the room and held Samantha down until her touch calmed her craving.

"Here, drink this," said Annabelle, handing her a cup of blood. Sitting up, Samantha drank it down quickly, without a breath, whilst Annabelle continued her touch.

"Grayson, you should have known better… you can't feed her at the moment. Not until she is fully transformed. Your blood just about sent her into blood lust, because you are craving each other," said Annabelle, with a furrowed brow, as she looked him in the eyes. "Are you out of your mind?"

"Shit… thanks, Annabelle. I got swept up in the moment and completely forgot about all that side of things. Luckily I had you here to help us," said Grayson, sitting up and ruffling his hair.

"I won't say anything to William about this episode, but you had better get your shit together, man," said Annabelle.

Samantha's thoughts become clearer after drinking the A+ blood.

"God, that was awful. I couldn't control myself. I am so sorry, Grayson," said Samantha, looking into his eyes.

"Don't apologise, Samantha. I should be the one saying 'sorry'. I plainly forgot about the blood lust when you are transforming," said Grayson, still running his hand through his hair, distressed.

"Well, I think you two need to get dressed and come down for breakfast," said Annabelle, getting up off the bed.

"Thanks, Annabelle. We will be down soon," said Grayson.

Walking into the dining room, William said to Grayson and Samantha in a heated voice, "I want to see you both, now."

Following William into the sitting room, they both knew what this was going to be about.

"What were you thinking Grayson? You know that you shouldn't have given Samantha your blood whilst she was still transforming. Are you seriously fucking stupid, you moron? You could have made Samantha go into blood lust, and then we would have had to stop her, which would not have been pleasant at all."

"I am sorry, sire. This won't happen again," said Grayson, bowing slightly. *Fucking Annabelle, she must have blabbed.*

"You are damn right this won't happen again. We all will all be keeping an eye on you both," said William frowning.

"I am sorry too, William. I won't drink from Grayson whilst I am transforming, I promise," said Samantha, as the tears formed in her eyes.

William approached Samantha and placed his hand on her right shoulder. "It's all right, Samantha. I am just sorry that you have had to go through this. You are and will always be like a daughter to me, Samantha, so I will always look after you and your well-being."

She hadn't heard those words spoken to her since before her father had died. Taken back by what William had said to her, she said, "Thank you, William. That means a lot to me. I hope I won't disappoint you. I have missed have a father figure to look after me again."

William looked at Samantha with adoring eyes like a father would and said, "Now… you both need to get some food into you to keep your strength up. Off you go."

Even though William was a warrior and the leader of the France Lepidopteras, his heart and intentions were always in the right place, when it came to his coven family.

Walking out of the sitting room, William gave Grayson a nod and thought, *She is a great lady Grayson, so don't fuck this up, or you will have me to deal with.*

Grayson nodded at William and thought, *I have waited far too long to find my life partner, so I won't stuff this up.*

At breakfast, Samantha couldn't believe her appetite. "God, at this rate I will be a good year blimp in no time at all if I keep eating like this."

"That's one good thing about being a vamp, Sam; you can eat as much as you like and don't put on weight," said Annabelle, smiling at her across the table.

"Yeah, it's definitely a perk… Samantha…what about after breakfast if I show you around the house, whilst William talks to everyone else about patrol tonight?" said Renee.

Looking to Grayson for reassurance, Samantha placed her hand in his, under the table. *Will that be all right?*

You'll be fine, thought Grayson to Samantha, as he held her hand firm.

"Thanks. That will be nice," said Samantha to Renee.

With William instructing everyone to meet in the operations room, Renee took Samantha for a tour around the house.

"You have a beautiful home, Renee," said Samantha, looking around.

"Thank you, Samantha," said Renee.

"Thank you for asking me to stay," said Samantha.

"Well actually, we were hoping that you would like to live here with us permanently. I am sure you already know that

Grayson loves you, and he too would like to have you move in here on a permanent basis," said Renee.

"Yeah I know. I… well… I am not sure. I am still getting used to this vampire thing," said Samantha, with a creased brow, as she waved a hand over her own body. "What would happen if I decided to stay at my apartment?"

"One of us would have to guard you, day in, day out. It would put a lot of strain on our coven, but in the end, your safety is all that matters, dear," said Renee, placing her arm around Samantha's shoulders and pulling her in close.

"Hmm… right. But how can I contribute to a house like this, Renee? I don't have combat experience, and I don't even know if I could kill someone either," said Samantha. Breathing a heavy sigh, she lowered her head.

"Come… let's take a seat," said Renee, steering Samantha over to the steps that lead out to the back lawn area. "Don't worry about all that kind of stuff yet, dear. None of us used to be trained in combat or could kill anyone at first. But over time, you can acquire these skills."

God, what have I gotten myself into here? I don't want this life. I wish this was all a dream, thought Samantha.

Renee listened to Samantha's thoughts and remembered back to the day she was told she was a vampire and how scared she was, too.

"Unfortunately, Sam, it's not a dream. There is one thing I can tell you though; you will belong to not only a powerful family, but also a family that will protect, love, and care for you always."

"That is nice to know. I do miss having family around. My mom, well, she lives in Chicago, and as you know, my dad, he passed away. So I don't have any family here in France," said Samantha, staring straight ahead, and feeling overwhelmed.

"Well, before you make your decision, Sam, why don't you stay for a few days and then see how you feel. You never know, we may make a good impression," said Renee, looking into her eyes, with a loving expression.

"Thanks, Renee," said Samantha.

"Let's go for a walk and I can show you around the grounds," said Renee.

Walking arm in arm around the beautifully manicured gardens, Samantha listened as Renee spoke about the time when the France-based Lepidopteras all moved to the house they were currently in, and how it was purposely built for the Gramaze family. She also explained the importance of keeping their kind a secret from humans and about the Debauched vampires.

Deciding to go back inside the house, they started to walk toward the back patio area. As they reached the limestone steps, Grayson was waiting for them.

"Hello, ladies," said Grayson.

"Hello," said Samantha, with a grin from ear to ear.

"Hi, Grayson. Finished already in there?" said Renee, surprised.

"Yes. For now, anyway," said Grayson.

Turning to Samantha he said, "It really is beautiful out here, isn't it?"

"Yes," said Samantha, nodding.

"So… are you feeling up to going for a drive somewhere?" said Grayson.

"Do you mind if we don't?… Sorry… I would prefer to stick around here today as I am feeling a bit out of sorts… well… not myself anyway. Could we just sit out here for a while and enjoy each other's company and the scenery?" said Samantha.

"Sure. That sounds good anyway. And don't be sorry, I totally understand that you are not feeling up to it," said Grayson.

"I will leave you two to chat," said Renee.

"Thank you for showing me around," said Samantha, giving Renee a hug.

"You are welcome, dear. Maybe we can catch up later on?" said Renee.

"I would like that," said Samantha, smiling.

"See you later then," said Renee, walking back inside.

Placing his arm around Samantha, Grayson steered her over to the patio area. "Let's go and sit down over there," said Grayson, pointing to the sofa.

The wood-framed double seated sofa they sat on looked out onto the green grass area and the gardens.

"I hope you weren't too disappointed when I said I wanted to stay here?" said Samantha, cuddling into Grayson's shoulder.

"No... I could never be disappointed in you Samantha, and I do understand how you are feeling. I would rather stay here anyway and cuddle up for a while," said Grayson.

Kissing him on his cheek, Samantha snuggled back into his shoulder and they enjoyed their time together. Not a word was spoken, but they could hear each other's thoughts. As Samantha relaxed, she became tired and it wasn't long before she was asleep on Grayson's shoulder.

Grayson picked her up in his muscular arms, and carried her back to his bedroom so that she could rest for a while. Watching her sleep, he knew that he was the luckiest man alive, especially now that he had found his life partner.

Samantha woke up disoriented. How she even got in Grayson's room, let alone his bed, was a mystery to her. Looking around, she found Grayson sitting next to her in bed. "Hello," said Samantha, sitting up and wiping the sleep from her eyes.

"Hello, my love. You must have been tired, because you fell asleep in my arms. So I brought you up here to rest," said Grayson.

"God, you are gorgeous and thoughtful. I think I am falling for you, Grayson," said Samantha, stroking his face gently.

"I feel the same way, my love. Hey, would you like a drink?" said Grayson, kissing her on the forehead.

"Yes please. Can I have a Coke this time? I don't feel the need for any blood at the moment," said Samantha.

"Sure. I'll go down to the kitchen and get one for you," said Grayson. "I won't be long."

Lying on the bed and looking up at the ceiling, Samantha closed her eyes to relax. All of a sudden, she heard a voice saying, *Come to me, my daughter.* Opening her eyes, she sat up and looked around the room, but there was no one else in the room, besides her. Deciding that she was hearing things, she lay back down again and closed her eyes.

Come to me, my daughter.

Sitting up, she followed the voice in a trance-like state down stairs to the basement. Standing in front of a door, she heard the voice again. *Come to me, my daughter.* She turned the door handle, and pushed the door open slowly. To her surprise, sitting inside, at the back of the room, was the most stunning woman she had ever seen. She stood in the doorway in awe, looking at her for a few moments, before she entered the room.

"Hello, my darling daughter. It's nice to see you again," said the woman, as Samantha entered the room. Her butterfly-like elegance was magnificent.

"Hello. What is your name?" asked Samantha, mesmerised by her beauty.

"Talitha," she said.

"It's nice to meet you, Talitha. So who are you? You keep referring to me as your daughter," said Samantha, frowning.

"I am your birth mother. I am pleased you are all right," said Talitha, smiling and patting the seat next to her. "Come sit with me, dear."

Samantha was taken back by her answer. She wasn't sure what to do, so she decided to keep her distance and stand in the door entrance.

Seeing how unsure Samantha was, Talitha decided to explain about how Samantha was born and why she had to give her up at birth.

"That must have been hard for you to give your children up at birth," said Samantha.

"Yes dear, it was. But it was for a good reason. I am sure you will agree," said Talitha.

"Yes, I do agree. You know, most of my life I have always felt like something was missing. I didn't seem to fit in anywhere, and I didn't have any close friends. It was like I had a big 'L' painted on my forehead for loser. I have always been a loner. Do most of the female Lepidoptera feel the same way?" said Samantha.

"Yes, most have commented that they feel the same way as you. It's very common. And the reason is because you are a vampire, not human. Tell me, since you have been at the Gramaze house, have you felt like part of the family?" asked Talitha.

"Yes. But how did you know?" said Samantha.

"It's because you are with family of your own kind. The Lepidoptera give off a scent, especially the females, that only our own kind know, which in turn makes you feel comfortable and welcomed. You will understand what I mean in time, dear."

Listening to Talitha speak about her future and of her destiny as a Lepidoptera was comforting and it opened her mind up to many possibilities.

"So why do you live down here instead of a more comfortable life inside the house above?" said Samantha, looking around at her small apartment-style room.

"Because if I live above ground the Debauched vamps will be able to feel my power and once they find me they will kill me and everyone else who lives here," said Talitha.

"That must be a lonely life, Talitha. I am so sorry that you have to go through this for all of us," said Samantha. "Is there anything that I can do for you?"

"Oh no, my dear. I am cared for well by William and Renee already," said Talitha.

"So, I see you two have met already," said William, walking into the room.

Samantha was startled when she heard his voice, as her back was to the basement. Turning around and composing herself, she said, "Yes. I heard Talitha calling me." She noticed Grayson was standing in the doorway as well.

"How are you, William?" asked Talitha, walking towards him.

"I am well today, my queen. I am glad you are back home safe and sound from your trip," said William.

"Thank you, William. Rome is lovely this time of year. How has everything been here with the Debauched?" said Talitha.

"Nothing has changed, my queen," said William, disappointment on his face. "And you, how have you been?"

"I am well. And finally, I have met my lovely daughter, Samantha," said Talitha.

"Would you like us to leave you and Samantha alone to talk some more?" asked William.

"Yes, that would be great, William. Don't worry Grayson, I will have her back to you in no time at all," said Talitha.

Grayson nodded and William said, "I will be back later on, my queen, to speak with you. Samantha, we will see you later on for dinner, OK?"

"Thank you, William," said Talitha.

"OK. See you both later," said Samantha, smiling nervously.

"Come and sit over here, my dear, and we can get to know each other a bit more," said Talitha, walking back to her seat.

Samantha had so many questions for her birth mother, and by the time day had turned into night, the queen had answered all of Samantha's questions and more.

At around 7.30 Talitha said to Samantha, "You haven't had any blood for a while, my dear, and it is now dinner time at the Gramaze house, so I think that will be enough for one day. You can always come back another day."

"Yes, I am a bit thirsty. Thank you for today, Talitha. Things are a lot clearer to me now and I now know what I need to do. Is there anything I can get you before I leave?"

"You are a kind child for asking, but no, I am all right. Go now, as I am sure Grayson is missing you," said Talitha.

"Is it OK if I give you a kiss on the cheek goodbye?" said Samantha, standing.

"Yes, that is fine, my dear," said Talitha.

Samantha leaned in and gave her a hug first, and then a kiss on her cheek. "See you again soon, I hope," said Samantha smiling.

"I am sure we will, dear," said Talitha.

Closing the door, Samantha started for the stairs.

I need to speak with Grayson, thought Samantha.

When she looked up to the top of the stairs, Grayson was waiting for her. "You called," he said.

"Can we sit down after dinner and talk about things?" said Samantha, walking up the stairs.

"Yes, my love," said Grayson.

"Could I please have some blood? I am feeling a bit strange again," said Samantha, feeling her forehead.

"Sure... come on. Let's go to the kitchen," said Grayson, taking her by the hand.

Samantha and Grayson sat next to William and Renee at the dining room table.

"What did you think of Talitha?" asked William.

"I like her. She actually explained a lot and helped me make up my mind about a few things today," said Samantha.

"Anything in particular?" asked William. But he already knew from Samantha's thoughts what she was going to say.

"Well... she explained that I'd probably transformed so quickly because I met Grayson so soon after the Debauched attack. She also made me understand why I need to be here and how important I am to your coven. Talitha explained everything to me really well. And... umm... I would like to ask if I could stay here permanently," said Samantha.

"You are welcome to stay for as long as you want to," said William.

"Thank you, William; and don't worry, as soon as I am able to, I would like to help make some sort of contribution around here," said Samantha.

"We don't have to rush things, my dear. But when you are up to it, we will start to teach you combat training. At least you will be able to protect yourself. And don't forget you are now part of our family, and family take care of each other. Welcome to our home, Samantha," said William.

"Thank you, William. I am very grateful to be a part of your family," said Samantha.

Grayson kissed Samantha on her temple. "I am so glad you are going to stay with us, my beautiful lady. Maybe tomorrow we can go and get the rest of your stuff from your apartment," said Grayson.

"Sounds like a good idea," said Samantha. "I sure will miss my apartment. But I feel that my place is here now."

After dinner was finished, Grayson and Samantha went up to Grayson's bedroom. Lying in each other's arms on the bed, Samantha said, "After speaking with the queen today, I now understand why things are done a certain way and how things work for a Lepidoptera. Like how you and I eventually met and how we were instantly attracted to each other. But there is one thing that I wanted to ask you, Grayson."

"What is it, my love?" said Grayson.

"Do you ever want to get married one day, or would you prefer to just stay life partners?" asked Samantha.

"None of us get married, Samantha. We all seem to just stay as life partners. I don't know why though. Are you a bit concerned about that?" asked Grayson.

"Yes, I am worried about that," said Samantha, sitting up and looking him in the eyes. "All my life I have wanted to get married to someone that loves me, like you do. But I fear that this won't ever happen for me now."

Grayson wasn't prepared for what Samantha had just said to him. He wasn't sure what to say. "Umm… do you need an answer about this now, Samantha? It's just… well… I have never thought about this before, and I don't know how to answer your question. And really… I don't want to upset you by saying something I haven't even had time to think about yet."

"That's OK, Grayson. I don't expect an answer straight away. But I would like an answer, someday, so that I know what to expect," said Samantha.

Grayson nodded and placed his arms around her waist. "I love you, beautiful lady. Never forget that."

Chapter Nine

Where has the weekend gone? Violette thought, opening her locker.

"Thanks for the lift, Annabelle. See you this afternoon."

"Have a good day, Vi," said Annabelle, waving goodbye as she walked back to her car.

Violette checked her timetable, which was taped onto the inside of her locker door, and noticed she had Maths first, and Science next. Taking the books out of her locker, she wondered what her week was going to be like, now that she had moved into the Gramaze house.

"Good morning, sis," said Danielle, poking her head around the door of Violette's locker.

"Hi Dan," said Violette, giving her a hug. Even though it had only been a couple of days, Violette had missed her sister.

"How was your first weekend away from us?" asked Danielle.

"It was really good, sis. I missed you though. We will have to catch up for a girls' night out one weekend," said Violette.

"Sounds like a plan," said Danielle. "So what's up with you cancelling your birthday dinner yesterday?"

"Yeah, sorry about that. I just didn't feel well yesterday," lied Violette.

"Are you still going to have a birthday dinner at all?" asked Danielle.

"Yeah. Just not sure when," said Violette. "Emily is checking when the restaurant is available next for me."

"Oh, that good. I was looking forward to going," said Danielle, opening her locker and getting her books out.

The school bell sounded for the first class to start.

"See you later on," said Violette, closing her locker.

"OK. Chat to you later," said Danielle, watching Violette walk away.

Violette's first two classes went by fast, and before she knew it, Science was over. Busting for a toilet break, she put her bag and books into her locker and ran for the ladies' toilets. Coming out of the toilet stall, she walked over to the basin to wash her hands. Not even realising that anyone was in the toilets with her, Violette felt someone strike her from behind. Falling to the floor, she lay there clutching her head. The pain was intense as she tried to focus.

She felt a needle being jabbed into her arm. Feeling the solution being injected into her body, she tried to get up off the floor. But it was no good. She couldn't move because the drug started to take effect straight away.

When she finally woke, her head was groggy and her strength had disappeared. Finding herself shackled by the hands and feet to a wall in a locked cell, she realised she had been kidnapped. She was paralysed and couldn't fight or even mind talk to anyone and her mind kept falling in and out of consciousness. Not knowing how long she had been here, or who had kidnapped her, all she could think of was Michael, and how much she loved him and wanted to see him again.

Arriving at her locker, and glad Monday classes were over with, Danielle spotted Annabelle waiting for Violette to arrive.

"Hi Danielle. How was your day?" asked Annabelle, leaning against Violette's locker door.

"Hi… yeah, not a bad day… but I have a heap of study tonight though," said Danielle, opening her locker. "Actually, I need to get a wriggle on as I am meeting some of my friends in the library to do some study. You here to pick up Violette?"

"Yeah," said Annabelle.

"She shouldn't be too long," said Danielle, closing her locker door. "Well… I had better go. See you later."

"Yeah. See ya," said Annabelle, watching her walk away.

Time went by, and Annabelle started to wonder where Violette was and why she hadn't turned up at the lockers. Annabelle folded her arms over her chest and watched other student walk by, as a feeling of dread came over her. Looking at her watch, she then realised that it was now thirty minutes after the last bell had rang. Taking her phone out of her jacket, she tried ringing Violette's mobile phone.

But it went straight to voice mail.

Opening Violette's locker with her mind, she noticed her bag was inside. Something was wrong.

Pressing the direct dial button on her mobile, Annabelle rang the Gramaze residence.

"William… I think we have a problem. Violette hasn't turned up at the lockers and I can't seem to find her anywhere."

"Check her timetable in her locker and see what classes she had today and then find out what class she attended last. Also, have you looked around the grounds, Annabelle? Report back to me when you know more or if you find her," said William, authoritatively.

"Yes, sire," said Annabelle, and hung up the phone. Opening the locker again, she pulled out the time table. She then turned around and noticed Michael standing in front of her.

"We will check each class and see which one she attended last," said Michael.

"OK," said Annabelle, with a creased brow.

They started at Maths and then Science. Each professor said that Violette had attended their class that day. But when they got to the third class, the professor checked the names of the students who had attended on the roll call sheet, and Violette's name was not there.

Standing outside the classroom with Michael, Annabelle rang William straight away with the news.

"William, she has disappeared after Science and we can't seem to mind talk to her either. So I would assume she has been taken."

"I want you two to get back here now, so we can figure out a plan on how to find her," said William.

On the way back to the Gramaze residence, Michael listened for Violette's thoughts.

"Why can't I hear her mind talk? …But hang on, I do sense something."

"Are you sure?" asked Annabelle, as they pulled up at the front gates and waited for them to open.

With his head tilted to one side he said, "Hmm, I am not sure if it's her or not, because it's different to her usual pull on me."

Parking at the front of the Gramaze home, Annabelle and Michael quickly exited the car and headed for the house. As they stepped through the front door, William met them in the foyer.

"Everyone is down in the operations room. Let's go and join them."

Entering the operations room, William called them all to order.

"Can you sense her at all, Michael?" asked Grayson.

"I feel something. But it's not her usual pull on me so I don't know if it's her or not," said Michael.

"It must be her, Michael. She is the only one who has a pull on you," said Talitha, as she entered the room.

They all bowed and couldn't believe the queen had come into the operations room. This had never happened previously, let alone her leaving her basement apartment for anything else, except for her protection.

"Your number one priority is to find Violette, and we all know why. She is a multi-coloured vampire who is the only one of us who can give the Debauched vamps new life. Brock, do you have a track on her mobile phone or not?" said Talitha, impatiently.

"Yes, Queen. I have a lock on her phone now," said Brock, checking his computer screen.

"Well what are you waiting for, you idiots? Go and get your princess now!" commanded Talitha, in a heated voice.

Within minutes, everyone except for William, was driving out the gates to find Violette.

As they got closer to the address Brock had given them, Michael said, "I can feel Violette's pull. Fuck... she isn't in a good way."

The Debauched vamps were draining Violette of her blood and isolating her DNA. They had been draining her for over two hours and Violette was now unconscious. Michael knew that if they drained her of all her blood, she would die. Violette was very close to death now.

"Sire, the woman is just about fully drained. What would you like us to do with her once she is dead?" said Prometheus.

"I want her body burned in the incinerator outside and then we will be out of here. I want all the blood and vials with the DNA stored in the special refrigerators in the van outside. Make sure all evidence is either burnt or taken with us because I don't want anyone of the Gramaze coven knowing we were here. I don't want them knowing that I am alive either, and that we are the ones who took their princess," said Nicholas, knowing what would happen to him if they caught him.

As Nicholas gave the instruction, there was an explosion outside, which sent a fireball into the night sky.

"Get outside and find out what is happening out there now!" screamed Nicholas. "Campbell, make sure all the blood and vials are put in the back of the van, so that we can leave."

"Yes, sire," said Campbell.

Grayson and Michael entered the front of the house. To their surprise there were five Debauched vamps waiting for them. Not hesitating for a moment, Grayson and Michael ran straight for them and cut their heads off. It was like a massacre, and there would be no mercy, until they found their princess. The rest of the family went around the back of the house and fought the other Debauched, whilst Michael went in search of Violette.

Feeling her pull, Michael frantically followed her scent to where he found Violette in the dungeon. She was chained and shackled by her feet and hands to the wall. She was slumped over like she was dead. Michael ripped the shackles from her body and placed her on the floor.

"Violette… Violette!… Are you OK?" screamed Michael. There was no answer from Violette. Michael felt her wrist for a pulse, but it was weak. Scooping her up in his arms, he ran with vampire speed up the stairs to find the medical van, which was parked outside. When he laid Violette on the bed inside the van, the medical team inserted a cannula drip into Violette's arm and hooked up a bag of A+ blood. Sitting on the side, as he held Violette's hand, Michael cringed as he finally noticed how many bruises she had on her face. As the medical team ripped the bloodied clothes from her body to ascertain her injuries, Michael saw just how bad of a beating she had taken. She was black and blue all over. From what Michael could remember when William had told him about his abduction, it looked like Violette had been treated the same way.

After a few minutes, the head of medical staff said, "Michael, we are not sure she is going to make it. She has been just about drained of all of her blood. Plus with the abuse she has had to endure, she is too weak."

"Is there anything we can do?" said Michael, frustrated, as he held her hand and looked at her battered face.

Talitha then entered Michael's mind and said, *Get Violette back to me and I will give her some of my blood. Hopefully this will help her heal.*

Knowing that Violette and Michael were connected as life partners, Talitha knew if she kept an eye on Michael, he would lead her to Violette and she would be able to give him advice on her treatment, if Violette was wounded.

Looking at the two medical staff, who were treating Violette, Michael said, "Take her back to the Gramaze residence. Quickly… someone will be waiting there for you to help heal her. Are you understanding me?"

"Yes, sire," they both said together, as one of them hopped in the front driver's seat of the van and started the motor, whilst the other took care of Violette.

Standing in the driveway, watching the van leave with his life partner, Michael felt powerless. There was nothing more he could do but wait to hear from Talitha, as Grayson had instructed him to stay and help with the clean-up.

"She will be OK. The queen will be able to save her, Michael," said Annabelle, placing a hand on his shoulder.

"Hmm... I hope so," said Michael, watching the car drive out of sight.

Grayson approached Michael and Annabelle and said, "You're not going to believe this... I have found out it was Nicholas that drained Violette. The bastard and his soldiers have escaped though, once again."

"What the fuck? That bastard is dead. I saw it with my own eyes, when William beheaded him," said Michael, bewildered.

But before Grayson could acknowledge his astonishment too, Brock joined them and said, "William has tracked a van that left here about the same time we got here. He told me to tell you the van is now on route nationale 1, travelling north. We need to stop that fucker now."

"Right... Michael, I know you want to go and see how Violette is, but we need to stop that van. We couldn't find any blood in the house, so I am surmising that the van will probably have Violette's blood in it," said Grayson.

"OK. What are we waiting for? Let's go!" shouted Michael.

Once they were on the road, William mind talked to Grayson, telling him where the van was at all times. He was tracking them via satellite.

At high speed, the Gramaze's SUV raced around the mountainous cliff side until the Debauched vamps' van came into view. As they got up behind the van, Brock, who was driving the Gramaze SUV, rammed the back of the Debauched van and tried to steer it off the road. When this didn't work, Brock drove up beside the Debauched van and tried to ram the side of the van. Swerving to miss them, the Debauched van tipped over and started sliding down the road. Brock then rammed the van again, and this time it went over the road railing and off the cliff. When it hit the rocks below it exploded into a fireball.

"Suck on that, you fucking blood stealing bastards," said Brock.

Brock pulled over to the side of the road, and they waited a few minutes to make sure there was no survivors. Grayson got out to look down over the cliff, but the van had been destroyed. He walked back to the SUV and said, "Let's get out of here Brock, before the police come."

"No problem," said Brock, steering the SUV away from the cliff.

Arriving at the Gramaze house, Michael jumped out the car quickly and ran inside. "How is she?" he asked William, as he entered the foyer.

"Go see for yourself. She is in your bedroom," said William, sadly.

Running up the stairs two at a time, Michael was hoping she was going to be all right. Reaching his bedroom doorway, he stood there for a minute watching her. Violette's eyes were closed and she was propped up in bed with a blood drip attached to her arm. Michael approached Violette with caution, not knowing what to expect. As he got closer to her, he noticed again how her face was badly cut and bruised with huge contusions, from the torture she had endured. Sitting on the bed, he cupped his hands over Violette's right hand and watched her sleep.

Opening her eyes slowly, Violette's vision was blurred. Where the eye ball should have been white, it was now bloodshot.

"Michael… I thought I was never going to see you again," said Violette softly. Her voice was raspy as her larynx had been damaged. As the tears welled in her eyes and spilled over onto her cheeks, she started to sob.

"Don't cry, my beautiful lady. You are home safe now and everything will be all right. How are you feeling now?" said Michael, not knowing whether to hug her. He didn't want to cause her any further pain.

"I am in a lot of pain. I have bruising to about eighty per cent of my body, and it hurts to breathe. I was told that I had lost just about all of my blood. But I think my blood is just about back to normal now, thanks to Talitha. Renee has called in Susan to come and heal me. She should be here soon," said Violette, slowly pulling back the covers so Michael could look at her injuries.

"Oh my god, Violette. I am so sorry. That looks painful. Is there anything I can get you?" said Michael, with a furrowed brow, as he held her hand.

"No. But thank you for offering. Talitha told me that I was lucky to be alive. She said that if you all didn't get there when you did, that I would have been totally drained and probably would have died. You know she gave me some of her blood to help heal me," said Violette.

"Yes, I know. She sure is a wonderful queen. We are so proud to have her with us here," said Michael.

"Knock, knock. May I come in?" said Susan, standing in the doorway.

"Hello Susan. Come in. Thank you for coming on such short notice," said Michael, standing.

"You are most welcome. Hello Violette," said Susan, walking over to the bed.

"Hello Susan," said Violette softly.

"Now let's see what I can do to help you heal faster and get rid of those bruises and the pain," said Susan, sitting next to Violette on the bed. Placing one hand on Violette's shoulder and the other on her stomach, she started the healing process.

Violette winced in pain at first, but once the pain subsided, she felt a sense of warmth and rejuvenation as Susan's power started to heal her body.

"How's that feeling, Violette?" said Susan, after about fifteen minutes.

"Better. Thank you," said Violette, looking into her eyes.

"Great… looks like my job here is nearly done. Well, I will leave you for a little while to see if your body naturally heals itself. I will come back later on tonight and check on you. OK?" said Susan.

Violette sat forward, and hugged Susan. "Thank you."

"You are most welcome. See you later then," said Susan, standing.

"Bye," said Violette, watching her walk towards the doorway.

"Thank you, Susan," said Michael.

Susan smiled, nodded once to Michael, and left the room.

Sitting next to Violette on the bed, Michael said, "Now that you are feeling a bit better, would you like to have a bath or a shower? I can wash your hair for you, if you want."

"Yes please, Michael. I would like to have a bath. I feel filthy," said Violette.

"OK," said Michael. Once he had filled the bath, Michael carefully undressed Violette and then carried her over to the bath and placed her slowly in it.

As Violette adjusted to the hot water on her skin, she sat still with her eyes closed, whilst he washed her hair and then bathed her battered body.

"Would you like to stay in there for a while and relax? It might make you feel a bit better," said Michael, kneeling next to the bath.

"Only if we can empty the water and put some clean water in," said Violette.

"Sure."

Pulling the plug on the bath, Michael lifted Violette out and sat her on the side of the bath. Wrapping a towel around her wet hair and placing a bathrobe around her shoulders, he gave the bath a rinse and refilled the claw foot tub with water and some bath bubbles, whilst Violette watched. Once the bath was full of warm water he took the towel and bathrobe off Violette and lifted her back into the bath again.

Leaning up against the end of the bath, with her legs out straight, she said, "Thank you for looking after me."

"You're welcome," said Michael.

"Can you hop in too, so that I can cuddle into you, Michael? I just want to hold you and feel safe," said Violette, looking up at him.

Nodding, Michael undressed and hoped in behind Violette. He put his back up against the back of the bath and Violette then cuddled into his chest.

"You will be OK," said Michael, as he stroked her hair.

After about twenty minutes, Michael sensed from her deep breathing that she had gone to sleep. Lifting her out of the bath, he dried her off quickly and then put her into their bed. As he watched her sleep, he thought about how lucky she had been that afternoon, and how he could have lost her. *I never want to go through another day like today, ever.*

Whilst she was asleep, Michael could see her body twitching. He knew she was having some bad dreams, because she was talking and crying out in her sleep. Lying down beside her, he cuddled into her back, hoping that this might subconsciously make her feel safe.

What a horrible ordeal she must have been through today, thought Michael. *You are safe, my love, you are safe*, he chanted through his mind to her mind.

Downstairs, William called his coven to a meeting in the operations room.

"This could have gone differently today, and I am so glad it didn't. So that this doesn't happen again, a student by the name of Sharina is coming to live with us and she will attend the same classes as Violette. That way, Violette will be protected at all times. Sharina will be arriving from Brussels with her life partner, Stephen, tomorrow. Renee, I will need you to get a room ready for them, as they will be living here permanently.

"As you all know, Stephen is Violette and Danielle's brother. So if Danielle comes to the house, you will need to remember to mind talk to everyone and let them know she is here. We don't want or need Danielle to find out her brother is here or even alive. This must remain a secret until I say otherwise. As you all know, Danielle is not one of us, so she is not to be told anything. Do I make myself clear on this subject?" said William authoritatively, as he looked around the room.

They all nodded in agreement.

"The rest of the times for guarding Violette will remain the same each day and night. Susan has told me earlier that Violette will take about two days to heal, so Renee, I will need you to ring the school tomorrow and let them know that Violette will be away for a few days, and to also provide a story to Emily and Adrian, so that they don't get worried and come over unexpectedly. We don't need them seeing Violette as she is. Annabelle, I will also need you to speak with Danielle and give her the same story that Renee is giving Emily and Adrian, so that she doesn't turn up unexpectedly either.

"Now... as for that bastard Nicholas, I have found out this evening that he had a twin brother. And it looks like that when I thought I had killed him, it wasn't actually him, but his twin, Maliyah. But I believe now, from speaking with Grayson earlier, that Nicholas was in the van that exploded on impact, when it slid off the side of the cliff. Anyway, I would say that the Debauched vamps are at loose ends at the moment. They will need to choose a new leader. So keep your eyes and ears open whilst you are out on patrol. Now that they know there is a multi-coloured female vamp, they will try again to take Violette. We will have to make sure that we double the protection for Violette. I am also going to ask the Rome leader if Christian can come and live with us permanently to help with this. Once that is sorted out, Renee, you will need to organise a room for Christian as well. Also, please alert the cook that we will need more food and blood stored," said William.

Renee nodded to William in agreeance.

Chapter Ten

Violette woke early the next morning, only to find Michael cuddled up behind her. His arms around her felt so reassuring. As she turned to face him, his eyes opened.

"Good morning. How are you feeling this morning?" asked Michael.

"Better. In fact, I am really hungry. Could we go down and make something to eat?" asked Violette.

"Sure. Would you like me to carry you, or are you able to walk?" asked Michael.

Violette sat up on the edge of the bed and tried to stand up. Her legs felt stiff and sore. Wincing, she said, "Could you please carry me? I am sure once I have something to eat and some more blood, that my legs will feel better. I am feeling a bit tired at the moment."

"No problem, my love. Susan has said it will probably take about two whole days before you are fully recovered, so don't worry," said Michael, sitting up.

"What am I going to do about school, Michael? If I don't turn up, then they will ring Emily and Adrian for sure. I don't need them coming over here to see me like this, or Danielle either," said Violette, panicking.

"It's OK, Vi. We have already rung the school and Emily, Adrian, and Danielle and given them all a story. They don't expect you back at school until Thursday," said Michael.

"Phew. Thank you. I was a bit worried there for a moment," said Violette, relaxing.

"By the way, I have some good news I want to share with you," said Michael.

"What is it? Tell me now; I want to know!" said Violette, all excited.

"After breakfast. That comes first, then I will tell you," said Michael, unhooking the bag of blood from her cannula.

"Oh, all right, teaser," joked Violette.

Picking her up in his arms, Michael carried Violette down the marble stairs and into the kitchen. Placing her on a stool at the island bench, Michael decided to make some scrambled eggs, bacon and some pancakes for both of them, and asked Violette to make the coffee whilst she sat at the bench.

"What would I do without you? You are so good to me. I love you very much," said Violette.

"I love you too, beautiful lady," said Michael, leaning across the bench, and kissing her lips tenderly.

Once Violette had her breakfast, Michael retrieved some A+ blood out the fridge for her. Drinking it down fast, she enjoyed the taste.

"So what is the good news? Don't keep me in suspense…" said Violette, excited.

"Well… as of today, you will now have more of us guarding you. Christian from Rome is going to be coming to live with us," said Michael.

"Oh, OK. Danielle will be happy about that as she has a small crush on him and she was really unhappy when Christian had to return back to Rome," said Violette.

"Right…" said Michael, knowing the problems that could arise from a vampire and human interaction.

"So who else will be coming?" said Violette, with a raised eyebrow.

"Sharina and Stephen," said Michael, with delight in his eyes.

"You mean my brother Stephen?" asked Violette, with a grin from ear to ear.

"Yes, and his life partner, Sharina," said Michael.

"How long are they staying for?" said Violette, ecstatic.

"At this stage, permanently," said Michael.

"Really. It sure will be great having my brother around again. I miss him a lot," said Violette, picturing Stephen's face and remembering how much fun she used to have with him when they were younger.

"Sharina is actually going to take the same classes as you at school so that you can be guarded there," said Michael.

Violette hugged Michael hard. "I can't believe I am finally going to get my big brother back in my life again. I suppose the worst thing is that I can't tell Danielle," said Violette.

"That's right. So if Danielle does come over, we need to mind talk and let everyone know. We don't want her bumping into Stephen unexpectedly," said Michael. "William said in the meeting yesterday, when you were sleeping, that we are not to tell Danielle anything until he says so, and he was very adamant on that, Vi."

"OK… I feel sad, knowing Danielle will never be able to see him again. She has told me just recently that she still misses him and thinks about him all the time. But I do understand William's instructions, and I will follow them, I promise," said Violette.

"Thank you, Violette," said Michael.

Yawning, Violette said, "Can you carry me back to bed, Michael? I really would like to cuddle up for a while and get some more sleep, if that's OK."

"Your wish is my command, my love," said Michael, bowing. Sweeping her up in his arms, he carried her back to their bedroom.

After Violette fell asleep and was peaceful, Michael had a shower, got dressed and went down stairs. As it was now mid-morning, Christian had arrived from Rome and was eating breakfast with Annabelle, Grayson and Samantha, when Michael walked in.

"How is Violette this morning?" asked Annabelle.

"She can't walk properly yet and is a bit weak, but she is healing nicely. She is sleeping at the moment though," said Michael.

"Man... I can't believe she even lived through what they did to her. She sure is one tough lady," said Christian.

"Thanks Christian. Good to see you again. We are all glad you are moving here permanently; welcome aboard, bro," said Michael, shaking his hand. "I hear from Violette that her sister Danielle has taken a liking to you, so you may have your hands full there, my man."

"My number one priority is to protect the princess. So don't worry, I won't be distracted, Michael, when it comes to guarding Violette," said Christian, seriously. "And anyway, Danielle is not one of our kind, so even if I did find her attractive, our laws on human and vampire relationships are not permitted, so I wouldn't even try."

"Wow, that's something else I didn't know until now. I mean I understand why this has to be, but how ridiculous is that? What would happen if you two fell in love with each other?" said Samantha, with brow furrowed and arms folded over her chest.

"Well, I would have to get William's approval first, and if he said no, then I would have to do as I am ordered. Laws are there for a reason, Samantha, and they are not to be broken whenever we want," stated Christian.

"I will remember that in the future, Christian. I still have a lot to learn," said Samantha, looking to Grayson for support.

Grayson gave Christian an intense look that said, *Shut the fuck up. Samantha is my woman and I won't hear you talk to her like that.*

Michael left them to talk, and went upstairs to see if Violette was awake. When he entered the room, he found Violette on the floor crying.

Rushing over to her, he said, "Are you all right?"

"I needed to go to the toilet. When I got out of bed I still couldn't walk," said Violette, through her tears.

"You should have just called me and I would have come to help you," said Michael. "Let's get you to the toilet and then in the bath, hey? You may feel a little bit better after a nice bath."

Feeling embarrassed Violette said, "Can you go to my drawer over there and get me my… umm… tampons, Michael?"

He nodded and thought to himself, *This must be so embarrassing for her to ask me.* Once he retrieved the tampons, he collected her and took her to the toilet, and left her there, by herself, for some privacy.

"Michael, you can come back in now? Can you please run me a bath with some bubbles?" said Violette out loud.

"Would you prefer a female to help you Vi, or are you OK with me doing this for you?" asked Michael, as he walked in the bathroom.

"I am a bit embarrassed, Michael… but I do want you to help me, as long as you are all right with that," said Violette, feeling her face turn red.

"No problem, my love. Whatever you need, you just ask me to get it for you," said Michael. After Michael ran the bath for Violette, he then lifted her in gently.

"This is lovely. The water is nice and hot and it's relaxing," said Violette, resting her head on the back of the bath.

"After your bath, would you like to go down to the dining room for lunch? Everyone is wondering how you are and would love to see you," said Michael.

"I'm not sure. It's just… well, I don't want everyone seeing me like this. I am feeling really insecure at the moment," said Violette.

"That's OK, my love. I will bring lunch up to you then," said Michael.

"Do you mind if I stay in the bath, while you go and get lunch for us?" said Violette.

"Are you sure you won't fall asleep if I leave?" said Michael.

"I never thought about that. You had better take me out and I will get dressed. I am so sorry to be a pain in the butt, Michael," said Violette.

"Hey beautiful… you are not a pain in the butt, and I am only too happy to help you," said Michael.

Lifting Violette out of the bath, he sat her on the bed and handed her a towel so she could dry herself. "What clothes would you like me to get out for you, Vi?"

"In that drawer there, I have some pyjamas, and I will need another tampon and some clean knickers as well, Michael," said Violette, pointing to the drawer.

Opening the drawer to get her pyjamas, Michael thought to himself, *She is trying to cover up her body and that's why she asked me to get her pyjamas out instead of clothes to wear outside. How am I going to get her out of this room, as she is so self-conscious about the bruising?*

Once he had helped Violette put on her pyjamas, he said, "I will be back in about fifteen minutes with lunch. Ok?"

"Thank you," said Violette, lying down on the pillow.

When Michael arrived in the dining room to get some lunch for Violette and himself, he noticed that Stephen and Sharina had arrived and were seated at the table.

"Hi Stephen, it's good to see you again," said Michael, shaking his hand. "Hi Sharina, my name is Michael, it's nice to meet you."

"Hello Michael. Nice to meet you too," said Sharina.

"How is she?" asked Stephen.

"Not good, bro. She won't come out the room because she can't walk and has so much bruising. And I don't know what to do," said Michael, feeling useless.

"Leave it with me and I will go and talk with her. Don't take her lunch up to her yet," said Stephen, getting up from the long table. "Just give me a few minutes. You will be able to read my mind anyway."

"Thanks bro," said Michael, taking his place at the table.

"Knock, knock. Can I come in?" said Stephen. He didn't wait for a reply, he just walked in and straight over to Violette, who was lying down in bed.

Violette sat up quickly when she saw it was Stephen. As he sat on the bed, she started to cry. Placing his arms around her tight, he held her in his arms and rocked her back and forth. "It's going to be OK, sis."

Violette sobbed into Stephen's chest, as he comforted her. When she finally quietened, he pulled her chin up to his face and said, "Come on, we need to get you dressed and out of this room. We don't have to go to the dining room, but you need to get some fresh air."

He then walked over to the wardrobe and pulled out a pair of track pants and a long sleeved top. "Put these on, sis."

He turned his back whilst she got dressed.

When she had finished getting dressed, he picked her up and took her downstairs and then outside to the patio area. As he was carrying her, she held onto him tight and cuddled into his chest, until he set her down.

Leaning back on the padded seat, Violette said, "Don't go. I need you to stay with me. I am not feeling myself. Please..."

"I am not going anywhere. I am here for you, sis," said Stephen, sitting next to Violette and wrapping his arm around her shoulder.

"Stephen, I have missed you so much. How long are you here for this time?" said Violette.

"I am here permanently to look after you... God, look at what those bastards did to you, Violette. You are lucky to be alive, kiddo," said Stephen, only just noticing her battered face.

"Really... permanently... kiddo...? I haven't heard you call me that for years. I have missed that, Stephen," said Violette, as she tried to hold back her sob.

"Don't cry. Everything will be OK," said Stephen, hugging her.

Michael... can you bring Violette's lunch outside to the patio area? thought Stephen to Michael.

I'll be there in a minute.

"Here we go my love, some lunch and A+ blood to keep your strength up," said Michael, standing in front of Violette with a tray and placing it on the table. "I will leave you two to talk."

"Thank you, Michael," said Violette.

Whilst Violette ate her lunch, she listened to Stephen tell her again about his life since he had left her when she was a child. How he met Sharina, and how much he missed her and Danielle when he became a vampire. As Violette listened to

Stephen, she could tell he must have had a hard time of things when he first left home. But now life was a lot better for him, especially as he now had a life partner, Sharina.

"I would love to meet Sharina. I want to see who has been keeping my brother happy," said Violette.

"She is inside if you want to meet her, sis. Do you want me to ask her to come out here now, or maybe tomorrow when you are feeling better?" said Stephen.

"Tomorrow, Stephen. I am not comfortable with people seeing me like this," said Violette.

"OK. Sorry, sis. Actually, I am going to have to go in a minute. I have some business to take care of this afternoon, and need to do it before the bank closes. Did you want to stay out here or should I take you back to your room?" said Stephen.

"You can leave me out here, Stephen. I will ask Michael to come out and sit with me. Thank you so much for being here for me today. I needed my big brother to give me some reassurance," said Violette.

"You are welcome, kiddo. And don't worry, I am not going anywhere. I will see you later on," said Stephen, standing.

"OK. Bye," said Violette, watching him walk inside.

Violette sat under the patio area, looking out into the beautifully manicured gardens thinking about how much she wanted her life to get back to some sort of normalcy.

"You feeling like some company yet?" asked Michael.

Violette looked up and said, "I am sorry I have neglected you today. Please... sit down."

"That's OK. I understand that you need time alone. Especially as it was with Stephen. How are you going, anyway? asked Michael, sitting down next to Violette and placing his arm around her shoulders.

"A bit better. Thank you for today. I am glad you asked Stephen to come and see me. I needed my big brother to comfort me. But I didn't mean to make you feel like you were left out or that you couldn't console me. It's just that I have a connection with Stephen, and as my brother, he makes me feel good about myself."

"I was worried about you, Violette. And when I couldn't do anything for you, well... it made me feel useless. But I do understand the connection you have with Stephen, and I am glad he has made your day better, anyway," said Michael.

Looking up, he noticed Annabelle walking towards them. "Looks like you have a visitor."

"Would it be OK to come and sit outside with you, Violette?" asked Annabelle.

Startled by her voice, Violette looked over in Annabelle's direction and noticed that Grayson and Samantha were with Annabelle too.

"Sure, guys. You don't have to ask to come out here. This is your house," said Violette.

"We just didn't want to upset you, that's all, Vi," said Annabelle, as she sat in front of Violette at the table.

"I could do with some cheering up, anyway," said Violette.

By the time the sun was setting in the back field, everyone was sitting outside with Violette, trying to talk with her and make her feel good about herself. Even though her injuries were confronting and embarrassing for Violette to experience, most of the Gramaze coven had been through this previously with other Debauched battles, and knew what to expect. In the end everyone told Violette about their worst or first beating they took from the Debauched, which made her feel at ease.

Before they all went inside for dinner, Violette cleared her throat and said through tears, out loud, "Thank you everyone for trying to cheer me up today. I am glad to be a part of this family, and thank you for sitting outside here with me today. I really appreciate it."

"You're welcome. We are all here for you… now, are we eating inside or outside tonight? It's your choice, Violette?" asked Renee.

"Inside would be nice, Renee. I will have to ask Michael to carry me in as I still can't walk properly, though," said Violette, looking to Michael for support.

Later that night, Susan came to see Violette again to heal her. After Susan used her ability to heal Violette some more, she said, "You should be able to walk again by tomorrow. The bruising will eventually go. But if you need me to come again, please don't hesitate to ask William."

"Thank you Susan," said Violette.

"You are welcome. Actually, I will be going back home tonight, as I am starting at a government home for disabled children in Berne tomorrow. I am really looking forward to starting there, as I am hoping to be able to heal some of these children. I feel that they don't deserve to go through life with the challenges that they face," said Susan.

"That is really nice of you Susan. What a lovely gift you have," said Violette.

"Well, you have that ability too, Violette. It's just that you have not crafted it as yet. But it will come to you soon. Actually, once all your powers kick in, you will be a very valuable asset to the Gramaze family. It's not often that we find a multi-coloured female," said Susan.

"Mmm, I know. Though, I am a bit frightened to tell you the truth, Susan. I just don't want to let anyone down," said Violette.

"You won't let anyone down, my dear. Once your abilities kick in, then you won't feel like this. We all felt like you do in the beginning. But as time has gone by, things have gotten easier. Eventually, you will feel more comfortable in your own skin," said Susan.

"Thanks, Susan. You sure know how to make a girl feel good about herself," said Violette.

Chapter Eleven

Nearly a month had gone by without any trouble or word from the Debauched vamps. William knew that they had to choose a new leader soon, so he doubled the patrols at night and everyone was instructed to keep their ears and eyes open. There was word on the streets that it was Clause who had taken over as leader, but it wasn't confirmed as yet. William knew Clause from the old days, and he knew how unscrupulous Clause was. If Clause was up to his old predictable habits, then they would see more drugs being sold on the streets, and more humans attacked for their blood. In the past, the Lepidoptera vampires were always cleaning up after the Debauched vamps. It seemed the norm these days as well. The Debauched didn't care one bit if the humans found out that vampires existed, but William knew how hard life would be if humans did find out. All Lepidoptera vampires would be categorised the same as the Debauched, and humans would not distinguish between the two enemies. William also knew that Clause would not rest until he found the multi-coloured female Lepidoptera, which meant Talitha and Violette had to be double guarded each day and night.

As William stood in the operations room with Grayson, who was his second in command, Vincent came up on the screen.

"Good evening gentlemen," said Vincent.

"Vincent, my friend. How are you and your family going in Brussels?" said William.

"We are fine here, and there is no word yet on the streets as to who has replaced Nicholas over here," said Vincent.

"We have heard it is maybe Clause, but that is not confirmed as yet," said William.

"Hmm… I hope it's not Clause, William. He is one motherfucker I would not like to go up against. But if push came to shove, we will band together and destroy him," said Vincent.

"The reason I have called this meeting is to ask you if you could release Jack, Theodore and Harrison? We would need them for a while to help guard the queen and princess," said William.

"How long would be a while, William? You have to remember these men all have life partners, and if they come, then their partners follow; that's if they are there for months at a time," said Vincent.

"Yes, I understand that Vincent. We do have room here for them all. I just don't want to leave you with not enough men to watch over your own coven in Brussels," said William.

"For the time being we will be all right. We will take it day by day for the moment," said Vincent.

"I will send a plane for them all, then," said William.

"I will make sure they are ready and waiting at the airport when your plane lands, William," said Vincent.

"Thank you, Vincent. I will always remember your kindness to my family, and I will repay you for this one day soon, my brother," said William.

"No need, my brother. I still remember the old days when you and your family saved my coven from being attacked. If it hadn't been for you and your family, I wouldn't be here today and nor would my family," said Vincent.

"After this is all over Vincent, we must get together and catch up," said William, remembering the old days.

"Are Stephen and Sharina settling in all right over there?" asked Vincent.

"Yes they are going really well here, Vincent, and I thank you for releasing them to us. They have been a real asset, and besides that, they have become part of our family now," said William.

"I am happy about that. Well, I will sign off for now and go and get everyone organised to meet you at the airport," said Vincent.

"Good, and thank you again," said William.

The screen went blank.

Anxious, apprehensive, nervous; that's me. I wonder what will happen, when Emily and Adrian come over today, thought Violette.

"Stop worrying so much, Violette. Everything will work out," said Michael, placing his clothes in the dirty clothes basket, as he listened to her thoughts.

"Easy for you to say," said Violette, with her hands on her hips, as she stood in the walk-in wardrobe trying to choose what she was going to wear for their visit.

It was the big day. One month had passed by since she had moved into the Gramaze residence and Emily and Adrian were coming to discuss how the living arrangement was going.

"If I have to go back to living at Emily and Adrian's house, then guarding me is going to become a logistical nightmare for everyone; you know that."

"Well, William and Renee did say that if Emily and Adrian said 'no' to you staying on a regular basis here, then they would seriously have to think about mind controlling them into changing their minds, right? But William was hoping it wouldn't come to that," said Michael, standing in the doorway of the walk-in robe.

"I can't say that I would be happy with Emily and Adrian's being mind-controlled," said Violette, with a creased brow.

"Look… we may be worrying about nothing at this stage. So let's just wait and see what they have to say first," said Michael.

Arriving as scheduled at 1pm, Emily and Adrian seemed very happy to see Violette. Walking to the sitting room, with her arm around Violette's shoulder, Emily said, "How are you going here, Violette?"

"I really like it here. And as promised, I have kept my grades up," said Violette.

"Yes, we know that, dear. But how are you and Michael going?" whispered Emily.

"We are going good. He is such a lovely boy," said Violette, grinning.

"I'm glad," said Emily, taking a seat on the sofa next to Adrian.

"Can I get you something to drink Emily and Adrian? Coffee, tea…" said Renee, sitting across from them.

"Nothing for me," said Adrian, leaning back into the sofa.

"No, thank you," said Emily.

"So how are things going, Violette?" said Adrian.

"Yeah, good, I was just saying to Emily that I am enjoying living here. Also you will be pleased to know that I have kept my grades up," said Violette.

"Great," said Adrian. "We would like to thank you William and Renee for having Violette in your home."

"She has been no trouble at all. We love having her here," said Renee.

"Michael, we can see from the last month that you have been true to your word, and have proved to us how much you care for Violette. But we want to know what your intentions are?" said Adrian, looking from Michael to Violette.

"Why are you asking this, Adrian?" interrupted Violette. "You know what Michael's intentions are."

"Well… the reason I ask is that we actually have some big news of our own… we are thinking about going back to LA again for four months and we need to know Michael's intentions because we are going to leave you here with the Gramaze family whilst we are gone That's only if it's OK with William and Renee."

William nodded and said, "Yes, that will be all right with us, as Violette is like a daughter to us."

Violette looked from Michael to Emily and Adrian, and asked, "So why are you leaving Bagnolet, and for four months?"

"Well what's happened is, my work has asked me to transfer there and take over a position whilst another gentleman is on leave. And if all goes well, then we should be back in three to four months, at the most," said Adrian.

"And as both you girls have settled in Bagnolet, we didn't want to uproot you again. So we decided that this would be the best plan," said Emily.

"What about Danielle? Where is she going to stay?" asked Violette.

"She will be staying with some friends of ours. Danielle has made good friends with their daughter, so I am sure that will all work out," said Emily.

"Ah, OK. Just as long as I can still see her; that's all that matters to me," said Violette.

"Will you shut the house up again? What will happen with the staff and cook?" asked William.

"We were going to ask you and Renee if you could find jobs for them here, until we get back in four months. If that's OK?" said Adrian.

"That's fine, Adrian. I will have plenty of work for them all here. We have guests from out of town staying for a few months and will need more staff to accommodate them, so that will work out well, all round," said William.

"Great," said Adrian.

"I can't believe I won't be seeing you for four months, I will miss you both a lot," said Violette, astonished they were leaving. But at the same time, she was glad she was now able to stay at the Gramaze residence on a more permanent basis, until they returned.

"You can always either ring or Skype us, you know, and we will also do the same each week. We are going to miss you and Danielle too," said Emily.

"When are you both leaving?" asked Violette.

"We will be leaving for LA in a couple of days, and I would say we will be back around January," said Adrian.

"As this maybe the last time we see you before you go to LA, would you all like to come for dinner tonight? We can have the cook make something special." said Renee.

"That would be lovely, Renee. I will contact Danielle now and let her know as well," said Emily. "Actually, Renee, I was wondering if we could do a birthday dinner for Violette tonight. It's just... well... she never got to celebrate her seventeenth birthday at all, and I, we feel terrible for not doing anything about it for her."

"Oh don't worry about that Emily. I am not bothered about missing out on a birthday celebration. That was a month ago anyway. Its' all good," said Violette, trying to dismiss it, as she looked from Emily to Adrian.

"I think that would be a lovely idea," said Renee, smiling. "I will have our cook make something special for dinner, Violette. Hmm, seventeen. You kept that quiet."

"Yeah, it's only my seventeenth. No biggy…" said Violette.

"Nonsense… every birthday is important, Violette. Anyway, in answer to your question Emily, I will make it happen," said Renee.

"Thank you, Renee," said Emily.

"Well now that is settled, we had better head off. We have a lot to do before we go to LA. What time did you want us to come back tonight Renee?" asked Adrian.

"Say around 7.30. Does that sound OK?" said Renee.

"Yes, that sounds good," said Emily.

Watching Emily and Adrian car pull away from the house, Violette felt sad knowing that after that night she wouldn't be seeing them for four months. But she was also happy to be able to stay with Michael at the Gramaze house. It had now become her home and she loved her new-found family.

Walking back inside, William said, "Well, that has worked out well, then. I will let everyone know that you are here for at least another four months, Violette."

"OK. Thanks, William," said Violette, wondering what her life would be like in four months' time, as it had already changed so much in the short time she had been in Bagnolet.

When the doorbell rang, Violette raced down the marble staircase at vampire speed to open the front door for Emily, Adrian, and Danielle. She was excited to see them and part of her missed the normal life she used to have with them.

Opening the door, Violette said, "Hello. Come in." She took their coats from them and hung them in the foyer closet. "Renee and William will be down soon."

Michael came towards them from the kitchen. "Good evening. Welcome. Come into the sitting room," indicated Michael.

"Hello, Michael," said Adrian, shaking his hand and following him.

"Hello, sis. How's it going?" said Danielle.

"Hi. Yeah, I'm good, and you?" said Violette, giving her a hug.

"Yeah, much the same. Big news hey, about Emily and Adrian moving?" whispered Danielle, as she leaned into Violette.

"Mmm… it's going to be strange not seeing them for four months," said Violette, following everyone into the sitting room.

Once everyone took their seats, Michael asked, "Would you like something to drink, or will we wait for Renee and William to come down?"

As he said this, William and Renee came in.

"Sorry we weren't here to greet you. We have had a busy afternoon and our business took longer than expected," said William.

"No trouble at all, William, we only just arrived anyway, and Violette and Michael were here to greet us," said Adrian, standing to shake William's hand and give Renee a hug.

"So what would everyone like to drink?" asked Michael.

As everyone gave their drink requests to Michael, Christian came in the front door. He had just been on patrol and needed a shower. He was grubby from a Debauched battle.

Walking past the sitting room he stopped, and said, "Good evening, everyone."

Scanning the room to see who the guests were, he noticed Danielle and held his breath. Feeling that his cheeks had turned red, he quickly averted his eyes. Christian could feel her watching him, but he dared not look back.

God, she is lovely. I wish I could have her as my girl. Her lovely skin and those legs… she looks hot, thought Christian, knowing he shouldn't even contemplate the idea.

"Sorry I am late. I had to work back. I will just go and have a shower and be back soon."

"No problem. Take your time," said Renee. *Are you mad? Don't let William hear your thoughts.*

Christian nodded to Renee once and ran off to have his shower.

Feeling her heart skip a beat, Danielle watched to see if Christian made eye contact with her before he left. *I wish he liked me. But he never seems to notice me.*

Danielle stared at the door way, impatiently waiting for Christian to return.

With a smirk on her face, Violette leaned into Danielle's shoulder and whispered, "He won't be too much longer."

Danielle smiled at Violette, and said, "What… who are you talking about, sis?"

Snickering, Violette said, "Christian. I see you looking at him. Or should I say ogling at him."

"Yeah… right," said Danielle, with a creased brow. "Hey… it sure will be different not having Emily and Adrian around for four months. I sure am going to miss them. Do you mind if we can spend some more time together whilst they are away? You are the only family I have left here."

"Of course we can. Maybe you can come over for sleepovers. I do miss you, Danielle, and the fun we used to have together," said Violette, remembering her childhood.

"Me too, Vi. Can we plan something soon?" said Danielle.

"I will check it out with Michael first and let you know when," said Violette.

"Cool."

Sitting down to a three-course dinner in the dining room, which was set up with a white linen table cloth, silver cutlery, and sparkling glassware, everyone waited for the cook to serve their meals.

Christian took longer than usual in the shower, trying to calm himself, and finally returned to the dining room as the first course was being served. Sitting next to Danielle at the table, Christian noticed William giving him a stern look.

She is off limits, thought William.

Christian nodded at William and thought, *I am quite aware of that, William. But I don't want to ignore her either, as that is rude.*

William's nostrils flared. *Don't be coy. You know the rules, Christian.*

Yes, sire.

Happy for Christian to be sitting next to her, Danielle gazed into his big brown eyes, as he spoke to her with his Italian accent.

"Good evening," said Christian, leaning into her shoulder.

"Hi…" said Danielle, breathing in his aftershave scent. Rolling her eyes, and looking away from him because she couldn't find the words, Danielle tried to pluck up the courage to speak. "Sorry… it's not every day a good-looking guy sits next to me. How have you been since I saw you last time?"

"Not bad. And you?" asked Christian, quite taken back by her statement.

"Well; thank you," said Danielle, smiling from ear to ear. *Oh, God he is hot. I would love to be snuggled up to him somewhere. But I bet he isn't interested.*

When Christian read Danielle's thoughts, he didn't know what to think. Glancing over at William, whose jaw was clenched and nostrils were flaring, Christian rolled his eyes. But it wasn't just William who heard her thoughts. In fact, every vampire in the room heard.

Cut her short… NOW, thought William to Christian.

Yes, sire, thought Christian.

Listening to William and Christian's conversation about her sister, Violette tried to change the discussion to another topic.

"Michael, do you think that we may be able to go out to a night club or do something with Danielle next weekend? I promised her I would spend more time with her whilst Emily and Adrian are away." said Violette.

"I can't see why not. I will have to ask William for his permission first," said Michael. "It will also depend on who we can get to guard you both."

Violette nodded and then smirked at Christian to see if he heard the conversation. Secretly, Violette wanted Christian to guard her, so he could spend some time alone with Danielle. But Violette wasn't about to say it out loud, let alone think about it, for everyone else to hear.

Christian frowned and shook his head at Violette. Leaning across the table, he said, "Not going to happen."

Violette raised her eyebrows at Christian and then smiled.

Lifting her glass in the air, Renee said, " Here to you, Violette. Happy birthday. May you have many more."

Everyone raised their glasses in the air and toasted Violette.

"Thanks everyone. And thanks for the lovely dinner you organised Renee," said Violette.

"You are most welcome," said Renee.

Emily, Adrian, and Danielle stood in the foyer of the Gramaze residence, waiting for the chauffeur to bring their black limousine up to the front door.

"I am going to miss you both, very much. Make sure you ring me when you land in LA," said Violette, as she looked from Adrian to Emily.

"We will. I am going to miss you too, Violette," said Emily, giving her a hug.

"If you need anything whilst we are away, please don't hesitate to ring. Be good, won't you. I will miss you, Violette, very much indeed," said Adrian, giving her a hug.

"Don't worry about Violette. She will be fine here with us, and we will take good care of her. And if you like, we can check in on Danielle as well, to make sure she is going all right?" said Renee.

"That would be good, Renee. Much appreciated," said Adrian.

Violette gave Emily and Adrian a final hug goodbye and said, "I love you both very much."

"We love you too, Violette. We will ring you when the plane lands in LA. Please keep in touch," said Emily, as she walked over to the limousine with Adrian.

Brazenly, Danielle took the opportunity to give Christian a hug and kiss on his cheek goodbye. With her heart beating fast as she pulled away from him slowly, she lingered for a few seconds to look into his eyes adoringly.

But Christian didn't bat an eyelid. Rigid, he knew he couldn't show any emotion to this girl, for fear of punishment from William.

"Good night, Danielle."

As Emily, Adrian and Danielle drove out the driveway Violette had tears in her eyes. "I miss them already."

"The four months will go quickly and they will be back before you know it, Violette. At least you still have Danielle here," said Renee, placing her arm around Violette's shoulder.

"Speaking of Danielle, Christian, I want to see you in the operations room, NOW," said William, in a demanding voice.

"Yes, sire."

Walking into the operations room, Christian knew he was about to get a lecture. As he approached, William said, "What the fuck was all that about tonight? You know she is human, so why do you pursue her? You can see she was attracted to you, but you still strung her along. I don't want you anywhere near her by yourself."

The rage inside Christian was overwhelming. He didn't care for his new leader's aggression towards him.

"Listen William… I have never been in this situation before where I am not allowed to even talk, let alone touch a human woman. I don't see what the problem is if we are not life partners," said Christian, with clenched fists.

"I don't care what you want or have done in the past, Christian. Whilst you are here and working in my coven, you will do as I bid," said William, sternly.

"Yes, sire. I apologise for my outburst. It won't happen again," said Christian, as he bowed his head to William.

"I can see you do have some feelings for this girl, and she for you. But as Danielle is human, nothing can come of it, so why do you pursue her, and more to the point why are you so attracted to her?" said William, trying to understand his new boarder.

"I can't answer why I have an attraction to Danielle, William. It's certainly strange. I have not felt like this for a human girl before," said Christian, anxiously.

"If I let you and Danielle get together, and she finds out we are vampires, but can't accept it, then we will have no choice but to wipe her mind. Then you are left with the attraction still. It doesn't work out well for you both, either way," said William.

Christian bowed his head, and said, "Yes, sire. I will try to do as you ask."

William put his hand on Christian's shoulder and said, "Danielle is a nice girl and I know this will be hard for you, but I am counting on you to be a gentleman with her and not to pursue this, Christian."

"Yes, sire," said Christian. He nodded and walked outside to get some fresh air.

Chapter Twelve

Lying in bed, looking at the ceiling and thinking about the events of the night before, Michael decided he needed to get dressed and go downstairs to speak with William. He knocked on the wooden doors to the operations room, and waited for an invitation to go in.

"Come," said William, looking through the paperwork on the table.

"Sire… are you busy?" asked Michael.

"What did you need, Michael?" said William, impatiently.

"I wanted to speak with you about Violette, sire," said Michael, wondering what had made William so irritable this morning.

"Well, spit it out, man. I don't have all day, you know," said William.

"William…" said Michael, hoping he would look up from his work.

"Yes, what is it? Just spit it out," said William.

"I wanted to know if Violette, Danielle, and myself could go to a night club tonight," ask Michael.

William opened his mouth to give Michael an answer, but Michael said, "I know what you are going to say… that we are putting Violette in harm's way. But she needs to have a night out with her sister, sire. You know, sisterly bonding and all that stuff."

"That's not a good idea here in France, Michael. You know there are too many Debauched vampires that know who Violette is, and I don't think they would stop at anything to abduct her right now, let alone kill any one of you who is protecting her," said William, looking up from his work.

"Yes, sire," said Michael, letting out a sigh.

With hand on his chin, William looked straight through Michael as he thought about his decision. He knew it wasn't a good idea to keep the princess locked up in the house all the time.

"What about taking the girls somewhere else, like, say, Rome? Christian knows his way around the city, and you could take the family plane there and back. Also, I could ask the Rome leader to see if he could release some of his men for the night to help guard them," said William.

"Hmm, not a bad idea. I am sure Violette and Danielle will love it too. Although are you sure you want Christian coming along with us, knowing how he feels about Danielle?" asked Michael.

"Listen, Michael… we have to trust Christian to do the right thing, so yes, I think it would be a good idea. But I want you to keep an eye on the situation," said William.

"I will go and talk with Violette and let you know. And William, thank you, we do appreciate this," said Michael, shaking William's hand and walking out of the operations room.

Entering his bedroom, Violette was nowhere to be seen. He could hear the shower running and knew from her scent, she was in the bathroom. Stripping off his clothes, he headed into the bathroom. Violette had her head under the water, and was enjoying the heat it provided, when Michael opened the shower door. Opening her eyes, she was surprised until she saw it was Michael and he was naked.

"Hi, gorgeous. Mmm… don't you look good enough to eat," said Violette, reaching to touch his enlarged penis.

Closing the door behind him, Michael leaned up against the tiles as she bent down in front of him and started to caress his cock with her tongue. Moaning, he felt like his insides were going to burst at any minute from the torment she inflicted on him. Pulling his cock in and out of her mouth rapidly, she continued the pleasure, nipping at the head of his cock and grazing it with her sharp fangs. Breathing heavily, he pulled his cock swiftly out of her mouth. He then picked her up and placing her on top of his cock. Now it was his turn to give her some pleasure. He fucked her wildly and vigorously, and she moaned with each stroke, as he slammed into her sex. When he finally came, he bit into her neck and sucked it hard. Breathing heavily and excited from the taste of her blood, he moaned as he sucked her neck even harder. Once he had enough, he pulled away from her and said, "Would you like to drink from me too?"

"Yes, please," said Violette, pushing his head to one side and biting down hard onto his neck. Excited by the taste of his blood, and the fact that she felt his penis had become hard again, she started to move up and down on his cock, whilst he held her in his arms. When her drinking stopped, their rhythm continued, and it wasn't long before he came, once again. Exhausted from their love making session in the shower, they both washed each other with the strawberry flavoured body wash. Turning the shower off, Michael carried Violette to their bed.

"I spoke with William this morning, and he said instead of going to a night club here in France, why don't we take the family plane and go to Rome and see a night club there? He even said Christian could come with us to show us around. William will also organise extra security for you as well. What do you think?" said Michael, cuddling Violette.

"Wow… that sounds fantastic. I will need to ring Danielle and confirm with her that this is OK, but I can't see why she wouldn't want to go. Thank you, Michael," said Violette, sitting up.

"You are welcome, my sweet lady," said Michael, sitting up and kissing her forehead.

Picking her mobile phone up from the side table, Violette rang Danielle and confirmed the Rome trip. As she hung up, she smiled and said, "Could you hear her screaming on the other end of the phone? Man, was she excited!"

Nodding, Michael said, "Yes. I sure could."

"She couldn't believe that Christian was coming as well. I told her we would pick her up on the way to the airport and that I would ring her later to confirm the time," said Violette.

"OK. I will go and tell William and Christian that we are going and organise for the plane to be fuelled," said Michael, getting out of bed and pulling on his jeans and a t-shirt.

"Tell William I said thank you and we really appreciate him doing this for us," said Violette.

"OK… why don't I meet you in the kitchen for breakfast in about thirty minutes?" said Michael, walking towards the door.

"Sounds good," said Violette.

Sitting in front of the mirror putting her jewellery on, Violette thought about what clothes she could wear that night to the club in Rome. She was really excited about going, as this was the first time she would have been out in weeks.

Sometimes I miss being human. It's not all it's cracked up to be, being a multi-coloured female Lepidoptera, because it has way too many restrictions, thought Violette.

Making her way down to the kitchen, Violette heard Samantha's thoughts, as she entered the room. Samantha was in there making herself some breakfast.

"Hi, Samantha," said Violette.

"Good morning, Violette. Would you like a coffee?" said Samantha.

"Thanks. That would be great," said Violette, sitting at the island bench. "How are you going? Are you adjusting OK with the change and everything?"

Samantha placed Violette's coffee in front of her and sat down at the island bench. "To be honest with you; it's all going really well. It's just that sometimes I wish I could go back to not knowing about our world. I don't like the restrictions we have. Don't get me wrong, I love the family and most of all Grayson, but my old life didn't suck that much you know," said Samantha.

"I know what you mean, Sam. I love it here too, but I am missing my old life as well," said Violette.

Both girls were very new to being Lepidoptera vampires, and this type of lifestyle would certainly take some getting used to, especially for Violette.

"At least we have each other to talk to when we need to talk about this, Samantha," said Violette.

"I agree. I am not sure the others would understand," said Samantha.

"Good morning, ladies. How are we both this morning?" said Annabelle, walking into the kitchen.

"Good morning," said Violette.

"Yeah, I'm good," said Samantha.

"Sorry to eavesdrop on your conversation just now, but I wanted to say to you both, that we all have felt like what you are feeling at the moment. It takes a long time to forget your old life and then to embrace this world. If you ever need to talk, I am here for you. Don't hesitate to ask me anything."

"Thanks, Annabelle," Violette and Samantha said together.

"Would you like a coffee, Annabelle?" asked Samantha.

"Yes thanks, Samantha," said Annabelle.

As the girls were chatting Michael came into the kitchen and greeted them all.

"How is everything this morning, Michael?" asked Annabelle.

"Not too bad, Annabelle," said Michael.

Placing his arms around Violette, he said. "I have made all the arrangements. We are ready to go whenever you want."

"Where are you both off to?" asked Annabelle.

"We are going to Rome," said Michael.

"Lucky things. How exciting," said Samantha. "I would love to go there one day."

"Yeah, I am excited. Can't wait… well I had better go and pack. What time will I tell Danielle we will pick her up?" said Violette.

"Tell her in about two hours. That should give you both plenty of time to pack and get ready," said Michael.

Violette took her phone out of her pocket and confirmed the time and details with Danielle. As she put her phone in her pocket of her jeans, she said, "Well, I will see you tomorrow, ladies. Take care whilst I am away."

"Have a great time, Violette," said Samantha.

"Thanks," said Violette. "I will."

"Yeah, have a good time guys," said Annabelle.

"I am sure we will," said Michael.

Chapter Thirteen

The jet sat on the tarmac waiting for instructions from the tower to take off, as Michael, Violette, Danielle and Christian walked up the metal stairs to board the plane.

Greeted by the steward, they heard the captain say over the loud speaker, "Please take your seats and prepare for take-off."

Excited, Violette took her seat next to Michael and fastened her seat belt. Looking across the aisle, she noticed Christian had taken a seat next to Danielle and could feel the nervous tension between them.

Fastening her seat belt tightly, Danielle looked out the window and realised that the plane had started to taxi out to the runway. "I don't like flying," said Danielle, hanging onto the armrest, her breathing rapid.

"You will be all right," said Christian, patting her hand.

"I can't wait to see Rome, though," said Danielle, trying to change the subject. They hadn't even taken off yet, but she couldn't wait to land.

"Rome is a beautiful city, Danielle. I am sure you will love it," said Christian.

With the plane about to take off, Christian could hear Danielle saying to herself, *Calm yourself. It's only a short plane trip and nothing is going to happen.* She repeated it over and over in her mind.

Placing his hand over hers and squeezing it, Christian looked into Danielle's eyes and said, "It's OK, Danielle... take a deep breath and you will be all right."

"Thank you, Christian. I always get nervous when I fly. I don't know why."

"If it makes you feel better, you can put you head on my shoulder and close your eyes if you want," said Christian, leaning into her.

Placing her head on his shoulder, she closed her eyes.

"Thanks Christian. This is nice of you."

"You're welcome," said Christian.

Michael looked across the aisle at Christian, and couldn't believe what he was seeing. *What do you think you are doing? You know that's not allowed*, thought Michael to Christian.

She is scared to fly. What was I supposed to do, just sit here for two hours, ignoring her? Even you wouldn't do that, Michael, thought Christian.

Nodding his head, just once, Michael thought to Christian, *As long as that is all there is to it, Christian.*

I know the rules, Michael…you don't have to explain them to me, thought Christian, as his nostrils flared and he rolled his eyes. He was sick and tired of hearing it.

Finally relaxing, as she lay her head on Christian's shoulder, it wasn't long before Danielle was asleep. As her breathing slowed, Christian placed both of their seats back to rest, until it was time to land.

"Wake up, sleepy head," said Christian, rocking her a little bit. "We have landed in Rome."

"Hmm... already? That was quick," said Danielle, sitting up straight and wiping the sleep from her eyes. "Thank you,

Christian, for the use of your shoulder. Was really nice what you did for me, and I do appreciate it."

"You are welcome," said Christian, smiling.

When the plane came to a stop at the terminal, the captain said over the PA system, "Ladies and gentlemen, we have now landed in Rome and you can take your seat belts off."

As the plane door opened, Michael stood in the doorway, with Christian, ready to protect their princess and Danielle. Walking down the stairs, onto the tarmac, Michael noticed a black limousine was waiting for them, and a black SUV with two other Lepidoptera guards, who were standing at the front of the van. As he reached the bottom of the stairs with Christian, he motioned for Violette and Danielle to depart the plane.

"How exciting is this, sis?" said Danielle, carrying her hand luggage.

"I know, right? I can't wait to see Rome," said Violette, smiling at Danielle. Reaching the bottom of the stairs, both girls handed their bags to the driver, stepped into the limousine and took their seats.

As it was still daylight when they landed, there was plenty of time to do some sight-seeing, so Christian instructed the driver to take them to all the famous monuments in Rome. Driving through Rome, Christian explained about each place in detail, and even when they got out the car to go inside to have a look, Christian informed them on the history of each piece of art, artefact and building. Michael was on guard the whole time they were out.

"I am sorry you can't enjoy yourself more because you have to guard us," said Violette quietly to Michael, as they were walking back to the car.

"That's OK, my love. I've been to Rome before, and anyway, I can enjoy myself more tonight as we will be in one place and have extra guards, who will be keeping you safe," said Michael.

As the day became night, Christian knew he had to keep a watch out for the Debauched vamps. They mostly only came out at night and he knew they wouldn't be safe. "I know of a really nice restaurant near here. Would you all like to go get some dinner?" asked Christian.

"That's sounds good. I am famished," said Danielle.

"Let's go. I am starving," said Violette.

Arriving at the restaurant, Michael sensed that the owner was a Lepidoptera vamp. He looked at Christian and thought, *Good call, bro.*

Christian nodded and followed the waitress to their table.

Seating them at their table, the waitress handed them all the menus and then put some glasses and bottles of water on the table. She advised them of the daily specials and spoke about the flavours of the food.

"Mmm, can't wait to try the spaghetti bolognaise here," said Danielle.

"Yeah, I think I might have the lamb casserole. That sounds good," said Violette. "What are you having Michael?"

"The crumbed veal and vegetables sounds good," said Michael.

"Mmm, I might have that too," said Christian.

Returning about fifteen minutes later, the waitress took their drink and food orders and returned to the kitchen.

Whilst waiting for their meals to come they all spoke about what they had seen during the day, and what they thought of Rome.

Danielle looked across the table at Christian and asked, "Have you lived here all your life?"

"No. I have only lived here for about five years," said Christian.

"It's certainly a lovely place. You must miss it now that you are living in Bagnolet?" said Danielle.

"I do a bit. But I also like Bagnolet a lot, too. It's a beautiful country, France. I would like to settle down there one day," said Christian.

"What type of work did you do here, Christian?" asked Danielle.

"I work mainly in security," said Christian.

"Do you feel like we don't exist?" whispered Violette to Michael, as she listened to Danielle and Christian's conversation.

Nodding, Michael said, "Sure do."

"So where are we going to go after dinner?" asked Michael, trying to distract Christian and Danielle. Just as Michael asked this, the waitress returned with their meals and drinks.

Watching everyone receive their meals, Christian said, "Well, I was thinking we could do some more sight-seeing. Rome is beautiful at night. And then maybe we can go to a night club."

"Sounds good, bro," said Michael.

"Yeah, I am excited about the night club," said Danielle.

"OK. It's sorted then," said Christian, taking a bite of his food.

Christian instructed the driver to take them to the night time tourist attractions. As they drove along Violette and

Danielle both looked out the windows and commented how the sights at night were so beautiful.

Not as beautiful as you, Danielle, Christian thought to himself.

"Driver… can you please take us to the night club now?" said Christian, looking at his watch.

"Yes, sir," said the driver, looking at Christian in the rear-view mirror.

It was around 10.30 when they all arrived at the night club. The limestone building had a long line to get in, but as Christian knew the vamp on the door they all walked in straight away. The room was filled with cigarette smoke and the coloured lights bounced off a mirror ball, and people danced to the loud music around the night club.

"Did you want to dance or get something to drink?" shouted Christian over the music.

"Dance," said Danielle and Violette both at the same time.

Christian grabbed Danielle's hand and said, "Come on, let's go."

Michael and Violette followed them onto the wooden dance floor.

An hour later, Christian shouted to Danielle over the music, "Would you like to go and get a drink?"

"Yes, please. I need a drink to cool me down. I'll have a Coke, please," said Danielle, leaning into Christian, whilst she continued to dance.

"You guys want a drink?" asked Christian to Michael and Violette, who had their arms around each other's shoulders, slow dancing.

"No, thanks," said Violette.

"Nah. I am OK, bro," said Michael. *You go ahead. I'll keep guard.*

Leaving Michael and Violette to keep dancing, Danielle followed Christian to the bar, and waited for him to order the drinks.

As she stood drinking her Coke, she turned to Christian and said, "Can we go sit down?"

He nodded and quickly scanned the night club for a vacant seat.

"Ah... there's one," shouted Christian to Danielle, as he pointed to the back of the night club.

Sitting in a four person booth next to Danielle, Christian asked, "Are you having fun? What do you think of this night club?"

Looking into his eyes as she sipped her drink, Danielle said, "Yeah, it's great. They play pretty good music in here as well."

"You know you have the most beautiful eyes, Danielle," said Christian.

Feeling her face heat up, and her heart beat quicken, she said, "Thanks... but..."

She didn't get to finish her sentence.

Learning in, Christian kissed her lips softly. He could feel that she enjoyed the moment just as much as he did.

When they came up for a breath, Danielle said with raised eyebrows, "Mmm... that was unexpected, Christian. I didn't think you wanted to be anything more than friends. So what has changed?"

"I have wanted to do that for a while, Danielle. But I have hesitated because... well... William spoke to me and said that I am not allowed to date you because he doesn't know if I will be staying in Bagnolet or coming back to Rome. He said he didn't want to see you get upset, that's all. The Gramaze family are very protective, when it comes to you and Violette."

"So, if that's the case, then why did you kiss me now, when you know the consequences?" said Danielle.

"I can't help myself, Danielle. I just want to be with you, and I don't care about the consequences any longer. I am sick and tired of all the rules," said Christian, looking into her eyes adoringly.

"I have liked you for a while too, Christian, and I am glad you have broken the rules for me," said Danielle, placing her arms around Christian and putting her head on his shoulder. When she eventually pulled away, Christian kissed her lips, once again, with as much passion as he could muster this time.

Realising that they hadn't seen Danielle and Christian for a while, Michael started to panic.

"Can you see them anywhere, Vi?" asked Michael.

Violette scanned the night club quickly.

"No, I can't."

"Let's go," said Michael, taking her by the hand and walking off the dance floor. As he walked through the night club, Michael leaned into Violette and indicated to the back of the room. "They are over there in the booth. Fuck…"

Violette looked to where Michael was pointing and spotted them. At first she thought her eyes were playing tricks on her, until she looked again. Christian and Danielle were entwined in each other's arms and kissing.

"What are we going to do, Michael? If William finds out about this, Christian will be in big trouble," said Violette, worried.

"Well… Christian knows the consequences… and I don't want to get involved. We knew they liked each other, so it was only a matter of time before they got together. They can sort this out with William when we get back home," said Michael, sick and tired of worrying about it all.

"You're right, Michael. I am not going to say anything; my lips are sealed," said Violette.

Standing next to the booth, waiting for them to look up, Violette said, "Finally, you two have gotten together."

What are you fucking doing, Christian? thought Michael, as he sat down with Violette in the booth.

Christian pulled away from his kiss with Danielle and scowled at Michael. *If you breathe one word...*

Realising Michael and Violette had sat down in the booth on the other side, Danielle said, "Hi. How's it going?"

"Good. But I think your night is going better," teased Violette.

"Sure is. We have both liked each other for a while. But I am a bit worried as Christian has told me that William said that we can't be together," said Danielle, leaning across the table.

"Yeah, I know. He is only looking after your well-being sis. That's why he said it," said Violette.

"You mean you knew about this and said nothing to me?" said Danielle, heatedly.

"Sorry sis," said Violette, with a creased brow.

"Enjoy yourself tonight, because tomorrow there is going to be one big shit fight with you and William, I can tell you," said Michael to Christian and Danielle, taking Violette by the hand and pulling her away so they could go and dance some more.

Confused and dismayed by it all, Danielle looked sadly at Christian and said, "Are you sure you want to go through with this, just to date me? I wouldn't blame you if you didn't want to."

"You're not going to give up on me that easily, are you? And after you have waited so long? Don't worry, I will speak with William as soon as we get back and try to sort something out," said Christian, running his hand down the side of her face.

Danielle placed her arms around Christian and kissed him passionately.

"Does that answer your question?" said Danielle.

Smiling, he nodded and kissed her back.

"Let's go dance some more and forget about all this talk," said Christian, pulling her out of the booth and onto the dance floor.

As the night progressed, the four of them enjoyed themselves so much, that they didn't want the night to end. Before they all knew it, it was time to head back to the airport to fly back to France.

Calmed by his presence, once again, Danielle slept most of the way back home, in Christian's arms.

How am I going to explain this to William? I hope he doesn't send me packing back to Roma, thought Christian. He knew he was going to be in a lot of trouble when they got back. But he was going to try to explain himself, because Danielle was worth the fight, even if she was a human.

"Thank you for taking me to Rome, Michael. It was nice to get out the house for a change. I feel like I have been cooped up forever, even though it has only been one month," said Violette, as she cuddled into his side on the plane.

"You're welcome," said Michael.

"I have thoroughly enjoyed myself, and it was also good to spend some time with my big sis again."

"Life sure is different for us now, Violette. Who would have thought that we would meet? I know you are still coming to terms with being a Lepidoptera vampire and are struggling with the restrictions it has for you in particular, but I will try to make life for you as normal as possible along the way," said Michael, looking into her adoring eyes.

"What did I ever do to deserve a guy like you, Michael? Sure, my world was turned upside down, but I wouldn't have it any other way. I love you so much and never want to be without you in my life," said Violette.

Michael placed his arm around Violette and pulled her in close. Lifting her chin up, he kissed her lips passionately.

Chapter Fourteen

"Hey… sleepy girl, we have landed," said Christian, as the wheels touched down and the plane landed at the airport. Danielle opened her eyes as Christian kissed her forehead.

"Thank you for a lovely time in Rome. I had so much fun," said Danielle, yawning.

"You are welcome, sweet lady. I enjoyed spending time with you," said Christian, looking into her eyes.

"Why do you look so worried, Christian?" asked Danielle.

"It's because I don't know what William is going to say or do about us being together in Rome," said Christian, with a furrowed brow.

"Why don't we face him together then?" said Danielle.

"I'm not sure that would be a good idea, Danielle. William can be pretty frightening sometimes. I think I would be better off going to see him first and explain what happened and ask for his approval, before you talk with him," said Christian.

"Well, you know him better than me, so I will leave it up to you. But if you need my support, let me know and I will be there in a heartbeat," said Danielle.

Christian leaned in and kissed Danielle on her lips, sensually. "Even though we have only known each other for a while, I know in my heart already that I want to be with you, Danielle, and I would do anything for you," said Christian.

"I feel the same way," said Danielle.

Waiting for them on the tarmac as they disembarked, were Grayson and Samantha.

"Hi, everyone. How did the trip to Rome go? I bet you all had a great time," said Samantha.

They all nodded and agreed that they did have a good time. On the way back to the Gramaze house everyone talked about what they done and seen and how sad they were when it ended.

I can't believe we didn't even run into any Debauched vamps! That was a first. Night time in Rome, they are usually out in the dozens causing trouble that we have to clean up afterwards. Makes you wonder what's going on and why they are so quiet, thought Christian.

It's been pretty quiet here whilst you were all gone too. Maybe you are right Christian. Maybe something is going on with them. Oh, and William would like to see you all in the operations room when we get back. He just wants a debrief; don't panic, thought Grayson.

"Can you please give your new home address to Grayson so that we can drop you off?" said Christian to Danielle.

"Sure," said Danielle.

Pulling up at the house where Danielle was staying whilst Emily and Adrian were away for four months, Christian hopped out the car quickly and retrieved Danielle's overnight bag out the trunk of the car.

"See you later, sis," said Violette, hugging Danielle.

"Bye. And thank you for taking me to Rome. I had such a wonderful time," said Danielle, hugging her back.

"You are welcome," said Michael.

"We will see you around," said Samantha.

"Yeah. Thank you for the lift," said Danielle, stepping out the car.

"No problem. Bye," said Grayson.

Christian was waiting for her at the front door. Placing his arms around her waist, he pulled her into his chest for a cuddle.

Pulling her chin up to meet his gaze, he kissed her lips passionately. Danielle thought her mind was going to explode from the intensity of his lips.

"Mmm, that was nice. I don't want you to go, Christian," said Danielle, with a creased brow.

"I will give you a ring later on and let you know what William has said. But no matter what he says, I am not going to give you up without a fight," said Christian, cuddling her tight. Kissing her once more, he then headed for the car.

"When did those two get so close? I can see there is going to be trouble when we get back home. William is going to be furious that Christian defied him," said Grayson.

Samantha slapped Grayson on the leg and gave him a look and said, "You can't hold back true love."

Arriving at the Gramaze house, they all put their bags away and then headed for the operations room where everyone was waiting for them.

"Good… I am glad you are all back," said William, watching the rest of his family walk through the doorway. "We need to talk about what has been going on. Last night was pretty quiet out on the streets here. I have been speaking with some of the other leaders today and they are all saying the same is happening in their areas as well."

"It was pretty quiet in Rome as well, William. We didn't even see one Debauched vamp," said Christian.

"This must mean that they were meeting their new leader, I think," said William, rubbing his chin.

"Do we have anyone on the inside who can let us know, William?" asked Violette.

"Funny you should say that, Violette. I am going to give our source a ring soon to see if we can find out anything. When you are out on patrol tonight I want you all paired up. No one is to be by themselves. I don't care what the situation. Am I clear?" said William, authoritatively.

They all nodded.

Once William gave out the patrol roster for the night, they all left the operations room, except for Christian.

"William, I know you are busy, but do you have a minute to talk?" said Christian.

"What is it Christian?" said William, in a heated breath.

"I don't know how to say this, sire. I have made a mess of things and have defied you," said Christian, nervously.

"What is it, man? I am busy. Just spit it out," said William.

"Well, I have kissed Danielle, and sire, I like her a real lot. I am asking you for your approval to go on seeing Danielle," said Christian, worried about his reaction.

William turned around from what he was doing, and pushed Christian up against the wall. With his hand at Christian's throat, he said in a heated voice, "What the fuck were you thinking? I gave you strict instructions. You told me you could be trusted, and now you have defied me." Squeezing Christian's throat with his hand, William nostrils flared, as he put his face closer to Christian's. "I can't believe you have done this. I will not tolerate your defiance."

"But sire… I have strong feelings for her," said Christian, struggling for breath.

"You will do as I have requested. Either you stop seeing Danielle, or I will send you back to your Rome leader and he can deal with you," said William, releasing the hold on Christian's throat.

Christian put his head down and nodded.

"Yes, sire."

"In fact, Christian… I am now going to change your patrol duties so that you don't have time to see her. This should put a stop to it once and for all. You are now on patrol every night from 7.30 until dawn. You will have the days free to do as you want and to also keep up your combat practice, but I don't want to hear or see you anywhere near Danielle. ARE WE CLEAR?" shouted William.

"Yes, sire... perfectly clear," said Christian, with his head down.

"Now get the fuck out of here, Christian... I am busy with more important stuff than this bullshit," said William, turning and shaking his head as he walked away.

Michael and Grayson were waiting for Christian when he came out of the operations room.

"Sorry man... at least you tried," said Grayson, walking along side Christian.

Michael put his hand on Christian's shoulder and said, "Come on, let's go let off some steam somewhere."

"Thanks, guys... I appreciate the offer, but I need to ring Danielle first and tell her what William has said... I just don't understand why he didn't even want to consider it, that's all," said Christian, feeling gut-wrenchingly miserable.

"We will catch up with you later then," said Grayson, shaking his hand.

"Yeah, bro. It will eventually sort itself out," said Michael.

"Catch you both later," said Christian, taking his phone out of his pocket and walking outside to the patio area.

"Hi, handsome. How did things go?" asked Danielle when she answered.

Christian took a deep breath and sighed.

"It didn't go well, Danielle. William has told me that he forbids me to see you and if I try, then he will send me back to Rome. He has also given me more shift work, so that I have to work long hours at night."

Danielle couldn't believe what she was hearing.

"What about if I ring Emily and Adrian and ask them for their permission? Do you think William would change his mind then?" asked Danielle.

"It won't work, Danielle. William told me that under no circumstances am I to pursue you. And even if Emily and Adrian did say yes, William has told me that he is going to keep me so busy that I won't have time to see you anyway," said Christian.

Danielle couldn't contain her feelings any longer. Her tears spilled over onto her cheeks. She couldn't speak, but Christian could hear her crying.

"I am so sorry, Danielle. I should have never acted on my feelings for you, and we wouldn't be in this mess. Please don't cry," said Christian.

"I have to go, Christian. Sorry... but I can't talk anymore. I know it's not your fault and I do have strong feelings for you... sorry, I have to go," said Danielle, through her sobs. She hung up abruptly.

Christian sat on the steps with his head in his hands. Saddened, tears spilled over onto his cheeks. He didn't know what to do. Sometimes he hated being a vampire with all the rules they dealt out.

Walking outside for some fresh air, Renee noticed the state Christian was in. Sitting next to him on the step, she put her arm around him and said, "Give it time, dear. It will get easier."

"He didn't even want to give us a chance, Renee, and that's just not fair at all. I can see his reasoning. But to not give us a chance? I don't understand why."

"When things like this happen, William has to think about how this will affect us all, not just you, Christian. So I would say this is the reason why," said Renee.

"I know… but I have strong feelings for this girl, and what if we are meant to be together. What then?" said Christian.

"Give it a few days. Once William has calmed down about this, I can try to talk to him for you. But I can't promise you anything, Christian. Usually when William has made up his mind, he won't change it, especially as you have defied his trust in you."

"Thank you, Renee. I would appreciate if you could talk to him," said Christian.

"You are welcome… well, I need to go and speak with the staff about dinner. Will you be OK?"

"Yes. I will be fine," said Christian.

"OK. I will see you later on for dinner," said Renee, walking back inside.

Grayson and Michael found Christian outside.

"Come on, bro. Let's go and let get some practice in," said Michael, from behind.

"Sure," said Christian, turning around.

The three of them went down to the combat room and put on their gear to practice their skills. Michael and Grayson took it in turns to fight Christian so he could try to get rid of his pent-up anger and rage. Once Christian was exhausted and couldn't take anymore, they all had showers and went to dinner in the dining room.

Violette had overheard what had happened with Christian and Danielle and decided she would give Danielle a ring to see if she was all right. She knew from Danielle's thoughts just how much she liked Christian. Taking her phone out of her pocket, she dialled the number and waited for her to answer. When there was no answer, she decided to ring again.

"Hello…" said Danielle sobbing.

Violette could hear in her sister's voice that she had been crying. "Hi, Danielle. Is there anything I can do for you?"

"Hi, Violette… thank you for ringing. I don't think there is anything anyone can do, as William has forbidden us to be together… is it possible for you to come over?" pleaded Danielle.

"I will have to go and ask Renee if it's OK for me to come over Danielle. I will ring you back in five minutes. OK? Bye," said Violette.

"OK. Bye," said Danielle.

Violette hung up and went to find Renee. Walking into the kitchen, she found Renee helping with the evening meal preparation.

"Would it be all right if I go over to Danielle's place? She is really upset and needs someone to talk with," asked Violette.

"I can't see that being a problem. You will need to take Annabelle and Harrison for protection with you," said Renee.

"Thanks, Renee. I will go and find them now," said Violette walking out the kitchen with her phone on redial. "Hi Danielle. I will be there in about twenty minutes."

"Thank you. See you soon."

Once Violette had organised for Annabelle and Harrison to guard her, she then asked the chauffeur to take her over to Danielle's place.

Knocking on the door, Violette waited in anticipation for Danielle to open it. When the door opened, Violette couldn't believe the state of her sister. Danielle's face was all red and blotchy. Her mascara had run down her face as well, not to mention the red eyes from crying. Hugging her, Violette said, "Come on, let's go inside and we can talk."

Placing her arm around Danielle's shoulder, they went up to her room.

"I just can't stop crying, Vi. I can't concentrate on anything else but the thought that I won't be able to see Christian, ever again," said Danielle.

Violette pulled her sister into a consoling hug and rubbed her back until Danielle stopped crying.

"I am so sorry that this has happened to you, Danielle. I wish that I could do something to ease your pain," said Violette.

"Thanks, Vi. I appreciate you coming over to help me through this. I don't know what I would do if you weren't here," said Danielle, wiping her tears away.

The longer Violette stayed and chatted with Danielle, the better Danielle felt. But before they knew it, it was time for Violette to go back home. Annabelle and Harrison also were getting impatient about being outside.

"I had better head off as I have homework I need to do for tomorrow at school," said Violette.

"God... so do I, Vi. I just hope I can concentrate on it," said Danielle. "Why do I always fall for the impossible, Vi?"

Violette shrugged her shoulders and said, "I don't know. But I am sure things will get better soon."

This doesn't make sense. Why are Christian and Danielle so attracted to each other? They definitely aren't life partners, thought Violette.

Walking to the front door, Violette said, "I am only a phone call away if you need me to come over. OK... just try keep yourself busy, as that always seems to work when you are feeling like this. I will see you tomorrow at school." Violette hugged Danielle goodbye. "Take care of yourself. Maybe have a bath to relax."

"Thanks, Violette. See you tomorrow," said Danielle, giving her another hug.

As Violette got into the car with Annabelle and Harrison, Annabelle said, "Poor girl. She has it bad."

"Yeah, but not much we can do for her though," said Violette, shaking her head.

When they arrived back at the Gramaze house, William asked Violette to come into the sitting room for a chat. "How is Danielle coping?" said William.

"She is understandably upset, William, and there is nothing any of us can do to console her," said Violette.

"I am sorry she has to go through this, Violette. But I have to think of the family when it comes to situations like this. Humans and vampires shouldn't ever be together, because the humans can't ever seem to get their minds around what we are. I just wished that I had listened to my third-in-command when he told me that I was making a mistake letting Christian go to Rome with you all," said William.

Violette looked bemused.

"Third-in-command. Who is that?" asked Violette.

"Sorry, Violette; I meant, Michael," said William.

Wow, I didn't know Michael was third in command here, thought Violette to herself.

"OK. Well there isn't much we can do about this all now, William. But I would like to ask you to maybe take a few days to reconsider how you feel about Christian and Danielle. I know it's not my place to say anything, and I should just shut my mouth, but I really hate seeing both of them so miserable.

You know in life we don't get too many chances for happiness…"

William put his hand up for Violette to stop talking.

"Violette, please don't ever think that you don't have a say around here, because you do. However, as I am leader, what I say must be obeyed by all. But thank you for your candour. I do appreciate it," said William.

Finishing up their conversation, William left the room leaving Violette thinking, *I sure don't understand that man sometimes.*

Violette was walking upstairs to her bedroom to do some study, when Michael caught up with her to tell her dinner was being served. When she turned around, Michael could see how upset she was and said, "Are you all right, my love?"

"No, I am not, Michael. I am sad for Danielle. Would you mind if I eat my dinner in our bedroom this evening, as I just want to be alone with my thoughts? Plus I do have a bit of homework to do as well," said Violette.

"Sure. Do you mind if I sit with you?" said Michael.

"Of course I want you to sit with me. I just need to cuddle up to you and to stare off into space for a while," said Violette.

"OK. I will go and get our dinner, and meet you in our room in about say ten minutes. Does that sound all right?" said Michael.

Violette hugged Michael, and said, "I love you. What would I do without you?"

Michael smiled and said, "Thank you, beautiful lady. I love you too, and I too would not know what I would do without you. I couldn't even imagine you not being in my life now." Pulling her in close to him, he then kissed her.

Violette continued up the stairs to their bedroom, where she got undressed and into her PJs. It wasn't long before Michael came upstairs with their dinner and drinks.

As they sat there on the bed eating their dinner Michael said, "Is Danielle going to be all right? How was she when you went over there today?"

"It was a terrible sight, Michael. She just does not cope well with rejection or hurt. I haven't seen her like this in a long time and I am hoping she will be OK. I will have to keep an eye on her that's all... you know when our parents died, we had each other to console us, but because she is living away from me now, I think she feels like she has no one she can talk to about Christian. Even though I did say to her she can ring me anytime," said Violette.

"This is such a stuffed up situation. I wish there was something I could do," said Michael. Secretly, he was also annoyed with Christian for even perusing Danielle and for disregarding William's direct orders.

After they had eaten their dinner, Michael took their dishes downstairs to the kitchen, whilst Violette tried to catch up on her homework in their bedroom. Violette didn't get far with her homework before she was interrupted by her phone ringing.

"Hello... are you OK?" Violette said, as she answered the phone. It was Danielle, and she was crying and sobbing.

"Can I come over and just sit and hug you, Violette? I need someone for support." said Danielle sobbing.

"Yes, of course you can. But I will need to ask Renee to ask the people you are staying with if that is OK first, Danielle. If they say 'yes', then I will send someone over to collect you. Give me five minutes and I will ring you back," said Violette, hoping off the bed and walking towards the doorway.

"OK. Thanks, Vi," said Danielle.

Violette ran down stairs in search of Renee. She found her in the kitchen speaking with Michael.

"Renee, would it be OK if Danielle stayed the night in my room with me? She has just rung me and is upset. I told her yes, but I said that I would ask you to ring the people she is staying with to ask them if this is all right. And that she can't just get up and leave," said Violette, anxiously.

"Firstly dear, I will have to ask William if that is all right. And only if he says 'yes', then I will ring the people she is staying with to ask if it is all right for her to stay here the night," said Renee.

"Oh, OK. Thanks, Renee. I did tell Danielle I would ring her back soon. So can you go ask him now for me?" said Violette.

"I will go and find William, now. But don't get excited as he may say 'no'," said Renee, walking out the kitchen.

"How about if I go and bunk with Christian tonight, Vi? That will give you and Danielle some space to talk and she can then go to sleep in our bed with you," said Michael.

"Thank you, Michael, for being so understanding. I just hope William says yes."

He smiled at her.

"Anything for you, my beautiful lady."

Walking into the kitchen with Renee, William approached Michael and Violette with a serious look on his face. Lately, it was never possible to tell if William was in a good mood or not. Standing in front of them with Renee by his side, he said, "I believe from speaking with Renee, that you would like Danielle to stay tonight."

"Yes, sire. Will this be OK?" asked Violette.

"As long as she doesn't think that by staying here, she will be able to be together with Christian. I want that made quite clear to her, Violette," stated William.

"Yes, William. I will make that quite clear to her," said Violette.

"What about if we ask the people that Danielle is staying with if she can stay here for a few days, or just until she is feeling better about things? It's not likely that she will run into Christian here anyway as he will be out on patrol at night and she will be at school during the day," said William.

"Thank you, William. I really appreciate you letting me do this for Danielle. Her voice on the phone was so miserable, and I haven't heard her talk like that since our parents died last year. So understandably, I am really concerned."

"I will go and ring the Brisket family, where Danielle is staying, and ask them if it is OK for Danielle to stay with us this week," said Renee.

"Thank you both," said Violette.

Violette watched Renee talk on the phone to the Brisket family about Danielle. They were happy for Danielle to stay at the Gramaze residence because they didn't know what they could do for her in the state she was in.

After Renee got off the phone, Violette rang Danielle and told her to pack her bags for one week.

Violette stood on the front step with Annabelle, and waited for Danielle. When the large wooden door opened, Danielle was standing there with the Brisket family, and Violette could see, from the look on Danielle's face, that she had made the right decision. Danielle's appearance was grey and numb, and even her lips were puffed up. Violette could only remember once in her whole life when Danielle looked like this: their parents' death. But the one thing Violette still couldn't work out was why Danielle and Christian were so attracted to each other. Especially as Danielle was human. It didn't make sense.

"Come on, let's get you back to our house and we can get you settled," said Violette, placing her arm around Danielle's shoulders.

"Goodbye Mr and Mrs Brisket. Sorry," said Danielle.

Violette mouthed, 'Thank you', to the Brisket family and then said, "I will be in touch during the week to let you know how she is doing."

"Thank you, Violette. Take care, Danielle. We are here if you need anything, dear," said Mrs Brisket.

Whilst Violette was out picking up Danielle, Renee had made sure that everyone, including Christian, knew that Danielle was staying for a few days because of what had happened. Christian was ordered by William to stay the hell away from Danielle whilst she was at the house.

Michael was waiting at the front door for them when they returned. Helping to take Danielle's bags upstairs, he watched as Annabelle and Violette took Danielle up to their room. Standing in the doorway, Michael said, "See you tomorrow, my love." He then gave Violette a passionate kiss good night. "Hope you are feeling better tomorrow, Danielle."

Danielle didn't even answer him. Sitting on the bed, she was in a daze. Annabelle had calmed Danielle with her touch when they were in the car.

"I love you, my gorgeous man. Sleep well, and thank you again," said Violette. He smiled at her and then shut the door behind him.

"Well… I might leave you two to catch up," said Annabelle. *Danielle seems to be ok. And now that I have showed you how to calm her, do you recon you will be able to do it yourself if she gets upset again?*

Violette nodded once. She had been practicing some of her abilities over the past month with Renee, Michael and Annabelle, and was now starting to get a handle on them.

"Oh, OK. Thanks for your help Annabelle." said Violette.

"No problem. Anytime," said Annabelle walking towards the door. *If you need me, just shout.*

"OK Danielle, why don't we get you out of these clothes and into a nice hot bath?" said Violette, holding her hand out for Danielle to follow her into the bathroom.

Whist they waited for the hot bubble bath to fill, Danielle said, "I don't usually fall head over heels for a boy I have only known for a few days. It sure is strange the feeling of loss I have for Christian. I can't seem to get him out of my mind and the attraction I feel for him is immeasurable."

"It's OK, sis. I am here to help you through it. I won't leave you," said Violette, turning off the water. Violette knew those feelings all too well. She remembered how she felt when she was apart from Michael in the beginning.

"Thank you, Vi. I don't know what I would do without you in my life. You are so kind and warm to me," said Danielle. Undressing, she placed her clothes on the chair next to the vanity and stepped into the bath. The water was hot when she first sat down, until her body adjusted to the temperature. Lying back against the bath, she closed her eyes.

"Mmm… this is just what the doctor ordered, sis. I feel like I am slowly relaxing."

"Glad to hear it. Did you want me to wash your hair?" asked Violette.

"Yes, please," said Danielle, sitting up. As Violette washed Danielle's hair they spoke about William's warning that Danielle was not to see Christian while she was staying at the Gramaze residence.

"I understand, Vi. It's not as if we will see each other anyway. I just want you around for some support, that's all," said Danielle.

Drying herself off and getting her PJs on, Danielle said, "Where am I sleeping tonight?"

"You are going to be sharing a bed with me, Danielle," said Violette.

"But this is yours and Michael's bed. Where is Michael sleeping?" said Danielle.

"It's OK. Michael is going to bunk with Christian tonight. We don't mind."

"I am sorry about this, Vi. But thank you, I do appreciate what you are doing for me," said Danielle.

"No problems. Would you like something to eat or drink before bed?" said Violette.

"No thanks. I couldn't stomach anything at the moment. I would just like to brush my teeth and go lie down, if that's OK," said Danielle.

"Sure, no problem. The toothpaste is in the cabinet under the vanity," said Violette, leaving Danielle to brush her teeth in the bathroom.

Violette waited in the bedroom for about ten minutes. Wondering what was taking Danielle so long, she knocked on the door and then went in. She found Danielle curled up in a ball on the bathroom floor sobbing and crying.

"Come on Danielle, let's get you into bed," said Violette, kneeling next to her.

Pulling the covers back on her bed, she helped Danielle get into bed and draped the quilt over her. Stroking her hair and the side of her face to try and calm her, Violette said, "I am going to go down to the kitchen and get you a hot cup of tea. I won't be long. OK?"

Danielle nodded and laid down on the pillow and closed her eyes.

Walking through the doorway to the kitchen, Violette was surprised to see Michael and Christian in there having a coffee. She smiled at them both as she walked in.

"How is she?" asked Christian.

"Not good, Christian. I let her go into the bathroom to brush her teeth, but when I went in to see what she was doing, I found her in a ball on the floor crying. I have just put her to bed and I have come to make her a hot cup of tea," said Violette, getting a cup out the cupboard.

Christian's face was forlorn and he didn't know what to say. He put his head in his hands.

"This is all my fault. If I had done what I was told, then this wouldn't be happening. Poor Danielle."

"Don't beat yourself up. You can't help the way you feel about Danielle," said Violette, pouring the hot water into the cup.

"You know Violette, I really like your sister and I am so sorry that Danielle is miserable. I will keep out of the way whilst she is here. I don't want her any more upset than what she currently is," said Christian.

"She feels the same way about you Christian. Well… I had better get this tea up to Danielle before she wonders where I am," said Violette. She gave Michael a kiss good night and went back to their bedroom.

As she got to the top of the stairs, she heard voices coming out of the room. Opening the door, she saw Annabelle had come in to talk with Danielle.

"Here we go, Danielle. A nice cup of hot tea to help you relax," said Violette. But Violette knew she wouldn't need the tea because Annabelle had her hand on Danielle's arm and this was soothing Danielle's troubles away.

Thank you, thought Violette to Annabelle.

She just nodded at Violette.

"Thank you, sis," said Danielle, as she took a sip of the tea, placed the cup on the side table and then laid back down. Within minutes, Danielle was asleep.

"Well, I had better go as I am meant to be out on patrol tonight. I will see you tomorrow to take you and Danielle to school," said Annabelle.

Violette gave Annabelle a hug and said, "Thanks again, Annabelle. See you tomorrow morning."

"You are welcome," said Annabelle.

After Annabelle left, Violette decided to get out her homework and finish it off.

Chapter Fifteen

Startled, Violette sat up quickly when she heard her alarm going off. Turning it off, she realised she had fallen asleep studying the night before. She yawned, stretched and turned to see Danielle was still sleeping. Not wanting to wake her yet, Violette went and had a hot shower and got dressed for school.

Danielle was just waking up when she returned to the bedroom.

"Good morning, sleepy head. How did you sleep?" said Violette.

"I slept like a log thanks, Vi," said Danielle.

"It's 7.30, why don't you have a shower and get ready for school? Then we can go and get some breakfast," said Violette.

"OK," said Danielle, hopping out of bed. After Danielle showered and did her makeup and hair, and dressed, they both went down for breakfast.

Lamiae was in the kitchen, cooking breakfast for everyone.

"Good morning, ladies. What would you like for breakfast this morning?" asked Lamiae.

"Good morning, Lamiae. I didn't know you were working here as well," said Danielle, smiling.

"Yes dear, I will be working here whilst Emily and Adrian are away," said Lamiae.

"Oh, OK. Could I have some scrambled eggs and pancakes as well? I am famished," said Danielle.

"I will have some pancakes, Lamiae. Thanks… there is coffee and tea over there, sis," said Violette. "Just get whatever you want. Sugar is on the island bench."

"OK. Thanks," said Danielle, walking over to the counter.

Violette hadn't seen Michael that morning, so she thought that he must have been still out on patrol. After breakfast, Violette, Danielle and Sharina waited outside at the front door for Annabelle to bring the car around to take them to school. Whilst they waited, Michael, Grayson and Christian pulled up in front of them. Letting Michael out the car, Grayson and Christian drove off to the back of the property to park the car.

Getting out the car, Michael walked over and gave Violette a passionate kiss. "Have a great day, my beautiful lady. See you later this afternoon."

Violette smiled and back handed Michael's bum as he walked away.

"Can't wait for later, my gorgeous man." *Mmm, sizzle.*

Pulling the car in front of them, Annabelle opened the door and said, "Let's go, ladies."

"You are so lucky, Violette. What I wouldn't do to have that," said Danielle, getting into the car and sitting next to Violette.

"I sure am lucky," said Violette, smiling and placing her hand on Danielle's hand. "Your turn is coming, sis. I can feel it in my bones."

Danielle smiled and said, "You are such a great sister. I love you."

"Ditto," said Violette.

Annabelle pulled up in the parking lot at the front of the school to drop Violette, Danielle and Sharina off. "See you this arvo, ladies. Have a good day."

"Wow… she is such a lovely person, and a great friend, isn't she?" said Danielle, as they all waved Annabelle off.

"She sure is," said Violette.

"Well… we had better get to our first class, Violette. See you later on, Danielle," said Sharina.

"Thanks. I will catch up with both of you at lunch," said Danielle.

"Chin up and keep your mind busy," said Violette, as she waved to her sister.

Busily getting her books out of her locker, Danielle didn't pay attention to what was going on around her, as her brain was still numb from what had happened with Christian. She didn't notice a teenage boy standing beside her until he cleared his throat.

"Hi… my name is Peter. Umm. this is my first day here and I was wondering if you would be able to show me where the main office is? I am a bit lost."

"Hi Peter. I'm Danielle. Give me a minute to get my books out and I will show you where it is."

"Come on," said Danielle, closing her locker door and gesturing for him to follow her.

Entering the slightly darkened, empty hallway to the main office, Peter made sure no other people were around, as he pushed Danielle into the wall and held his hand to her throat. Grabbing her by the hair, he then put his hand over her mouth so that she couldn't scream.

"Keep quiet, bitch," said Peter, in a low, husky voice.

With her eyes wide and wondering what was going to happen to her, Danielle tried to scream, but to no avail. She felt a prick in her neck, and tried to wriggle free, but instead collapsed into his arms.

Peter carried her limp body over his shoulder, out of the school grounds and into a waiting white van, which had blacked out windows. He opened up the back door and lay her body inside. Hopping into the van and closing the door from the inside, he said to the driver, "Let's get out of fuck out of here, before they notice she is missing."

Watching Danielle sleep as they sped away, Peter rang his master.

"Sire… I have the girl. We are about thirty minutes away."

"Good. Did you leave the phone and letter as instructed in the sister's locker?" asked Clause.

"Yes, sire. When she wasn't looking, I put it in there," said Peter.

"Good," said Clause and he hung up abruptly.

At lunch time, Violette and Sharina waited at the lockers for Danielle to turn up, but she didn't show. Worried, Violette asked some of Danielle's friends if they knew where she was, but they just said that they hadn't seen her that morning.

"That doesn't sound right. They should have at least seen her in some of their classes that they share together. I will ring William to see if she has returned home," said Sharina, getting her phone out of her bag.

"No, she is not here," said William, when Sharina explained what had happened. "When was the last time you saw her?"

"First period this morning, sire. What would you like me to do?" said Sharina.

"Find out if she attended any of her classes today and then get back to me. Also check the nurse's station and ladies' toilets," said William.

"Fuck."

Violette quickly grabbed the phone from Sharina and said to William, "I have just found a phone and note in my locker. Them fucking Debauched bastards have taken her."

"I will send Annabelle to collect you both now," said William.

Arriving back at the Gramaze house, William ordered a meeting in the operations room straight away.

"What does the letter say, Violette?" said William.

Violette read the letter aloud so everyone could hear:

> *I have taken your sister, Danielle. If you don't want her to get hurt, you had better not warn the authorities. I have left a mobile phone in your locker. So when I call, you had better answer it, otherwise Danielle will die. I will ring you at 4pm, so you had better take my call, bitch.*
>
> *Clause*

"Clause... that motherfucking bastard... he will not get away with this. We have two hours before he calls, and he won't know that we are prepared either. I want each and every one of you to get into your combat gear, equipment ready and sharpened. It is going to be an all-out fight to the death, this time. We do not take any prisoners. Do you all understand what I am saying?!" said William, slamming his closed fist on the desk.

They all nodded in unison.

"Violette, after you have taken the call, I will need you to give Brock a hand in the operations room with the surveillance and tracking of the car that took Danielle," said William.

"Yes, sire," said Violette.

"Samantha, you can help with loading of weapons and sharpening of knives prior to us leaving," said William, looking in her direction.

"Yes, sire. Is there anything else I can help with?" said Samantha.

"Just stay at the house. We will need some medical help when we all get back from this fight," said William.

"OK," said Samantha, with a creased brow. *What is going to happen?*

Grayson was standing behind Samantha and he could hear her thoughts. Placing his arms around Samantha he thought, *Don't worry, my love. I will be all right.*

She turned to look at him and hugged him back. *I hope so. I don't want to lose you now… I love you.*

Before they knew it, it was 4 o'clock and the phone that had been placed in Violette's locker, rang.

"Hello," said Violette, in a shaky voice.

"I see you got my message, Violette," said Clause, in a surly voice.

"Why have you taken my sister, you fucker?" Violette's breathing was erratic, as her nostrils flared.

"Feisty one, aren't you? But don't think you have the upper hand here, bitch. I do." Clause smirked. "I want you to come to the park near the Eiffel Tower at 5.30 and when I see you have arrived by yourself and alone, I will then release Danielle. You see you are giving your life for hers."

Violette couldn't believe what she was hearing.

"Right. I will be there."

"Like I said, dear, if I see one vampire from your coven I will kill your sister, on the spot. Do you hear me, bitch?" shouted Clause.

"Yes… as I said, I will be there. But she'd better be alive and not harmed," said Violette.

Hanging up the phone, Violette couldn't hold back the tears any longer.

Standing beside her, Michael pulled her into a hug and she buried her head in his chest.

"Don't worry, we will fix that bastard," said Michael, as he looked at William.

"I have a lead on them, William," said Brock, looking up from his computer screen. "After checking the satellite surveillance cameras, I have followed them from the time they abducted Danielle at the school, to the place where they are currently holding her. They still have her captive there now. The house is only forty-five minutes from here, so we should make it in time to get these motherfuckers before they leave for the Eiffel Tower."

"Once we get to the property outskirts, I will give the orders. But I want to make it clear right here and now, that I don't want any Debauched vamps left, and if they have any experimental labs or gear there, I want it blown sky high," said William.

They all said, "Yes, sire."

Watching them drive out the front gates, Violette said to Samantha, "I hope that they haven't hurt my sister. If they have, I will not rest until each and every one of those bastards pays for what they have done."

Samantha put her arm around Violette and said, "Let's get the medical supplies ready, and keep ourselves busy whilst they are gone. We don't want to worry about something that might not happen."

"Thanks Sam. You are right, of course. Let's go," said Violette.

As the Gramaze family coven was travelling to the Debauched vamps' house to rescue Danielle, Brock was checking on his satellite surveillance cameras to make sure that they didn't leave with Danielle prior to them arriving.

Pulling up at the outskirts of the house which was in a bushy area William said, "Renee, I want you to stay here with the car. Grayson and Annabelle, you will go in through the back door and look for Danielle. Theodore and Harrison, I want you both to make an explosion outside the front gates and then again inside the front gates and I want lots of flame-throwing fire-power as well. Michael, I want you with me as we are going to find Clause and his army of soldiers inside the house, and kill each and every one of them. Jack, you can set the explosive inside the house once everyone is out. Now that everyone has their orders, let's go and kill these fucking bastards. Remember our number one priority is to get Danielle out alive."

Clause flinched as he heard the first explosion outside.

"Go check it out and report back!" shouted Clause to his two henchmen, as he heard the second explosion. Ordering his soldiers outside to check out the explosions was a bad move, because Michael and William were waiting for them on the front porch as each soldier exited the house. Beheading them with their long swords, was no effort, as the unexpected Debauched guards couldn't have imagined their fate.

Grayson and Annabelle stormed the house, with their swords drawn. Checking out each room as they walked through the house, they came upon four vamps in total. But the Debauched were no match for the Gramaze family and came off second best, eventually turning to ash.

"Go see if you can find Danielle in the house. She has to be somewhere in here," said Grayson to Annabelle, as he watched for any Debauched to surprise them.

"OK," said Annabelle, running off.

Grayson joined up with Michael and William to find Clause and his guards. Searching the entire house, there was no trace of them to be found.

"Most of these old places have a running creek down the back of the property and usually there is a jetty, which would give them a point of escape. I think we had better go down there and check it out. We don't want them fuckers escaping," said William.

With vampire speed, William, Grayson, and Michael took off to the back of the property. It was there that they saw three vamps escaping in a jet boat down the river. Standing next to the jetty, William put the fully loaded rocket propelled grenade launcher onto his shoulder and fired it at the jet boat. The first shot missed, so William reloaded. Firing it again, this time it hit the jet boat with full blast. It exploded from the impact, and they watched to see if any vamps survived the fallout. They kept watching for a few minutes but didn't see a Debauched vamp in sight.

"That fixed those fuckers," said Michael.

Inside the house, Jack was setting the explosives and waiting for everyone to get out so that they could blow it sky high.

Annabelle searched through the house for Danielle, ending up down in the basement, which was set up like a laboratory. Entering the room, she found syringes, funnels, cryogenic containers and other types of drugs which were stored in the fridges. At the back of the room, chained to the wall and slumped over, was Danielle. Annabelle ran over to Danielle and checked for her pulse. It was weak but she was still alive. Ripping the shackles and chains off Danielle, she carried her limp body upstairs. Once outside, she took Danielle over to the medical van.

Danielle was in bad shape and needed some blood. She was bruised all over her body and face, and Annabelle figured she had been beaten badly. But what Annabelle noticed first, was that Danielle had track marks on both her arms, which meant the Debauched vamps had pumped her with some of the manufactured drugs.

"Shit," said Annabelle, as realisation hit her. *Jack... don't blow the house yet. We need to get some samples of the drugs in the laboratory down-stairs. Danielle has been injected with some type of drug. We need to know what it is she has been drugged with.*

Right... got ya. We'll box them up, thought Jack. Once the vials, and canisters were boxed up, Jack took them outside and put them into the SUV.

Are we all done here? thought William to his coven.

Just putting the last of it into the van, sire, thought Jack.

Excellent... let's get out of here. Jack blow this joint now, thought William.

Driving away from the house and stopping in the next street, they all watched as the house and its contents exploded into a fire ball, sending debris everywhere.

Looking out the darkened window, Michael thought to Violette, *We have Danielle and are on our way back.*

Thank you, thought Violette.

Arriving at the Gramaze residence, the medical team carried Danielle into the house on a stretcher. Passing Violette and Samantha in the foyer, they headed for a room that was set up for any medical emergencies the Lepidoptera had.

Violette stood in the doorway, with her hand to her mouth, watching the medical team connect a cannula into Danielle's battered body and attach a bag of blood to the drip.

This is all my fault.

"No, it's not. Don't blame yourself," said Samantha, listening to her thoughts, as she placed her arm around Violette's shoulder.

Violette leaned into Samantha and said, "If anything happens to her, I will never forgive myself."

"Nothing is going to happen. Don't think like that Violette. She is in good hands here," said Samantha, as she watched the medical team work on Danielle. But just as she said it, the heart rate monitor made the sound that no one likes to hear. Danielle's heart had stopped and she was in cardiac arrest.

"Oh my god… Danielle!" shouted Violette, as she ran into the room and looked at her sister's lifeless body.

"Get her out of here," said the oldest doctor, who was treating Danielle. Ripping open Danielle's blouse, and placing the defibrillator pads on her bare chest, he then charged the machine ready for electric shock.

"Clear!" shouted the second doctor, as he picked up the electrodes and shocked Danielle's heart. But there was still a flat line on the monitor.

"Clear!" he shouted again, and watched the monitor for signs of life. As the monitor started to beat and show her normal heartbeat rhythm, the two men breathed a sigh of relief.

Waiting outside the doorway, with her back to the wall and looking towards the ceiling, Violette prayed for her sister's life and sobbed. All she wanted was her sister back. She didn't care about anything else.

When the oldest of the two doctors approached her, she said, "Danielle… is she…?"

Placing his hand on her shoulder, he said, "She is alive."

"Is she going to be all right?" asked Violette, her face tear stained.

"We are not sure, at this stage. She has been through a lot. We have taken some samples of her blood and will do some tests on it to see what she had been injected with. We have also hooked her up to some fluids and are giving her blood through intravenous drip. At the moment, she is comfortable. We will just keep an eye on her and see how she goes for the next few hours."

"Thank you… can I see her?" asked Violette, with a creased brow.

"Yes. Come this way."

Violette followed him into the room. As she approached the bed, she noticed they had propped Danielle up in bed and she looked like she was sleeping.

"Here's a chair," said the doctor, as he placed it next to the bed for Violette to sit on.

"Thank you," said Violette, pulling the chair close to the bed. As Violette studied her sister's bruised face, she watched her eyelids flutter from side to side.

"What's happening? Is she dreaming?"

"Were not sure, at this stage."

"Hmm…" said Violette, as she placed her hand over Danielle's hand.

Christian ran into the room at vampire speed.

"How is she?"

"Get out… you know you are not allowed near her," said Violette, through her heated tears.

"I am not leaving her. I want to be here when she wakes," said Christian.

"You will leave now. I won't ask you again," yelled Violette, as she stood up with her hands on her hips.

"Oh, what are you going to do, little girl?" grunted Christian. He was sick and tired of being told he couldn't see the girl he liked.

Violette was in no mood for his arrogance. With her nostrils flaring and her breathing accelerating, she held her hand out in front of her body in the direction of Christian, and forced him back against the wall with her powers. As he hit the wall with a thud, she curled her fingers in a ball, and he started to choke.

Christian eyes widened as he realised Violette was going to collapse his windpipe using her Lepidoptera abilities.

"Violette…" Christian said in a whispered voice, as he fought for breath.

As William approached the doorway he heard the commotion between Violette and Christian. Rushing into the room he said, "Violette… let him go, now."

As her focus was broken from William's command, she dropped to the ground in exhaustion.

"Christian… are you OK?" asked William, standing beside him.

"Yes, sire," said Christian, trying to catch his breath. Holding his throat and leaning back against the wall, his brow furrowed as he watched Violette get up off the floor.

William turned to see Violette standing. "Are you OK princess?"

"Yes…" said Violette, shaking. Composing herself, she held her head high. "I want him out of here."

"Get out, the both of you. How dare you stand here arguing and fighting whilst Danielle is unconscious?" said William, authoritively.

"Stop the noise… please. My head is hurting," said Danielle, waking from all the commotion.

Turning to see that her sister had opened her eyes, Violette said, "Danielle… how are you feeling?"

"I hurt all over, Vi. I feel weak. Those men who kidnapped me, they tried to get information out of me and when I wouldn't tell them anything, they bashed me until I was unconscious. I think they also injected me with some drug," said Danielle, speaking with a coarse voice.

"God, I thought you were going to die, Danielle. I am so glad you are going to be all right," said Violette, through her tears, as she walked over to the bed.

Looking around the room, Danielle put her hand out to Christian. "Christian, come over here," said Danielle.

Christian knew the rules. He looked to William for approval first and then gulped as he looked to Violette for her approval.

William nodded.

Stony faced, Violette's eyes narrowed.

Violette… don't push this. He has my approval and that is all he needs. Back away, now, thought William.

Violette looked from Christian to William, and tried to calm herself. She then bowed her head to William.

Christian ran over to Danielle and kissed her ever so gently on her forehead. "Can I sit with Danielle for a while, William?" asked Christian.

"Yes, that will be fine. But only one person at a time until she is cleared by the medical team," said William.

"I won't be far away, Danielle. I love you sis," said Violette, giving Danielle a kiss on the forehead. "I will come and see you later on."

Violette knew from Danielle's thoughts that she wanted to spend some time alone with Christian.

"OK… I love you too," said Danielle, watching Violette and William walk out the room.

I'm watching you Christian, thought Violette.

Christian swallowed hard and sat down on the bed next to Danielle.

Christian took her hand in his and kissed it.

"I love you, Danielle. I was so worried that we wouldn't find you alive. Now that we have a second chance, I am going to speak with William again to see if we can date," said Christian, looking into her eyes.

"I do hope he changes his mind. I really like you a lot, Christian," said Danielle softly, as she held his hand. "You know when those men were beating me, they asked me the most bizarre questions. Like, if I knew anything about a type of vampire race called the Lepid… I don't know, can't pronounce it. It sure was strange."

Christian didn't know what to say, so he just nodded and said nothing.

"Christian, I thought I was never going to see you ever again. But when they had me tied up, you were all I could think of. It's funny, but the feelings that I have for you seem to intensify more when they injected me with the drugs. I don't know what was in it, but it made me hallucinate that they were drinking my blood from my neck. It was weird," said Danielle, as she remembered being captured and tortured.

William could hear everything that Danielle was telling Christian about the Debauched vamps. He could also see how in love these two people were. He needed to get Christian out of the room, because Danielle would expect some answers, and sooner or later he knew Christian would tell her about their coven.

"I think Danielle needs her rest. It's time to leave now, Christian," said William, walking back into the room.

Christian gave Danielle a kiss on the forehead and said, "See you later."

"Bye," said Danielle. She was too weak to put up an argument.

Once Christian and William were in the hallway, William said, "We need to find out what she was injected with. I have my people doing tests on all the drugs we found at the Debauched vamps' house, and we should know some results soon. Until then, you need to keep away from Danielle. At this stage, she thinks she may have hallucinated what she heard and saw. And I don't need you telling her she wasn't hallucinating."

"Yes, sire. But after this is over I want to speak with you about Danielle and I going on a date. William, I have an attraction to this girl, and for some reason, I'm not sure why, I don't want to live my life without her," said Christian.

Even though Christian knew humans and vampires didn't usually have an attraction, like life partners did, he couldn't help but feel an emotional pull towards her.

"We will speak about this later," said William, walking off to see how the lab technicians were doing with the drugs they found.

When William entered the laboratory, the lab technician approached him and said, "I have some disturbing news, sire."

"What is it?" said William.

"I think that the drug they injected into Danielle was to make her a vampire. We have tested the drugs and a sample of Danielle's blood and they have the same ingredients. We then checked it against the Lepidoptera bloods we have on file here, and well, it is the same. It looks like the Debauched vamps have finally worked out how to turn a human into a vampire."

"Luckily we stopped them when we did then," said William, with raised eyebrows. Thank you for all your work you have done here today. You know this information is confidential, don't you?"

"Yes, sire," said the lab technician.

He knew if word got out, there would be hell to pay, and his life would end.

Walking out of the lab, William couldn't believe what he had just been told. *I wonder if there are other labs around the world, in which the Debauched have finally mastered the transformation from human to vampire.*

Meeting in the operations room, Gramaze coven, thought William to everyone.

Once everyone was assembled in the operations room William called the room to order.

"First of all, I would like to say good job, on the rescue of Danielle tonight. Hopefully she will recover after a few days… next … now that the new Debauched leader, Clause, has been exterminated, they will be looking to replace him, so keep your eyes and ears open when you are all out on patrol. Finally, there is something I need to bring to your attention… you all know about the drugs we found at the Debauched vamps house… well, our lab technician has informed me that the drugs we found actually can turn a human into a vampire."

Most of the Lepidoptera's were bewildered that a drug this powerful could be manufactured. Some were astonished at the thought of a human being able to be turned into a vampire. A hum went around the room as each Gramaze vampire considered the impact this could have to their future.

"Quiet…" said William, looking around the room. "By us stopping these fuckers today, we have in fact stopped this from happening to anyone else in the future."

"What do you mean by, anyone else, William?" asked Brock.

With his head held high, and taking a deep breath, William informed his coven about Danielle and how she had been injected with the drugs, and was transforming into a Lepidoptera.

Everyone in the room couldn't believe what William had just told them. Christian was hoping it was true for the obvious reasons, and Violette was also hoping it was true because she wanted Danielle and Stephen in her life fulltime.

"But how can we be sure of this, William?" said Harrison.

"Fortunately…"

But before William could finish his sentence, the big screen came alive and the California leader, Mason, came into view.

"Hello Gramaze coven. I have some news that may be of assistance," said Mason.

"Hello, my friend. It's been a long time since we have spoken. What news do you have for us?" said William, looking at the screen.

"Yes, it's been way too long, my friend… I believe that Clause, whose background is in chemistry, has manufactured a drug that can turn humans in vampires," said Mason.

"Yes. That's true… but he won't be a problem to us anymore. He is dead and we destroyed his lab," said William, proud of his coven's achievements.

"Well, I wouldn't be too sure of that, William. Word on the street is that even though Clause is dead, his work has been carried on by others," said Mason. "Apparently when Clause became leader of the Debauched vamps, he set up more labs around the world, to manufacture this drug. So there is no telling how many humans will be turned into vampires."

"Fuck…" said William, his nostrils flaring.

"William, we will be setting up a teleconference later on tonight with all leaders, worldwide, to discuss our plan of action. Can I count you in?" said Mason.

"Of course, my friend. I too, want to stop these bastards from wreaking hell on this earth," said William, with clenched fists.

"Excellent… in the meantime, get your coven ready for a battle with these fuckers," said Mason.

"We will be ready, don't you worry," said William. "Bye, my friend."

The screen went blank.

Turning around to face his coven, William looked around the room, and observed the rage in each and every one of their faces. With their nostrils flaring, and their fangs bared, each Lepidoptera was enraged by what they had been told.

"Fuckers won't stand a chance against us. William, I think we all need to be in on this teleconference," said Grayson.

"I agree. Once I find out when it is, I want you all back in here, so we can discuss, as a coven and with the other world leaders, a plan of attack," stated William, looking around the room at each of his family.

"Now… back to Danielle… Grayson, I want a fulltime guard on Danielle tonight and tomorrow. Please keep informed of any developments. She is not to leave this house, either," said William.

"Yes, sire," said Grayson.

"Violette, I want you to be on hand to help with Danielle, if needed," said William.

"Yes, sire," said Violette.

"For now… I want each of you to prepare for battle," said William.

They all said, "Yes, sire."

Filing out of the operations room one by one, they all headed for the combat room.

Chapter Sixteen

With his head resting on his folded arms on the side of the bed, Christian woke to feeling his hair being stroked gently. Sitting up quickly, he realised Danielle was awake and lying in bed staring at him. Christian had snuck into her room during the night to check on her and decided to stay.

"Good morning… how long have you been sitting there?" asked Danielle.

Yawning, he said, "Hi… most of the night. How are you feeling?"

"I feel much better, thanks, Christian. In fact, I was going to ask if I could get up, out of bed," said Danielle.

"Oh, right… hang on, and I will go and find someone for you," said Christian, standing and walking towards the doorway.

As he neared the doorway, the male nurse bumped into Christian.

"Whoops… Ah, Danielle is awake, and asking to get out of bed. Will this be OK?" asked Christian.

Walking over to Danielle, he said, "You're looking much better this morning. Let's check you over."

Placing the cuff around Danielle's arm, he pressed the button on the machine that took her blood pressure.

"Hmm, not bad. Let's check your other vitals."

After he checked the other machines, which was hooked up to Danielle, along with the saline and blood drip bags, he said, "All seems good, Danielle. But your release is up to William, not me. I am only here to make you feel better."

"OK. Thanks," said Christian, running off to find William. Searching the whole house at vampire speed, for William, Christian couldn't seem to locate him. So he headed back Danielle's room.

Upon entering Danielle's room, he found William sitting with Danielle. She was sitting up in bed and William was checking the back of her neck.

"Can Danielle be released back into the house today, William?" said Christian, as he approached them.

"Yes. I will have Renee make up a room for her. She still has to stay on the blood drip and we need to get some food into you as well, Danielle, to get your strength back to normal," said William, looking from Christian to Danielle.

"Yes, Mr Gramaze. I am really hungry, anyway. I think I could eat a horse at the moment," said Danielle, lying back down.

"We will get you taken up to your room in a few minutes, Danielle, and once you are there I will organise for the cook to bring you something to eat for breakfast," said William.

"Thanks, Mr Gramaze. I do appreciate all you have done for me. But I would like to talk with you later on today; if you are not busy… about what happened yesterday," said Danielle.

"We can talk later, dear, when you have eaten breakfast and feel well enough. OK?" said William, standing.

She nodded.

"Yes, sir."

"Well I have a bit to do, so I will come by and see you later on once you are settled in," said William.

"OK. Thank you," said Danielle, watching William walk out the room.

"Let's get you ready to move upstairs to a room," said the nurse, taking the monitor off Danielle's pointer finger.

"Is there anything I can help with?" said Christian, eagerly.

"Yes. Once we are sorted here, you could carry Danielle up to her room. She can't walk yet and needs to conserve her energy," said the nurse, taking the connecting bag of blood out of the cannula.

"Right… let's get you up to your room. Let me know if I hurt you when I pick you up," said Christian, placing his arms around Danielle.

Danielle leaned into Christian, and placed her head against his shoulder As his muscular arms picked her up out the bed, she winced in pain.

"You OK?"

"Yeah," lied Danielle.

When they entered her room, the bed covers had already been pulled back, so Christian carried Danielle over to her bed and set her down.

"Are you comfortable, or would you like me to put another pillow behind you?"

"If I could have another pillow behind me, would be good. I want to sit up for a while," said Danielle, as she tried to get comfortable.

Christian retrieved the other pillow from the chair and propped it in behind her.

"There you go."

"Thanks, Christian," said Danielle, leaning forward, and taking in his scent.

Entering Danielle's room, the nurse said, "Well… it looks like you are comfortable there. Are you in any pain at the moment?"

"It's not too bad at the moment. But my whole body is still aching. Could you leave some pain medication for me?" said Danielle.

The nurse nodded and placed some pain relief tablets for Danielle on her bedside table. He also brought in a jug of water for Danielle to sip on during the day and night.

"You need to keep your fluids up, Danielle, so please make sure you drink plenty of water. You will have the blood drip and saline drip in your arms for a few days though, and I will change these during the next twenty-four hours for you."

"Oh, OK. Thank you," said Danielle, watching the nurse leave the room.

"Are you feeling warm enough?" asked Christian.

"I am a bit cold, Christian. Are you allowed to sit on the bed with me and keep me warm?" said Danielle.

"I would love to Danielle, but I had better not. I don't want to antagonise William. I will get you another blanket instead," said Christian.

"That's OK. I understand," said Danielle.

As Christian put the blanket on Danielle he kissed her forehead and said, "I wish William would change his mind about us."

"Not much we can do about that. Maybe he might change his mind one day. We can only hope," said Danielle.

As they were talking there was a knock at the door and when Christian opened it, Lamiae was standing there with a tray full of food for Danielle.

"Here, let me give you a hand."

"Thanks, Christian," said Lamiae, handing the tray to Christian. "How is she?"

"See for yourself," said Christian, gesturing for Lamiae to come in.

Walking into the room, Lamiae's eyes opened wide when she saw the bruising and swelling over Danielle's whole face. Holding her hand over her mouth, Lamiae rushed over to Danielle.

"My dear girl! What have they done to you?" said Lamiae, as she sat on the bed and gave Danielle a warm hug.

"I will be alright, Lamiae. Mr Gramaze told me I was one tough lady to have endured what I had been through and come out alive," said Danielle, trying to smile, while she held Lamiae's hand.

"Lamiae has made you a nice breakfast," said Christian, placing the tray on the opposite side of the queen bed.

"Thank you for the lovely breakfast," said Danielle, looking at the tray.

"You are welcome my dear. Is there anything else I can get you?" said Lamiae.

"No thanks, Lamiae. This is great what you have made me for," said Danielle.

"If you need anything dear, see that phone over there? Just press 1 and I will answer and bring whatever you want. OK?" said Lamiae.

"OK. Thank you," said Danielle.

Lamiae kissed Danielle softly on her forehead and said, "I have to go back to the kitchen dear, but I will come by later to check on how you are going."

"Thanks again, Lamiae, for the lovely breakfast," said Danielle, watching her walk to the doorway. "Bye."

"I won't be able to eat all this food, Christian. I bet you haven't had breakfast yet. Would you like some of this?" said Danielle, as she picked up a piece of toast from the plate.

"Thanks Danielle. That's nice of you to ask. Are you sure you won't be able to eat all of it?" said Christian.

"I don't usually eat too much at all, Christian. So yes, you are welcome to share with me," said Danielle.

"OK. That will be nice, said Christian.

As Danielle was eating her breakfast, she said to Christian, "I really would like to have a shower or a bath and get cleaned up. Do you think you could ask Violette to come in and help me with that?"

"Sure. I'll go and see if she is free now, if you like," said Christian, getting off the bed and walking to the doorway.

"Thanks," said Danielle.

"I hear someone is wanting to get cleaned up," said Violette, entering the room, about ten minutes later.

Danielle smiled when she saw Violette.

"Yes please."

"How are you feeling, sis?" asked Violette, as she sat next to Danielle on the bed and studied her swollen face.

"I've had better days. I just want to get cleaned up. Could you please either run a bath for me or help me have a shower?" said Danielle.

"I think that maybe a bath would be better for you, Danielle. You should be able to wash yourself. But I can wash your hair for you," said Violette.

"That's sounds nice, sis. Thank you," said Danielle.

"Give me a minute and I will go run the water for you," said Violette, getting up off the bed.

After Violette ran the hot bath water, she helped Danielle detach the blood drip, which was still connected to the cannula in her arm. As Danielle swung her legs out over the side of the bed, Violette helped her stand.

"Wow, I feel dizzy," said Danielle, holding onto Violette tightly.

"It's OK. Take your time," said Violette, holding her up.

Leaning on Violette, Danielle said, "OK. Let's go."

Violette sat on the side of the bath and watched Danielle wash herself with the strawberry scented body wash. *The way Danielle is washing herself is like she has been violated by someone or something,* thought Violette as she watched Danielle scrub and scrub herself until her skin was red raw.

"You OK?" asked Violette.

"Hmm…um… no. I feel dirty," said Danielle, as the tears welled in her eyes.

Placing her hand on Danielle's soapy shoulder, Violette said, "Would you like me to wash your hair now?"

Nodding, Danielle said, "Yes."

As Violette washed Danielle's hair, the room was silent, as she remembered the times she had been taken and beaten and how she had felt violated by the Debauched.

Fuckers. I am gonna make them pay for what they have done to my sister. When I learn how to use my abilities, they won't know what hit them.

Once Violette had washed Danielle's hair, she asked, "Would you like me to get rid of the dirty water and we can put some clean hot water and bubbles into the bath for you and then you can relax? It should soothe your pain."

"Yes, please. That sounds nice, Vi," said Danielle.

Once the bath was full, Danielle relaxed against the back of the bath, in the clean water, with bubbles all around her, as Violette put her wet hair up in a towel. Watching her sister's eyes close and her body relax, Violette's memories came flooding back from her own ordeal, when she was kidnapped. She remembered that the hot water and bubbles soothed her pain away and made her feel a lot better afterwards.

As Danielle lay in the hot bath relaxing, she said to Violette, "Thank you for helping me, sis. I love you."

"You are welcome. I am just glad you are going to be all right and that I got to see you again," said Violette, as the tears welled in her eyes.

Once she was out of the bath and back in bed, Danielle felt relaxed, but tired. She yawned and said, "That bath was good. Just what the doctor ordered. I might just have a sleep for a while, Vi."

"That's OK, sis. You lie down and have a sleep. I will catch up with you later on," said Violette, stroking her blonde hair.

Turning over on her side, it didn't take Danielle long and she was asleep.

With lunch being prepared, Christian decided to go up and check on Danielle and to see if she wanted something to eat. Walking up the marble staircase, he thought he could hear screaming. As he neared Danielle's room, he realised it was her. Running into the room, he found her thrashing about in the bed. He sat on the side of the bed, and started to stoke her hair with his hand.

"Danielle… wake up, wake up! You are dreaming," said Christian.

He had to repeat it to her again until she came around.

As her eyes opened, Danielle sat up quickly. Her breathing was uneven and her body trembling, but she soon realised that Christian was sitting on the bed.

"Shh… it's OK," said Christian, rubbing her arm.

Putting her arms around Christian, she took some deep breaths.

"Oh, Christian… I was dreaming that I was kidnapped all over again. I thought it was real, until you woke me. Thank god you are here," said Danielle shaking.

"It's going to be OK... I am here for you always, Danielle. Any time you need me, I will be there," said Christian hugging her, and rubbing her back. "Shhh…"

Christian slowly pulled away from their embrace and asked, "Are you OK now?"

"Yes. Thank you, Christian," said Danielle, her face tear-stained.

"How do you feel about eating some lunch?" said Christian, as he looked into her eyes.

"I think I could eat a little bit," said Danielle.

"Would you like to eat up here or downstairs?" asked Christian.

"I don't feel up to going downstairs yet," said Danielle.

"That's OK. I will ring Lamiae and let her know that you are eating up here and she will bring us both some lunch. Does that sound all right?" said Christian.

"Sound good. Thanks," said Danielle.

After Christian got off the phone to Lamiae, he sat next to Danielle on the bed and said, "How are you feeling now? You certainly look better than last night that's for sure. You seem to be healing fast."

"I do feel better. But I have this godawful neck-ache and headache that just won't go away. The back of my neck is so itchy as well," said Danielle.

"Let me have a look. Maybe I can go and get some cream or something from the nurse to ease the itching and the pain," said Christian.

Pulling Danielle's long hair away from the back of her neck, he could see why she was in pain. She had the black outline of the butterfly appearing. In Christian's mind, he did a back flip and shouted hoorah. He knew that he now would be able to date Danielle because she was turning into a Lepidoptera vampire.

"I will go and see the nurse to see what we can put on your neck. Ok? I won't be long."

"OK. Maybe some headache pills as well," called Danielle to Christian as he walked towards the door.

"Sure."

Walking to the nurses' room, Christian thought to William, *Danielle has the black outline of the butterfly on the back of her neck starting to appear. Could we sit down with her and explain everything to her, including why she was kidnapped?*

I will come and see you both this afternoon and we can talk about it then, thought William.

When Christian got back to Danielle's room, Lamiae was just dropping off lunch for them both.

"Thanks Lamiae," said Christian, walking in the door.

"You are most welcome," said Lamiae, leaving them to enjoy their lunch together.

Christian sat next to Danielle on the bed.

"Can you lift your hair away from your neck and I will rub some ointment into the back of her neck," said Christian.

Lifting the hair from the back of her neck, Danielle felt the pain ease as soon as he rubbed it in.

"Thank you Christian. That is easing the pain and the itch," said Danielle, twisting her neck around to the side.

"You're welcome. I am glad it is working so fast for you. I will go and wash up and we can then enjoy lunch together," said Christian, walking to the bathroom.

When Christian returned, he put Danielle's food tray in front of her on the bed and then sat next to her with his own tray. They chatted away for a while, and after they had finished their lunch, Christian said, "How's the neck now?"

"A lot better. I don't even feel it and the headache has gone too," said Danielle.

"That's great. I'm glad," said Christian.

Knocking at the door, William and Violette asked if it was all right to come in.

"Hello, Danielle. How are you feeling this afternoon?" asked William.

"I am feeling much better. Thanks for asking, Mr Gramaze," said Danielle.

"That's good, sis," said Violette smiling.

"I would like to have a chat with you about yesterday, amongst other things," said William seriously.

"Sit down, Mr Gramaze. You too, Violette," said Danielle, patting the bed.

With the four of them now sitting on the bed William said, "What I am about to tell you, Danielle, may sound a bit unbelievable at first, but once you understand our kind a bit more, then it will all make sense."

Just spit it out. I need to know what is going on, thought Danielle.

"When you were kidnapped yesterday, it was by a group of individuals that over the centuries we have been fighting" said William.

"Fighting? What do you mean 'fighting'?" said Danielle, interrupting William.

Females…they sure are impatient, thought William.

"Just let me finish… you see, Danielle, we are a race of individuals called the Lepidoptera vampires, and the ones that kidnapped you are called Debauched vampires," said William, watching her reaction.

Laughing, Danielle said, "Vampires. Sure."

She looked from William to Violette and then Christian, and they all had serious faces. *He isn't joking.* With her eyes widening, she listened to William nervously.

"The Debauched vampires are a sadistic race of vampires, who thrive on drugs, and the blood of humans, whom by the way, they love to kill. Whereas the Lepidoptera vampires, which is everyone who lives in this house, are a respectable, decent kind of vampire, who are trying to save the human race.

"The reason the Debauched kidnapped you was because they worked out that you were Violette's sister. They thought that if they could take you, then Violette would come to rescue you. The reason they wanted Violette is because Violette is a multi-coloured female Lepidoptera vampire, who is the most powerful female vampire to our race. In fact, she is our princess."

Danielle frowned, as she tried to take in what William had just told her. Swallowing hard, she looked from William to Violette and said, "Is this a load of bullshit, or is this true, Vi?" Danielle started to shake.

"William is telling you the truth, and he is our leader, Danielle. He is over three thousand years old, so you need to listen to what he is telling you," said Violette, watching Danielle's reaction.

Three thousand years old, yeah right, thought Danielle.

"When you were kidnapped, do you remember being drugged by the Debauched vamps? And do you remember them sucking your blood out of your neck?" said William.

Thinking back to the previous day and the events that took place, Danielle remembered some of the things that they did to her.

"Yes, I do remember them drinking my blood… but I thought I was dreaming. I didn't know it was real. And yes, I do remember them injecting some type of drug into me," said Danielle, with a furrowed brow.

"The drug that they injected into you was one that they have been working on for a while. It actually turns humans into vampires. They were hoping by injecting you with their drug that they could turn you into a vampire," said William.

"Are you sure that they injected me with that type of drug? The reason I ask is because I don't feel any different, and I think I would know if I were a vampire," said Danielle.

"Yes, we are one hundred per cent sure that they injected the drug into you. We tested your blood against the drugs we found in the laboratory at that house where you were held captive, and it's the same," said William.

"You mean I am now a Lepidoptera vampire?" said Danielle, panic in her voice.

"Yes," said William. "Christian, go into the bathroom and get a hand-held mirror and bring it back here."

With vampire speed, Christian ran to the bathroom and returned with the mirror.

Danielle shook her head in disbelief as she watched Christian move so quickly. Her eyes couldn't adjust to the speed.

"Violette, please help Danielle over to the dressing table mirror and sit her down in the chair," said William, taking the mirror from Christian.

As Danielle sat in front of the mirror, William stood behind her with the mirror and pulled Danielle's hair up off her neck.

"Can you see this black outline of a butterfly on the back of your neck?" asked William.

Danielle had a good look at the mirror and as she noticed the butterfly outline she said, "Why do I have this on the back of my neck? I don't do tattoos."

"This black butterfly outline is the start of your transformation into a vampire. Once the outline has fully formed, it will then colour itself in. Each vampire has a different colour. When we know what colour you are, we can let you know what abilities or power you will have," said William.

Danielle nodded and tried to process all this information she was given.

"What if I don't want to be this Lepidot... oh, whatever the name is... vampire? Anyway, you can't force me. I want to go home," said Danielle anxiously.

"You won't be able to return home yet, Danielle. First we have to make sure that you don't want to drink from any humans. There is a transformation process to go through," said Christian, reaching for her hand.

Pulling away, she said, "I don't want any part of this. Please..."

"Danielle, there is more to my story than you know," said Violette. "You see, my real mother was a Lepidoptera vampire who gave me up at birth. When we arrived in Bagnolet, I kept seeing Michael everywhere I went and I had some sort of pull towards him. He also had an attraction to me and we couldn't keep away from each other. As our attraction grew, my butterfly tattoo started to come out."

"So are you saying that you and Michael were destined to be together, because you are vampire partners? I don't understand," said Danielle, with a creased brow.

"Yes, you are correct. But don't worry, I can explain that later to you. We want to talk more about what is going to happen to you first," said Violette.

"Now that we know you are transforming into a vampire, you need to be aware that at first you will need to drink blood every day until your transformation has taken place," said William matter-of-factly. "Then it will only be once a month. Yes, you do still eat food, and there are probably other things that you will need to learn about our race. But I am sure

Violette will be able to inform you more about that at a later time."

"Please… I don't want to be a vampire. Violette, help me," said Danielle, looking to Violette for some support or guidance.

"I would love to kill each and every one of those sick motherfucking Debauched vamps for what they have done to you. Sorry, Danielle, but unfortunately you don't have a choice. There is nothing I can do to change it for you. The only thing I can do for you is to help you understand what an honour it is to be a Lepidoptera vampire, and how to deal with it," said Violette.

"I know it's a lot to take in, but you do have a lot of support here. So if there is anything we can do, don't hesitate to ask. Oh, and by the way, I give my approval and blessing for you and Christian to date," said William.

"Hmm… now I know why you wouldn't let Christian and me date or see each other. It all makes sense. And you Violette, now I know why you wanted to move in here with them all," said Danielle, sickened by it all.

"Humans and vampires never work and I didn't understand why you two had an attraction for each other, anyway. I had to make a choice that was good for this coven," said William.

Coven, thought Danielle, frowning.

"Thank you, sire," said Christian.

"Danielle, how are you feeling now, about what we have told you," said William.

"I am not sure how I feel yet, Mr Gramaze. It's a lot to digest… Especially for a person like me who never believed in supernatural beings or make-believe as a kid, let alone vampires," said Danielle. Her heart was racing. "Would it be all right if I could talk with Violette alone?"

"No problem. Christian and I will leave you two to talk," said William, standing with Christian.

As the door closed, Danielle said, "Let's get out of here, Vi. I am scared."

"Don't be silly, Danielle. Everything will be all right," said Violette, holding her hand to calm her. "Come on, let's get you back to bed."

Whilst hooking Danielle back up to the blood drip, through the cannula, Violette heard a voice outside the door.

Let me talk with her.

"Danielle… there is someone waiting outside the door, who wants to see you. Can I let him in?" said Violette.

"I'm not sure I am ready for visitors. This is a lot to process, and I don't want anyone seeing me like this," said Danielle.

Violette placed the hand-held mirror in front of Danielle.

"If you are worried about what you look like, then don't worry. Your face is just about healed. It's one of the perks of being a vampire. Have a look," said Violette.

"Unbelievable… hey, this vampire thing could be a good thing," said Danielle, looking at her reflection in the mirror.

"Well, are you up for a visitor?" asked Violette.

"Oh, OK. Don't keep me in suspense," said Danielle.

There was a knock at the door. "Come in," said Danielle, looking up at the doorway.

As Stephen walked into the room, Danielle at first thought she was seeing things. Wiping her eyes, she took a deep breath and tried to focus.

"Stephen… is that you?" said Danielle, smiling from ear to ear.

"Hello, sweet cheeks. How are you?" said Stephen, as he reached the bed and sat next to her.

Danielle looked at Violette, and said, "How is this possible?"

"I am a vampire, just like you, Danielle. That's why I disappeared and you haven't seen me for all these years," said Stephen, taking her hand in his and smiling.

"I can't believe you are here, Stephen. God, how I have missed you all these years," said Danielle, as the tears spilled onto her cheeks and she hugged him tight. "You are in big trouble, Vi, for not telling me you had seen Stephen."

"I was forbidden to tell you. You were human," said Violette.

"Come over here, Vi. I need a family hug," said Danielle.

When they finally pulled away from each other, Violette said, "Stephen has a life partner too, and she lives here as well... actually, come to think of it, you have met her. Her name is Sharina."

"Unbelievable... what a day! First I find out that I am transforming into a vampire, and then I find out my big brother lives at the Gramaze house. So how long have you been living here, Stephen?" said Danielle.

"Well, we only arrived about six weeks ago. The reason we moved here was to protect, Violette, our princess. William needed more protection for Violette, so I put my hand up as soon as he asked my old leader for some help," said Stephen.

"Why do you all keep calling Violette your princess? I don't understand that. She is just Violette," said Danielle, confused.

"What you don't know is that Violette was adopted by our parents. Her birth mother is the queen of the Lepidoptera vampires, who happens to live in the basement here," said Stephen. "If you have a look at the back of Violette's neck you will see that she has a multi-coloured butterfly tattoo, which means she has a lot of power and abilities. When I say abilities, I mean like supernatural kind of abilities. Like healing, mimicry, element control, duplication of anything, the list is endless... show Danielle your butterfly, Violette."

Turning around, Violette lifted her hair from the back of her neck and showed off her multi-coloured butterfly.

"Oh, wow… that is beautiful," said Danielle, mesmerised by the tattoo.

"Isn't it just?" said Stephen, looking at the tattoo.

Letting her hair down, and turning back around, Violette said, "You see, our queen is also a multi-coloured vampire, and she is thousands of years old and very valuable to our kind. At this stage, the Debauched don't know where she is hidden, and we need to keep it that way, to keep her safe. If she dies, then our race will die."

"So now that Violette is a multi-coloured Lepidoptera vampire, she is the princess until our queen dies. Then she will take over as the queen when the queen dies. It's all a bit confusing, I know, but Violette is really a princess and this is why we have a lot of people here at the house guarding and protecting her and the queen around the clock. No matter where Violette goes, school, shopping, she is guarded 24/7 so that the Debauched vamps don't kidnap her. She would be very valuable to them if they took her. In fact, it did happen not too long ago and Violette nearly died. So this was another reason I moved here to protect and look after her," said Stephen.

"Really… unbelievable. You are certainly important to this race. Were you hurt when they kidnapped you?" said Danielle.

"Yes, I was hurt badly. Just like you, I had bruising everywhere, but they nearly drained me of all my blood and that is how I nearly died," said Violette.

Danielle then gave Violette a hug and said, "I'm sorry I didn't know. I wish I had've been here to help you."

"There is no way we could have told you, Danielle. Because you were human and we are not allowed to show humans who we are, ever. They can't seem to comprehend our race and what we do," said Violette.

"I sure have a lot to learn, don't I?" said Danielle anxiously.

"There is plenty of time for learning. Not even I know everything yet," said Violette. "And both Stephen and I are here for you."

"So what happens now to me?" said Danielle.

"Well, in the next couple of days, your butterfly outline on the back of your neck will start to colour itself in. Once we see what colour you are then we will know what ability you will have. Also, you will probably notice that you will have a need to drink blood. You do need to keep your blood supply up, because if you don't, then you will turn into a Debauched vampire who has blood lust all the time and wants to kill humans. There are other things you will notice, but we will talk about them as they appear," said Violette.

"Vi, I am not sure I can drink blood. The thought of it makes me feel queasy in the stomach," said Danielle.

"Don't worry, I felt like that before I drank the blood, too. Once you taste it for the first time, you won't feel like that ever again," said Violette, holding her hand.

"Well… I will leave you two to chat. I will come by and see you again later, Danielle," said Stephen, standing.

"Do you have to go?" asked Danielle.

"Sorry, Danielle. Yes, I do. But I will come back later," said Stephen.

"OK," said Danielle, as she put her arms out for him to give her a cuddle.

When he left, Danielle said, "Do you believe this, Vi? We are a family again. The three amigos."

"It's a nice feeling, isn't it, when you have family around? In fact, now that you are transforming into a vampire, everyone in this house is your family. The Gramaze house is full of vamps, or people as I call them, who care about you and treat you as their own kind. The love you feel, well, it's overwhelming," said Violette.

"I am not sure how I feel about being a vampire yet, Vi. But having extra family does sounds good, and it's something I have been missing since mum and dad died. As much as I love Emily and Adrian as our foster parents, I have never felt like I belonged. I don't know… it just always felt wrong; it's hard to explain. Who would have thought that we travelled all this way to France to become vampires?" said Danielle, shrugging her shoulders.

"I can't wait to find out what colour butterfly you have, Danielle. You know, I have wanted to tell you for a while that I was a vampire, but as we are forbidden to tell humans what we are, then that made it hard. This is why I had to move out as well; I found it hard to be around you all and not tell you. Oh, and besides the fact that Michael is my life partner. God, I love him so much. He is so perfect in every way. By the way, if Christian is your life partner, then you are going to have such a great life with him. I know for a fact that he really likes you."

Thank God I didn't kill him yesterday. I feel so bad for what I did to him. Luckily William stopped me. I have got to get these abilities under control, thought Violette.

"How will I know if Christian is my life partner?" said Danielle.

"When you are around him, do you feel an attraction to him? It's sort of like a pulling feeling, and you seem to know how he is feeling as well," said Violette.

"I'm not sure… I do like Christian and feel an attraction, but I can't say I have known what he is feeling," said Danielle, thinking back to all the times they had been together.

"Well, when he comes to see you next, try to see how you feel, and if the attraction you feel is more than just a teenage girl crush, if you know what I mean," said Violette.

Danielle yawned and said, "OK."

"You tired?" asked Violette.

"Yeah… do you mind if I have a sleep now?"

"No problem, sis. I will leave you to rest and come back later on," said Violette. Giving Danielle a kiss on the cheek, she hugged her goodbye and left.

Chapter Seventeen

Waking to the digital clock that was illuminating her darkened room, which was showing 6.30pm, Danielle sat up slowly, and placed her legs over the side of the bed. She took a deep breath, and tried to stand, but realised that her legs were still weak. Sitting back down on the edge of the bed, she contemplated how she was going to get to the toilet. *This is going to be interesting.*

Startled by a knock on her bedroom door, she looked up and was surprised to see Christian standing at the entrance.

"Do you need some help?" asked Christian, who had read her mind.

"Could you help me to the bathroom? I need to go to the toilet," said Danielle, a bit embarrassed.

"No problem," said Christian, walking over to Danielle and picking her up in his muscular arms.

"Thank you," said Danielle, snuggling into his chest.

"I am ready to come out now, Christian," shouted Danielle, after she had finished in the bathroom.

"All good?" asked Christian, standing in the doorway.

"Yep. All good now," said Danielle.

Christian placed her down on the bed, but Danielle didn't release her hold. As he tried to stand up straight, she pulled him closer, and tenderly kissed his mouth-watering lips.

"Mmm… I have missed this," said Christian, as he sat next to her on the bed. Kissing her passionately, his hand gently wandered over her body.

Pushing his hand away, Danielle thought, *I am not that easy.*

Christian pulled away from their embrace, took a deep breath, and said, "Sorry…"

"Don't be sorry. It's just… well… I would like to get to know you better first, that's all," said Danielle, feeling her face turn beetroot red.

"I can understand that," said Christian, realising her trust was to be earned and was not a given. "How are you feeling?"

"Still sore. But I could do with some affection from my man," said Danielle, teasing him, as she patted the pillow. She just hoped she wasn't giving off the wrong signals. All she wanted was to cuddle into Christian's chest and feel safe.

I wonder if she is well enough to make love… God, man, what are you thinking. She is still recovering. Don't even go there, thought Christian.

"Christian… I didn't see your lips move then, but I heard you speaking," said Danielle, with a furrowed brow.

"Forgive me, Danielle. I shouldn't have even thought it. This is one of the vampire abilities you are getting. It seems you can now read minds," said Christian, sheepishly.

"Humph… cool… what a great gift," said Danielle, amazed by what was happening to her. "In answer to your question though, I would like to make love to you, Christian, one day. But I don't think I am in any shape to be doing that, just yet."

"There is no hurry, Danielle. I can wait. I shouldn't have even thought about it either. It was selfish of me," said Christian, holding her hand.

"Christian… this morning Violette and I were talking about life partners. How do I know if you are my life partner or not?" asked Danielle.

"You obviously don't feel what I do yet. It's like a pull and a huge attraction and you can't think of anything else. That's how I feel about you, my beautiful lady," said Christian. Closing his eyes as he kissed her forehead, he drank in her scent. Rose.

"Why don't I feel that way then?" asked Danielle.

As he sat back to look into her eyes, he said, "It could be because you haven't fully transformed yet. But don't you feel something between us?"

"I do… but I don't feel a pull yet, not like you are describing," said Danielle.

"Hey… let's not overanalyse this, Danielle. Let's just enjoy each other's company at the moment," said Christian. "Would you like to come down to the dining room for dinner? Everyone is waiting for us."

"Umm, OK. But you will have to carry me," said Danielle.

"That's fine," said Christian.

When they entered the dining room everyone clapped and stood up. Danielle could hear them thinking, *Welcome to our family.*

Danielle felt overwhelmed by the fondness they were showing her. So much so, that she started to cry with joy. Looking around the room through her tears, she said, "Thank you everyone. I am so glad to be a part of your family."

She could also hear them all mind-talking to her, to congratulate her as well. She wasn't used to the mind reading yet, but it sure was nice to feel loved by a family again. She had missed this.

Christian placed her on a seat at the table next to Sharina and Stephen.

"What would you like to eat?" asked Christian, with his hand on her shoulder.

"I don't mind; you pick something for me. But not too much, as I am not that hungry," said Danielle.

As Christian was getting her food, Renee sat next to Danielle.

"I know you probably don't want to drink this, but you will need to have some blood soon, Danielle. Are you feeling a bit twitchy yet?" said Renee, handing her a cup of blood, with a lid on it.

"Hmm… but how did you know I feel like this?" asked Danielle.

"My dear, we have all been through the transformation and we all remember what it's like. The only way to fix it is to drink the blood," said Renee reassuringly.

Danielle took the cup from Renee and placed it on the table. Swallowing hard, she picked up again and sniffed the contents.

"That smells disgusting," said Danielle, feeling her stomach churn.

Closing her eyes, she took a few sips. Pulling the cup from her mouth, she shook her head and quivered all over.

"Drink it down fast, my dear," said Renee.

Putting the cup up to her lips, she closed her eyes and drank it down fast as she could, whilst holding her breath. When she had finished it, she opened her eyes, licked her lips and said, "Not bad. Could I have some more?"

Renee laughed. "Twitching gone?" she asked.

"Yup," said Danielle, smiling.

The first hurdle was over.

As they sat through dinner, Danielle was introduced to everyone at the table. Some she already knew, but there were some new faces at the table these days - ones who protected her sister, the princess.

"Mr Gramaze, I wanted to ask a question," said Danielle, leaning across the table.

"It's William… call me William…what is it?"

"Will it be OK for me to meet the queen?" said Danielle. She was intrigued and wanted to meet the monarch of all vampires.

Everyone in the room went silent as William answered.

"I will check with the queen and let you know when you can speak with her. I am sure she will be interested in meeting you, my dear."

"Thank you, William," said Danielle.

He nodded and continued eating his food.

Leaning into Christian, Danielle quietly said, "Ouch… the back of my neck is hurting again, Christian. Can you have a look and see what's happening, please?"

Christian pushed the hair away from the back of Danielle's neck. With his mouth open wide, he had to look twice. Her butterfly tattoo had coloured itself in and was half red and half green. With raised eyebrows, he looked at William, and said, "You need to see this. I have never seen a butterfly like this before and not sure I know what it means."

The room went quiet, as William pushed his chair back and went over and had a look at Danielle's butterfly tattoo. "This is what I thought might happen," said William, with raised eyebrows.

"What is it?" said Danielle.

"When any of us have becomes a vampire, we usually only have one colour on the butterfly, except for Violette, our princess, of course. Because the Debauched vamps manufactured this drug that turned you into a vampire, your butterfly is half red and half green. Now it's nothing to be worried about, so don't panic, Danielle. It just means you have more abilities because you have two colours," said William.

"Phew… what abilities do each of my colours have?" asked Danielle curious.

"Red has strength and the ability to change anyone's thoughts, and Green is for a healing power," said William.

Astonished by what William had just told her, Danielle sat quietly trying to take it all in. This was still new to her and she wasn't quite sure about anything yet.

Annabelle came over to Danielle and gave her a hug. "Wow… those are two great abilities to have. If I can help you to develop these powers, just ask."

"Thanks, Annabelle. You are too kind," said Danielle. "You know, even though I am a little bit scared about all of this, I think that with the love I feel from everyone here, I will make it through. Mind you, I don't know what we are going to tell Emily and Adrian when they get back."

"Don't worry about that now, Danielle. We will sort something out with them and it will all work out in the long run," said William. *Hmm, that is something else I will need to tell her. She doesn't know that Adrian is a warlock. Later…*

After a couple of days, Renee and William rang Emily and Adrian to see if Danielle could live with them permanently. Violette and Danielle sat nearby so they could talk with Emily and Adrian, too. As they dialled the number Violette said, "This should be interesting."

The call connected and Emily said, "Hello."

"Hi Emily, it's Renee and William here. How are you both?"

"We are well. How are you all going?" said Emily.

"Great, thanks. The reason for our call, Emily, is talk with you and Adrian about Danielle. Is he there with you so we can talk to you both on speaker phone?" said Renee.

"I'll just go get him," said Emily.

Returning with Adrian to the phone, Adrian said, "Hi, Renee and William. How are our girls going?"

"Violette is going really good. Part of the furniture now. We really wanted to talk with you about, Danielle," said Renee.

"Is everything alright?" said Emily, sounding a little apprehensive.

"Yes, she is fine, now," said William.

"What do you mean, now," asked Emily.

William and Renee looked at one another.

"William, Renee, what has happened?" asked Adrian.

"The Debauched... they kidnapped Danielle a couple of days ago," said William. "But don't worry, she is OK."

"Fuck... how did this happen?" asked Adrian.

Violette and Danielle looked at each other and frowned. They had never heard Adrian swear before.

"They took her from school... but don't worry, we have that covered now. And I can promise you it won't happen again," said Renee.

"Right... hang on... what are you not telling us?" said Adrian.

"Danielle was subjected to a terrible beating, and they injected an experimental drug into her, which now has consequences," said William.

"What consequences..." said Adrian.

William averted his eyes as he shifted in his seat, and tried to find the right words to describe what had happened.

"William... what consequences?" said Adrian.

"She is now one of us," said William.

"What... how is this possible?" asked Adrian, confused. He knew the Lepidoptera well and this was inconceivable.

"The Debauched have been experimenting for a while on this. They have been trying to turn vampire into human, but it never worked. So instead, they tried turning human into vampire, to strengthen their numbers, and this has succeeded," said William, looking at Danielle.

"Bastards... they will pay with their lives when I return. They want a war, I will give them one. Anyone who fucks with my foster daughter is going to pay," said Adrian.

Violette and Danielle smiled, knowing he had their backs as well as the Lepidopteras.

"Actually, if you go and see Mason whilst you are there, he will be able to keep you informed on what we have planned," said William.

"So the Lepidopteras have a plan of attack?" stated Adrian.

"You could say that. The Debauched won't know what has hit them," said William, smirking.

"I will contact Mason today and find out if there is anything I can do to help," said Adrian.

"Thanks, Adrian," said William. "Also, whilst we have you on the phone, we were thinking that as Danielle is now a Lepidoptera, can we have your approval for her stay here with us permanently?"

"She does seem a lot happier here and we will take good care of her. Oh, and we will make sure she is keeping her grades up at schools as well," said Renee.

"Hmm... I can't say that I am happy about this. But I know she will be cared for by you and your family, and that is all I can ask for," said Adrian. "Is it possible for us to speak with Violette and Danielle?"

"We are already here listening, Adrian and Emily," said Danielle, into the speaker phone.

"Hello, Emily and Adrian. How are you both going?" said Violette.

"We are going really well, girls... sorry you had to go through such an awful ordeal, Danielle. But I suppose one good thing that has come from this is, that you now have your family back. How is Stephen going?" said Emily.

"You're not wrong. And Stephen, well, he is going good. I was overwhelmed when I first saw him again. I have missed having my brother and sister around," said Danielle.

"So… I need to ask… how are both you girls coping with the Lepidoptera lifestyle and ways?" asked Adrian.

"Well… it's all new to me. I am not sure yet," said Danielle, looking to Violette for support.

"Don't worry, sis, I will look after you… as for me, I miss my old life, but I am slowly getting used to the Lepidoptera ways, and the promise that one day I will be their queen," said Violette.

"We are sure it will all work out for you both. We have had many dealings with the Gramaze family and we know they will look after you both," said Adrian.

"Well… we need to go now girls. We have some people coming over soon to go over some business with us. We love you girls very much and miss you a lot. Take care of each other… and thanks once again, Renee and William for looking after our girls. You are such good friends and we love you both for taking care of them whilst we are away," said Adrian.

"We will talk with you soon. Bye," said Emily.

They all said their goodbyes.

"Well… that went really good. I didn't think that they would say 'no' anyway, because Emily and Adrian have always worked well with us when it comes to finding our own kind," said Renee.

"So… are Emily and Adrian human? asked Danielle.

"Emily is. But Adrian is a warlock. They have been helping us for years, to find supernatural beings of all kinds and reunite them with their own kind. Just like you, Violette. Adrian knew from the moment he met you, that you were a Lepidoptera," said William, looking from Danielle to Violette.

"Warlock…" said Danielle, shaking her head. "I have a lot to learn, don't I?"

Nodding, Renee said, "Yes, dear. But don't worry about all that just now."

"Hmm… OK. Umm… when can we go and get my stuff from the Briskets' house?" said Danielle.

"Maybe tomorrow, Danielle. I don't think you are up to going over there and packing your stuff up, at the moment," said William.

"Sure… maybe you're right. I still do feel a bit weak," said Danielle.

"Yes, and maybe you will need to complete your transformation from human to vampire first, before you are around humans. We don't want you drinking from them," said Renee.

"Humph… right," said Danielle, raising her eye brows.

"Renee, can you speak with the Briskets', to let them know that she is moving in with us permanently and that she will be by sometime in the next couple of days to collect her things?" said William.

"Yes, my love. I will organise that now," said Renee.

"Now, you will have to excuse me, as I have some business to attend to," said William standing.

"Anything we can help with?" asked Violette.

"No dear, but thank you for asking," said William.

He left the sitting room and went down to the basement to talk with the queen.

Chapter Eighteen

Within weeks of Danielle's full transformation, the Lepidopteras worldwide had devised a plan together to destroy the Debauched and their experimental drugs for good. As the day got closer for the eradication, William heard rumours that a new Debauched leader had taken over from Clause. He didn't know their new leader, Diablo, and hadn't heard anything about him previously. But that didn't matter much to William, as his intentions were clear: kill all Debauched and save the human race.

Gathered in the operations room with his own coven, William and all the Lepidoptera leaders worldwide, who were on the flat screen, finalised their plans on how each state or country would destroy the Debauched and their experimental drugs. Even though the attack was scheduled for the next night at the same time worldwide, there were concerns that it was already too late for the humans who had been transformed into vampires from these drugs.

When the meeting had finished, and the flat screen had gone blank, William said to his coven, "Jack, Theodore, Harrison, Annabelle, I need you to stay back, so we can discuss a few things. You too, Grayson and Michael. Everyone else, you can go."

Grayson tightened his grip on Samantha's hand.

"See you later, my love."

"You sure will," said Samantha, hugging him goodbye.

"See you later on, sweet girl," said Michael to Violette, as he kissed her forehead.

"Bye," said Violette, soaking up his affection.

As the rest of the Gramaze coven filed out the door, William wrote on the whiteboard and discussed his plan of attack on a Debauched house nearby with his remaining warriors.

"Jack, Theodore, Harrison, I am sending you three soldiers out to destroy a poppy field, which is in a town nearby," said William, looking at each of their faces.

They all nodded.

"The police here don't or can't seem to stop the sale of this shit, and I am over all the drugs that are flooding our streets," said William, with flared nostrils.

"Would you like Michael and me to come along, as back up?" asked Grayson.

"No… you are both needed on patrol tonight," said William. "Annabelle, you will be driving, so you can act as look-out for Jack, Theodore, and Harrison."

"Yes, sire," said Annabelle.

"Grayson, I want you and Michael to make sure that the Debauched aren't aware of the attack tomorrow night. We don't need any surprises," said William.

"Yes, sire," said Grayson and Michael together.

"Assemble two others to go with you of course, but keep a low profile. We don't want these fuckers knowing what we are up to," said William.

"Right…" said Michael. "Let's get a move on, then."

Jack, Theodore and Harrison left the Gramaze residence, heavily armed and ready to burn down the poppy fields that were on the outskirts of Montreuil. It was only a ten minute drive away from Bagnolet, so all they had to do, once they arrived, was set it alight and drive back to the Gramaze house.

Arriving near the outskirts of a castle in Montreuil in their SUV with blacked-out windows, Jack, Theodore and Harrison jumped out the back of the van with their blow torches, ready to incinerate the poppy fields.

"You wait for us here, Annabelle," said Harrison, as he stood next to the driver's side window.

"I'll be here, ready and waiting," said Annabelle.

With vampire speed, the three Gramaze soldiers chose a secluded road, at the bottom of the castle wall, to stake out the poppy fields.

As Harrison stood back watching Jack and Theodore go check for Debauched up ahead, he heard a snapping of a twig behind him. Before he could look around, he was beheaded and his body disintegrated.

Standing over his ashes, the four Debauched then spread out in search for any more Lepidoptera. They knew their new leader, Diablo, would be pleased that they had stopped the burning of his crops.

Jack and Theodore crept through the hundred acre poppy field quietly and started to set the fires with their blow torches. As the plants caught fire, the flames seemed to spread quickly.

Harrison, where are you bro? thought Theodore.

There was no answer.

Jack... have you seen or heard from Harrison? thought Theodore.

There was no answer.

Fuck... where are you guys? thought Theodore. *Annabelle...*

Yes. What is it? thought Annabelle, as she waited for their return.

Are Jack and Harrison there with you?

No… fuck… get back here now, Theodore.

Within seconds Theodore was opening the passenger door of the SUV.

"What the fuck is going on, Annabelle…"

But before he could say another word, a Debauched vamp had pulled Theodore out the SUV and beheaded him.

Annabelle screamed as she watched her friend disintegrate. She planted her foot quickly on the pedal, but the wheels skidded in one spot, and she couldn't get traction to drive away. As her driver window smashed, she felt a hand come through, and try to drag her out. It was then that the van's wheels finally got traction and she pulled away, with the Debauched vamp hanging off her. Making the van swerve from side to side and trying to fight him off as she headed for the road, Annabelle took out her belt knife and stabbed the Debauched vamp in the eye. In pain, he finally let go, and she sped away, whilst watching the poppy field burn in the back ground. Even though her three friends were dead, they had done what they had come to do, and that was to stop the trafficking of drugs on the streets of Paris.

Pulling the van into the Gramaze driveway, Annabelle put the van into park, and pictured the three faces of her friends she had just lost. Holding her hands over her face, the tears she had held back started to cascade down her cheeks, and she cried uncontrollably, in their memory.

Oh, poor Nicky, Sherrie, and Temperance. They are left without their life partners. What am I going to tell them, thought Annabelle, wiping her nose on her sleeve.

As she looked up and tried to focus through the tears, she noticed Grayson standing in front of the van with Michael. Walking around to her door, Grayson opened it and gave

Annabelle a hug. She sobbed hysterically into his shoulder. Picking her up in his arms, Grayson carried Annabelle into the house, whilst Michael drove the van around to the back of the house.

This was a sad moment in the Gramaze house. They hadn't lost any of their coven for hundreds of years. Let alone three life partners in one night.

As the night turned into day, William grew more furious about the loss of his family. He wanted blood and Diablo was about to pay.

"Right… you all have your orders. Let's get the fuck out of here and kill these bastards."

Everyone cheered and filed out the operations room, ready for a fight to the death.

As William, Grayson and Michael kissed their life partners goodbye at the back of the property, William said, "Your job, ladies, is to keep the queen safe. No matter what happens, you must protect her at all costs. Renee, I need you to keep watch on Nicky, Sherrie and Temperance. We don't want them slipping out the house and taking matters into their own hands for the loss of their life partners Jack, Theodore, and Harrison."

"Yes, sire," they all said together.

"Come on girls, let's get set up inside," said Renee, looking from Violette to Samantha. "We can monitor the situation from the operations room. Danielle has it all set up for us."

Arriving a street away from their targeted house, William gave the orders to his coven on their plan of attack.

"Revenge is sweet," said William, as he took his sword out of its sheath and held it in the air.

The Gramaze coven all cheered in agreeance, and held their swords in the air too.

When the Debauched house came into view, Annabelle and Brock ran at vampire speed, around the back of the house, whilst William, Grayson, Michael, Stephen and Sharina walked in a straight line towards the front of the house. With no Debauched soldiers in sight at the back of the house, Annabelle and Brock quietly slipped in through the glass kitchen door and headed for the basement, hoping this would be where they found the experimental drugs. Finding a stair case, in a hidden door panel near the kitchen, they continued downstairs with their swords drawn and ready for action. Stepping onto the concrete floor in the basement, Annabelle and Brock looked at each other, unable to believe what they had found: humans, hundreds of them, kept in locked cells, all packed in like sardines. And at the end of the cells was a well-lit open room, which had a few fridge and freezer storage units, and benches, with swabs and syringes.

William, we are going to need a few trucks, thought Annabelle.

What for? thought William.

Literally, there are hundreds of humans down here. Not sure if they have been injected, or transformation has taken place. But you won't believe it, even when you see it, thought Annabelle, looking around the basement.

Unbelievable… trucks are on their way, thought William, as he took his phone out of his jacket pocket and called Renee.

As Brock and Annabelle got closer to the first locked cell, one of the women tried to grab Annabelle, through the bars.

"Help us. Please…"

"Help is on the way," said Annabelle, standing just far enough away from the people so they couldn't touch her.

"Thank you… the doors are booby trapped," said the woman.

"Right," said Brock, noticing the metal boxes connected to the cell doors opening. "Where are the keys?"

"I don't know. The other men took them with them," said the woman.

"Don't worry… we will get you out of there, and in one piece," said Brock.

William, Grayson and Michael waited on the front porch of the house, whilst Stephen and Sharina went in through the front flywire door. After looking through the house for a few minutes, Stephen thought to William, *There is no one in here.*

William frowned, and wondered where the Debauched were. It was never this easy.

Keep checking.

Hearing a noise coming from the side of the property, William directed Michael and Grayson to go have a look and report back.

Nearing the shed, Grayson and Michael noticed that a truck had pulled up. Watching in the shadows, they saw five Debauched herding some more humans into the shed.

William, you need to see this, thought Grayson.

William was there in no time. As he watched from the shadows, he gave Grayson and Michael orders to exterminate the Debauched. Knowing Grayson and Michael wouldn't need his help, he then walked around to the front of the house again. Just as he rounded the corner, he was confronted by a Debauched with a blow torch. Quickly stepping out of the line of fire, William pulled out his knife from his belt and threw it at the Debauched's chest. The blow sent the vampire backwards, and William threw himself forward and broke the Debauched's neck with his bare hands. As the soldier stumbled and fell to the ground, William then beheaded him, and watched his body disintegrate.

Hearing a sword swish through the air behind him, William stepped sideways in the hopes it would miss him. Turning to see who was trying to attack him, he lunged at the Debauched soldier with force, driving his own sword through the soldiers torso. Again, he was no match for William, who had three thousand years' experience. William beheaded the young soldier.

It wasn't long before all the Debauched who were guarding the house and its contents were dead, and the humans from the basement had been helped into trucks.

As William watched the last truck come towards him, he realised at the last minute, that the truck wasn't going to stop. Instead it ploughed into William and right through the front of the house. Coming to a stop inside the front lounge room, a Debauched driver jumped out the window of the smashed-up truck and tried to escape. Running out the back door of the house, he was stopped in his tracks when he noticed Michael standing in front of him, with his sword drawn.

"You think you can stop me? Come on… let's see," said the smug Debauched.

Lunging forward, Michael tried to stab him with his knife. But the driver jumped out the way.

"That all you got?" said the driver.

Michael's lips thinned and his nostrils flared, as he jumped into the air and kicked the driver to the ground with his foot. Stabbing him in his chest, he then beheaded the Debauched and watched his body disintegrate.

Running back inside the house, Michael called out, "William… you OK?"

No answer.

William, where are you? thought Michael. Looking around the crash site, Michael finally came upon William's dusty, limp body. Kneeling down beside him, he threw the rubble off William's chest. Michael bit into his own flesh on his wrist, and placed it over William's mouth and tried to drain some blood into it.

Drink… William, drink.

Within seconds, William forcibly grabbed Michael's arm and started to suck the blood from his wrist. As his eyes changed to a crimson red colour, Michael tried to pull away. But William was too powerful. Michael knew if he couldn't stop William, not only would Michael lose his life, but William would hit blood lust.

Grayson, thought Michael, just as he became unconscious.

Michael woke to someone stroking his face. At first, he was disoriented, but then he suddenly remembered the attack on the Debauched house and William trying to suck him dry. He sat up quickly.

"It's OK. You are home," said Violette, placing her hand on his shoulder.

"Is William all right?" asked Michael, as he looked at his wrist, which had already healed.

"Yes. He is fine," said Violette. "Now lie back and relax."

"I can't. I need to see William," said Michael, slipping his legs over the side of the bed.

"William is resting," said Violette.

Michael just ignored her, and ran with vampire speed out the door of their bedroom.

Renee, he is on his way, thought Violette.

As Michael got to Renee and William's bedroom door, the door opened and Renee stepped out.

"You can't come in here, Michael. He will see you later."

"Like hell," said Michael, pushing past her.

Leaning on the door frame, Michael's eyes adjusted to the darkened room.

"Leave… NOW!" shouted Renee, standing in front of him, baring her fangs.

"It's all right, my love. Leave us alone," said William, in a weak voice.

"Are you sure, William?" said Renee.

"Yes."

William watched Renee close the door behind her. As his vision focused on Michael, he said, "Don't come any closer. Blood lust has taken over me."

"Is there anything I can do to help you, sire?" asked Michael.

"There is nothing. I will need a few days to work through this by myself," said William.

"Did I cause this?" asked Michael.

"Yes… but you are not to blame yourself. I was pretty badly injured and basically you saved my life by giving me your blood," said William.

"Right…" said Michael, as he lowered his head.

Licking his lips, William guessed that his eyes had changed to a crimson red again. "You need to get out of here, Michael. NOW!" shouted William, as he grabbed hold of the sheets for control. "Get Renee to send for Susan."

"Yes, sire," said Michael, opening the door.

Closing the door, he noticed Renee leaning up against the railing, waiting for him to come out. "He said to send for Susan," said Michael, as he walked away, dazed.

"Michael…" said Renee.

He didn't answer. He just kept walking.

Pulling her phone from her jeans pocket, Renee gave Susan a call.

"William needs you, Susan. He has hit blood lust," said Renee.

"I will be there in one hour," said Susan.

"Thank you."

Michael went in search of Grayson. He needed some answers. Standing in the doorway of the kitchen, he noticed Violette was sitting next to Grayson at the island bench, and they were chatting with Lamiae.

"Can I speak with you Grayson, in private?" asked Michael.

"Sure... let's go outside for a walk," said Grayson, noticing how agitated Michael was.

Not even looking at Violette or Lamiae, Michael followed Grayson through the house and out onto the patio area.

"So what happened? I need a debrief," asked Michael, impatiently.

"Well... after all the humans were taken away in trucks, Brock set the charges and we blew the house, and the experimental drugs, sky high," said Grayson, as he looked out to the pool area.

"That's not what I am asking you about, and you know it," said Michael, with furrowed brow. "What happened with William?"

"You know what happened. He fed from you, hit blood lust and the rest is history," said Grayson, matter-of-factly.

"That's all?" asked Michael.

"Yes, that's all," said Grayson stiffly. "Now... can I get back to eating some dinner?"

"Sure..." said Michael, staring out into the darkness of the property. He wasn't sure if he believed Grayson.

Standing in the shower, Michael let the soothing water cascade over his shoulders and onto his back.

Violette opened the shower door, and asked, "How are you feeling?"

"Don't worry about me, I will be all right," grunted Michael, with his chin pointing to the tiled floor.

"But I am worried about you. What's wrong?" said Violette.

"Nothing… nothing at all. Except for no one around here is telling me the truth about what happened tonight," said Michael, as he looked Violette in the eyes.

"What… you think they are holding back on some sort of information?" said Violette.

"Yeah… and you know they are, Vi," said Michael, annoyed.

Taking a deep breath, Violette let out a heavy sigh.

"The only thing they haven't told you is about the experimental drugs and how William just about sucked you dry. He nearly killed you, Michael."

"William couldn't help it. He was injured and needed blood," said Michael.

"Yes… but you didn't have to give him yours. There were others there to help him," said Violette, with her hands on her hips.

"Yes, I do know that, Violette. It's just that I didn't want anyone else getting hurt," said Michael.

"If Grayson hadn't pulled you away from William's blood lust, then you would be dead. I would never forgive William for that, Michael," said Violette, handing him a towel as he turned the water off and stepped out the shower.

He raised his eyebrows, as the realisation his him.

"I suppose I didn't stop and think about the consequences, Violette. Or even how you would have been left without a life partner... sorry."

"Just promise me you won't do that again, and you'll think about the consequences of your actions," said Violette.

"I promise," said Michael, drying himself off. "So... what were you saying about the experimental drugs?"

"As William is not in his right mind at the moment, Grayson has taken the reins, so to speak. You know, being second in command and all."

"Yeah, yeah."

"Well... in the operations room tonight, Grayson spoke with all the other counterparts around the world about their attacks on the Debauched facilities. It seems that besides us, Rome and LA, nobody else was successful. Bad intel or something... apparently, when they raided the houses or warehouses, the experimental drugs had already disappeared, and there were no Debauched in sight," said Violette, with her hands on her hips.

"Strange... the leads we were given were meant to be good," said Michael, putting on his clothes.

"Yeah. And that's not all... on the news tonight, humans have been complaining of being bitten by other humans. They laughed off the idea of vampires on the news, but sooner or later, the authorities will figure it out."

"Shit. We will have to get back out there and find these humans that have been transformed and kill them. What other choice do we have?" said Michael.

Violette followed Michael into the bedroom.

"That is exactly what Grayson told us all tonight. That we would have to kill humans who have transformed, unless the Debauched had come up with a type of reversal drug. But I can't see them doing this, can you?" said Violette.

"Who knows, Vi? Fuck… it's gonna take a good chemist to manufacture that type of drug."

"Hmm, I know. Hey… what about Diablo? Why don't we capture him and see what information we can get out of him? I am sure he would probably know about a reversal drug. What do you think?"

"Good idea. But… I will speak with Grayson and see what he thinks first," said Michael, standing in front of Violette. He suddenly went pale, and grabbed onto her for support.

Michael had become weak, from lack of blood in his system.

"Would you like me to get you some blood from the kitchen?" asked Violette.

"That sounds good. Thank you," said Michael.

"I won't be a minute," said Violette, walking towards the door.

"Take your time, sweet lady.

As soon as she left the room, Michael went to find Grayson.

Entering the combat room, Michael found Grayson sparring with Brock.

"I need to speak with you. In private."

"Humph… what is it this time, Michael?"

Grayson was not in the mood for more questions. He had enough to worry about.

"I am sure you know what this is all about," said Michael, annoyed that Grayson didn't take him seriously.

"Can't you see that I am busy at the moment?" said Grayson, as he continued to spar with Brock.

"Can you just stand still for one moment…. I wanted to talk with you about Diablo," said Michael.

"What about Diablo?" said Grayson, as he stopped sparring and stood facing Michael.

"Do you think Diablo would have a reversal drug for the humans who have transformed?" asked Michael, in front of Brock.

"How did you know about that...? Oh, never mind. I can guess who told you. In answer to your question, I don't know. But that is a seriously good question. Hmm..." said Grayson, with his hand resting on his chin.

"One worth investigating though, right."

"Sure is... let's get to the operations room and call the other leaders," said Grayson.

Chapter Nineteen

Grayson's excitement about this new lead was short-lived. Even though the other leaders wanted to help with the capture of Diablo, and the prevention of any more experimental drugs being injected into humans, they weren't able to, because most of them had lost too many soldiers during the last attack, and couldn't afford to lose any more.

Frustrated, Grayson watched the big screen go blank. He knew that he needed to make a decision, and soon, if they were to stop the carnage on the streets, and protect their kind from being discovered by the humans.

"Stop what you are planning," said William, entering the operations room with Susan.

Looking up to see William walking slowly towards them, both Grayson and Michael, bowed their heads.

"Sire," they both said together.

"What are you thinking?" said William, coming to stand in front of them.

"Sire… we need to stop these fuckers, and…" said Grayson.

Interrupting him before he could finish his sentence, William said, "We don't have the manpower… let alone the knowledge of where Diablo is. You are forbidden to continue with these plans."

"But sire," said Grayson.

"There are no buts. We are stronger in numbers… you know this. Now get out of here," said William authoritatively, waving his hand for them to leave the room.

With his nostrils flared, and fists clenched, Grayson's rigid jaw ached as left the operations room with Michael.

Fuck…

"I'm going down to the combat room to let off some steam. You coming?" he asked Michael.

"Nah… might give it a miss, bro. I'll catch up with you later."

"Catch you later," said Grayson, walking off.

Michael walked up the marble staircase, taking two steps at a time. He was headed for his bedroom. Entering the darkened room, he was thankful that Violette was nowhere to be seen. He shut the door, and quickly walked over to his wardrobe.

Moving the shoe rack to one side, Michael pulled back the carpet to reveal a secret metal compartment, which had weapons inside a grey duffle bag. Michael unzipped it and pulled out a long sword, four knives, and throwing stars. Slipping them into the long pockets of his black, full length leather jacket, which was hanging up in his wardrobe, he was now ready for a battle with the Debauched.

Lying in wait across the road from one of Diablo's houses of ill repute, which he inherited from Nicholas, Michael hid in the shadows and waited, hoping to catch a Debauched and torture him for information on the whereabouts of Diablo.

Hearing a noise from behind, Michael turned around, with his sword drawn, only to see Grayson standing there.

"What are you doing here?" asked Michael, as he relaxed and slid his sword back in its sheath on his belt.

"I could ask you the same question. But I think I already know the answer," said Grayson, as he came to stand next to Michael.

"Are you by yourself?" asked Michael, looking around.

"Yes. William has ordered me to bring you back home," said Grayson.

"That's not going to happen. I am here to find Diablo and if there is a reversal drug. You can either stay and help me or leave. Your choice," said Michael, matter-of-factly, with his hands on his hips.

"You will stand down, soldier. That is an order," came a voice from behind them.

Looking around, Michael and Grayson were shocked to see William walk out from the shadows. He was in full battle gear and both men could hear from his gruff voice, that he was not in a good mood.

Bowing his head, Michael said, "Sire."

"You were given an order, soldier. I want you back at the house, NOW!" said William, coming to stand in front of Michael. Watching the defiance in Michael's eyes, William raised his drawn sword to challenge him.

"Stop," said Grayson, in a low voice. "We have company."

Looking over their shoulders, and past Grayson, William and Michael watched as three heavily armed Debauched walked out the side entrance of the club. Rugged, and walking with a proud swagger, the leader's bald head shone in the moonlight. With two dark-skinned henchmen in tow, he walked towards a parked four-wheel drive cruiser, which was waiting for them.

William's eyes narrowed as he watched them drive out the alley way.

"Roof top, NOW!" grunted William, to Grayson and Michael. With one swift move of their feet, the three Gramaze Lepidoptera's leaped up onto the roof.

Follow them.

255

Leaping from one roof top to another, and then onto the roadway, William, Grayson and Michael, followed the cruiser for a few miles, before stopping at a large warehouse down by the harbour. Crouching down behind some parked cars, the three Gramaze Lepidopteras waited for the three Debauched to enter the warehouse. William then gave the signal to Grayson and Michael, to search the warehouse.

Leaping up to the roof, William quickly crept over to the first clear skylight to see if he could get a better look inside the building. He spotted what looked like five big steel vats, that had stirring arms, mixing some sort of white power and liquid together. As he listened to the thoughts of the Debauched below, William soon realised that not only was the bald-headed guy, Diablo, but also that this warehouse was the one manufacturing the human to vampire drugs.

Grayson, Michael…

Yes, sire, thought Grayson.

Inside this building are nine heavily armed Debauched, and a handful of human helpers. From what I can see up here, they are manufacturing the human to vampire drug at this very location. We are outnumbered… I have requested Annabelle, Brock, and Renee, to come and help us. So you will sit tight until they arrive… are we clear? thought William.

Yes, sire, thought Grayson and Michael together.

Leaping to the roof, they waited until back up arrived, as instructed.

Sire, we are close by. What are your instructions? thought Brock.

Blow this warehouse to smithereens - its contents and the Debauched, along with their human helpers, thought William. *I want these fuckers to pay. But one thing I want to make clear… Diablo is inside the warehouse and we need him alive.*

Understood, sire, thought Brock.

Hearing William give the orders, all the Gramaze coven knew their mission and what it meant to their kind to keep Diablo alive.

When Brock, Annabelle, and Renee finally arrived, William gave orders to set up bombs around the perimeter, which would explode when an electronic signal was given by Brock. Once this was done, William then gave the order to storm the building.

With their swords drawn and ready for any action, the Gramaze coven crashed through the steel roof, and immediately took out six Debauched vamps. Watching the humans run towards Diablo's office for help, William gave the command to decapitate them as well.

Forcing the door open to Diablo's office, William, Grayson and Michael soon became aware that the two other guards and Diablo had escaped. Looking around the office, William spotted some paperwork that was on top of a grey desk. As he read through the paperwork, he soon realised that the answer to their problems was right in front of him. Folding the instructions up, William put them in his leather jacket pocket for safe keeping.

"Don't move, sire!" shouted Michael, holding his hand up. "You are standing on an explosive plate."

Looking down to his feet, William knew if he took one more step, he would be blown to pieces.

Brock… get in here, thought Michael, as he looked at William with a furrowed brow.

Within seconds, Brock arrived. As he was the Gramaze coven's explosives expert, Michael had every confidence in Brock to solve this minor hiccup. Bending down to access the situation, Brock said, "Hmm… pressure plate bomb. This is activated when you step off, William."

"Right…" said William, looking around the room. "Grayson… over there… that filing cabinet. How heavy is it?"

Rushing over to the cabinet and picking it up, Grayson carried it back over to William. "It's pretty heavy, sire. I think it will do."

Looking at William, Brock said, "Let's try this."

William looked at Grayson and said, "On three."

Grayson nodded.

"One… two…three," said Grayson, as he switched out the heavy filing cabinet for William, hoping they were the same weight.

William breathed a sigh of relief.

"Thank fuck for that," said William, feeling the adrenalin flowing thought his body.

Smiling, Grayson and Brock high fived each other, whilst Michael breathed a sigh of relief and rolled his eyes.

"Now that that has been sorted, I want a search of the building, before we blow it, to see if Diablo is hiding anywhere with his guards," said William.

"Yes, sire," they all said together.

They walked out the office, and into the factory, with their swords drawn, in hope that they would find Diablo. Suddenly, there was an explosion from behind them, and the four Gramaze Lepidopteras were thrown forward into the air. As debris and glass showered down on them, they all landed with a thud on the hard concrete floor.

Hearing the explosion, Annabelle and Renee rushed from the left-hand side of the warehouse to their family at vampire speed. As Annabelle reached Grayson, Michael, and Brock, who were lying next to each other, she noticed they were all knocked unconscious. She knelt down next to each of them, checked their battered bodies, and ascertained if their injuries were life threatening.

Eventually coming round from the explosion feeling dazed, Michael and Grayson's injuries soon healed, whereas Brock lay on the ground with a long piece of steel pierced through his shoulder.

Annabelle helped Brock sit up slowly, whilst balancing the piece of steel through his shoulder.

"Fuck… just pull it out, Annabelle," said Brock, holding his shoulder.

Without a word, she did as she was asked and watched him double over in pain.

"Aww," said Brock, as he watched Annabelle place her hand over the wound to soothe his pain. It wasn't long before his wound healed over.

When Renee reached William, he was on the ground, in a sitting position, plucking out pieces of debris from his body. He seemed dazed as she looked into his crimson red eyes. Baring his teeth, she could see he was about to hit blood lust, once again. Luckily Susan had warned Renee this may happen again, so Renee had brought along some blood from home.

Renee opened the door to the van, and reached in to retrieve the blood for William. Closing the van door, with the bag in hand, she turned to see William standing behind her. Yet in a way, he didn't seem like her life partner.

His eyes were a brilliant red and dilated. His fangs were extended, and his nostrils flared, as his breathing was rapid.

"Give me that," said William, pointing to the bag of blood and wrenching it out of her hands.

Renee watched him rip the bag of blood open and down the contents in one second. She knew he needed more, so she attempted to get the other bag. As she tried to open the door, he booted it shut and pushed her up against the van. Holding her hands, William tore into the flesh on her neck, and sucked her blood like a wild man.

Renee tried to push him away, but he was too strong. Screaming in pain, she called his name.

"William... William!"

He didn't hear her. Her blood was so intoxicating that all he could think of was draining her dry.

Renee was limp, and unconscious in his arms, but as he continued to suck the blood from her neck, William felt someone forcibly grab him from behind, and rip him from his prey.

Renee's body slumped to the ground.

With Renee's blood dripping from his fangs, Michael held William's arms behind him, whilst Grayson smashed William in the face and then the torso. As the fight continued, Grayson tried to convince William that he had hit blood lust. But William didn't want to know about it. Grunting, as Michael held him face down on the ground, with his hands behind his back, William tried to struggle free.

Annabelle watched on, as Michael and Grayson fought William, and tried to get him under control. Taking a deep breath, she thought to Grayson, *Let me help*.

Looking up, Grayson nodded, but held William down firmly on the ground whilst Annabelle knelt next to him. Annabelle's calming touch on William's back was enough to relax him and eventually put him into a deep sleep.

"Thank fuck for that. I don't think we could have fought him much longer," said Michael, looking at Annabelle and Grayson, and letting go of William.

"Hmm... you're not wrong, bro. How is Brock?" asked Grayson.

"I'm fine," said Brock, approaching them. "Let's just get William and Renee into the van and blow this fucking place sky high."

"I second that," said Grayson, as he turned William over to help carry him to the van.

As William lay flat on the floor, in the back of the van, Grayson noticed some paperwork sticking out of his jacket, and wondered what it was. Grayson took the folded up papers out of William's jacket, opened it, and read the contents.

"Fuck… do you believe this…? William found the reversal drug information and how to manufacture it."

"Really?" said Michael, snatching it from Grayson's hands and having a look at it for himself. "Well, at least one good thing has come from this mission."

Grayson looked at Michael with contempt.

"What mission? Bro… you disobeyed a direct order. You will explain yourself later to not only me, but to William as well… now, let's get out of here."

They drove away from the building, only to stop for Brock to press the button on the electronic detonator, then all watched out the windows, as the warehouse exploded. With debris scattering far and wide, and the smoke billowing from the building, the Gramaze family high fived each other and continued their journey home.

Epilogue

It had been two months since the Gramaze coven had destroyed Diablo's drug manufacturing warehouse, and it seemed, from all the whispers on the street, that the Debauched had gone into hiding. Even though the experimental drugs were destroyed and a reversal drug had been administered to most of the humans who had been turned into vampires, the Lepidopteras still expected some fallout from the Debauched worldwide.

Recovered from his blood lust, with the full support and help from his coven and life partner Renee, William was happy that his family was growing and that the Debauched lineage was finally diminishing in numbers. His next mission was to find Diablo and terminate him.

Concerned for the newest member of his coven, Danielle, William spoke with the queen.

"Do you think we should administer the reversal drug to Danielle?" said William, as he sat on the couch, in front of Talitha.

"Obviously, I think we should. But I have spoken with Danielle about this, and she wants to remain one of us. I have given her my assurance that we won't reverse the transformation," said Talitha, pouring a glass of blood for her and William. "I would like you to keep an eye on this situation. As you know... this is not the natural way to become a

Lepidoptera vampire and maybe later on, there could be consequences for Danielle. So please keep me informed."

"Yes, Queen," said William, nodding and picking up the glass.

Samantha, Violette and Danielle sat quietly on the steps to the combat room, and watched the rest of the Gramaze coven practise their battle skills on each other. Even though they each needed more practice, the three female Lepidopteras always liked to watch their men train.

Watching the sweat pour from her life partner, Violette thought, *There is something sexy about the way he moves... Mmm, it turns me on.*

"Mmm, I know what you mean, sis," said Danielle, watching Christian work out.

"Get a hold of yourself, you two," said Samantha, snickering, as she looked from Violette to Danielle. Looking back at her life partner, Grayson, she watched his every move.

"Looks who's talking," said Danielle, bumping Samantha with her shoulder.

Samantha laughed.

"Yeah, life sure is good at the moment."

"Agreed," said Danielle, with a raised eyebrow, watching Christian.

"So how are you settling in, Samantha?" asked Violette, as she leant forward to look at Samantha.

"Better now. Even though my life has changed, I am appreciative for what it has brought me. And the best news of all is, that I have been talking with William, and he said that I could go back to studying at university for my doctor's degree in children's medicine," said Samantha.

"Wow... that's awesome, Sam," said Violette.

"Yeah… I have checked into it and I am resuming my studies next week. Which means in two years I will be fully qualified and be able to start my own practice," said Samantha, excited.

"I bet you are thrilled," said Danielle.

"Sure am," said Samantha, remembering her conversation with William. "But I also feel the need and have spoken with William about becoming a valuable team player and helping with the patrols at night… I will always be indebted to William for what he is doing for me."

"I am glad things are working out for you, Sam," said Violette. "What about you, Danielle? How are you coping with being a Lepidoptera?"

Looking down at her feet, Danielle twitched her lips from left to right. "Umm, well, it sure has it perks, sis."

"Spill," said Violette, bumping Danielle's shoulder.

"You know… Christian, this house, being part of a family again. And to tell you the truth, I enjoy being a vampire and the advantages that come along with it," said Danielle. *Oh, and the sex, it's awesome. God, how that makes me feel. Never had so many orgasms in my entire life.*

"Really?" said Violette, with raised eyebrows, smirking.

"Oops, forgot you can hear my thoughts," said Danielle, shrugging her shoulders. "But I think another thing I am enjoying is the combat training, and I certainly am looking forward to becoming, just like you Sam, a valuable team player, who can repay William's kindness someday."

"That's great, sis," said Violette, as she placed her arm around Danielle's shoulder. "Hey… how did you go with our queen the other day, when you met her for the first time?"

"Good, I think. Was a bit scary at first, not knowing what to expect and all. But she spoke to me about how important a female Lepidoptera is and what my role is. I suppose I felt relief as well, when she told me that even though I became a vampire through drugs, that she accepted me as her own child and would love me unconditionally, like her own, for eternity," said Danielle.

"Wow… that is nice," said Samantha, looking at Danielle. "Do you believe how regal she looks?'

"Yeah… I know. I had to rub my eyes, twice. Her presence is like sunlight shining through a window on a gloomy day," said Danielle, smiling.

"Yeah… so… I hear from Grayson that Emily and Adrian aren't returning from LA for about a year because their business is going well," said Samantha.

"Yeah. And now they know that Danielle and I are Lepidopteras and are happy here, they're pleased for us both to stay here. Plus it would have been hard for us to live apart from our life partners, let alone try to guard us," said Violette.

"Yeah… that would have been a logistical nightmare. That's for sure," said Samantha, standing, as she watched Grayson, Michael and Christian walk towards her. "Hello, boys."

"Hello," they all said together, standing at the bottom of the stairs.

"Well… we have finished up in here. How about we go have our showers and meet up in the dining room?" said Michael, as he looked from Grayson to Christian.

Nodding, both men took their ladies' hands and continued out of the combat room and to their own bedrooms.

"You ready, my love?" asked Michael, holding out his hand.

"Yep," said Violette, standing and placing her hand in his.

Life had changed dramatically for Samantha, Violette and Danielle since meeting their life partners and becoming Lepidopteras, especially for Violette, who was next in line for the throne. But it was a life that they all accepted and felt that they belonged to now.

Check my website for when the third book in this series will be published. www.susanhoddy.com

For the latest news on Susan Hoddy visit:-

Facebook /susan.hoddy

Twitter @susan_hoddy

Instagram susanhoddy

ALSO BY SUSAN HODDY

Book One of the Lepidoptera Vampire Series

Acknowledgements

This book would not be here, resting in your hands, or on your e-reader if it weren't for the following people. I owe all of them my deepest appreciation.

My daughter, Samantha Hoddy, and my fiancée, Michael Houston. You have always given me time and space to write my books and have been interested in what I am writing. I could not have written this without your continued support and love. Thank you Michael and Sam.

My editor, Rebecca Freeman, whose continued advice and support has provided me with a much needed calming strength to keep going. Thank you, Rebecca.

Several friends, and family members, whom read my manuscript and gave me feedback on what they wanted to see in the storyline and book cover. Thank you all.

My book cover designer, Laura Moyer from the Book Cover Machine, who worked tirelessly to provide me with a truly awesome cover design. Thank you, Laura.